To Experi...
Girls W...

By Em...

Published by Emma V. Leech.

Copyright (c) Emma V. Leech 2020

Cover Art: Victoria Cooper

ASIN No.: B082MQRLX4

ISBN: 9798626477283

All rights reserved. Without limiting the rights under copyright reserved above, no part of this publication may be reproduced, stored in or introduced into a retrieval system, or transmitted, in any form, or by any means (electronic, mechanical, photocopying, recording, or otherwise) without the prior written permission of both the copyright owner and the above publisher of this book. This is a work of fiction. Names, characters, places, brands, media, and incidents are either the product of the author's imagination or are used fictitiously. The author acknowledges the trademarked status and trademark owners of various products referenced in this work of fiction, which have been used without permission. The publication/use of these trademarks is not authorised, associated with, or sponsored by the trademark owners. The ebook version and print version are licensed for your personal enjoyment only.

The ebook version may not be re-sold or given away to other people. If you would like to share the ebook with another person, please purchase an additional copy for each person you share it with. No identification with actual persons (living or deceased), places, buildings, and products is inferred.

Table of Contents

Members of the Peculiar Ladies' Book Club	1
Chapter 1	3
Chapter 2	13
Chapter 3	22
Chapter 4	37
Chapter 5	49
Chapter 6	62
Chapter 7	79
Chapter 8	87
Chapter 9	98
Chapter 10	112
Chapter 11	127
Chapter 12	136
Chapter 13	146
Chapter 14	162
Chapter 15	175
Chapter 16	192
Chapter 17	205
Chapter 18	223
Chapter 19	237
Chapter 20	248
To Bed the Baron	258
Chapter 1	260
Chapter 2	268

Want more Emma?	277
About Me!	278
Other Works by Emma V. Leech	280
Audio Books!	284
The Rogue	286
Dying for a Duke	288
The Key to Erebus	290
The Dark Prince	292
Acknowledgements	294

Members of the Peculiar Ladies' Book Club

Prunella Adolphus, Duchess of Bedwin – first peculiar lady and secretly Miss Terry, author of *The Dark History of a Damned Duke*.

Mrs Alice Hunt (née Dowding)–Not as shy as she once was. Recently married to Matilda's brother, the notorious Nathanial Hunt, owner of *Hunter's*, the exclusive gambling club.

Lady Aashini Cavendish (Lucia de Feria) – a beauty. A foreigner. Recently happily, and scandalously, married to Silas Anson, Viscount Cavendish.

Mrs Kitty Baxter (née Connolly) – quiet and watchful, until she isn't. Recently eloped to marry childhood sweetheart, Mr Luke Baxter.

Lady Harriet Cadogan (née Stanhope) Countess of St Clair – serious, studious, intelligent. Prim. Wearer of spectacles. Finally married to the Earl of St Clair.

Bonnie Cadogan – (née Campbell) still too outspoken and forever in a scrape alongside her husband, Jerome Cadogan.

Ruth Anderson– (née Stone) heiress and daughter of a wealthy merchant living peacefully in Scotland after having tamed a wild Highlander.

Minerva Butler - Prue's cousin. Not so vain or vacuous as she appears. Dreams of love.

Jemima Fernside – pretty and penniless.

Lady Helena Adolphus – vivacious, managing, unexpected.

Matilda Hunt – blonde and lovely and ruined in a scandal that was none of her making.

Chapter 1

I promised myself I would not write again, but it seems I have no self-control where you are concerned. Why did you not reply to my last letter? Do you have any idea how dull it is, always waiting for a reply that never comes?

I have been to balls and dinners and rout parties and made endless social calls and I am bored to tears. I wore the most glorious yellow gown the other night and everyone told me I looked very lovely, and I didn't care a bit for you were not there. Their compliments mean nothing to me. I would rather hear you reprimand my wickedness for kissing you than endure another poem dedicated to my eyes. Won't you at least reply and tell me what a wretched nuisance I am?

—**Excerpt of a letter from Miss Minerva Butler to Mr Inigo de Beauvoir.**

20th December 1814. Church Street, Isleworth, London.

Inigo stared at the letter in his hand and reminded himself of the promise he'd made.

He would not reply.

His heart gave an uneven thump, and he cursed Miss Minerva Butler. Wishing he'd never laid eyes on the provoking creature was all well and good, but it didn't solve the problem, and she *was* a problem.

The threat she'd written, with her pretty, extravagant handwriting, in the letter before this one had made his blood run cold.

> *I confess I have sighed most despondently over your assurances that you find nothing romantic in the invitation, but of course a man like yourself has more important things to think about than stolen kisses. I did steal that one after all, did I not? I cannot pretend otherwise. I am a thief and have fallen so far into my life of crime that I cannot be redeemed. So, you had best be on your guard and prepared to keep your assets under lock and key. There will be a villainess at large in Soho Square, and she intends to make a greater theft.*
>
> *Your heart.*

He ought never to have invited her to attend one of his lectures; had only done so because she'd threatened to turn up uninvited and cause heaven alone knew what kind of scene. His palms grew damp just thinking about it. He was thirty years old, a man of science, respected and admired for his work, he ought not be thrown into disarray by a pretty little blonde chit of a girl. He knew this. That he knew this, and yet it didn't change a thing, only made him furious.

If only Harriet Stanhope—now the Countess St Clair—hadn't fallen victim to lust and married another man, he might have been safe from such attacks. They would have had a perfectly satisfactory marriage based on mutual admiration of each other's intelligence and capabilities. Of course, Harriet would have it that she'd fallen in love. Inigo snorted in disgust. How such an intelligent woman could fall for that old chestnut was beyond him. Love was nothing but a series of chemical reactions and a deep-seated biological need to procreate, to keep humanity ticking along. The desire to mate was as instinctual to men and women as it was to dogs, birds, insects and any other variety of creature. To ascribe anything more meaningful to it was as ridiculous as suggesting chickens felt any romantic attachment to the cockerel.

Inigo would admit that human beings were far more complex creatures who felt the need to explain every aspect of their lives, whether inventing gods who demanded sacrifices, or using the rational approach to which Inigo was a slave. He understood the desire for explanation, could totally accept the need to know why things worked, but such understanding required cold, clear thinking and judgement, not emotion. Unfortunately, his ability to remain coldly judgemental and objective seemed to wither and die whenever the blasted young woman got anywhere near him.

No, it was worse than that. She didn't even need to be near him. These damn letters were enough, filled with flirtation and admiration and an obvious desire to tease him and drive him out of his bloody mind. She ought to be locked up, for her own safety if not his sanity. The foolish creature was playing with fire. He was a man, after all, flesh and blood and just as likely to fall victim to lust. If he forgot the rules of society, rules he did not even believe in, he could simply act on his desires and take everything she was offering. She was asking to be ruined and, no matter how many times he warned her off, she would not heed him. The only thing that held him in check was her idiotic belief that there *were* romantic feelings involved. It would be wicked to take advantage of a girl so obviously deluded as to the realities of life. If she kept on, however, he would have to open her eyes to the truth.

He had to face it, so it only seemed fair. Why should he be the only one suffering such torment? He couldn't sleep, as thoughts of her invaded his dreams. He could not concentrate on his work, as the memory of the kiss she'd stolen lingered. His mind, so adept at focusing on details, now obsessed over the softness of her lips, the impossible blue of her eyes, and the scent of jasmine and vanilla that intoxicated him more potently than any liquor.

Oh, God. He was doomed.

With a muttered curse, he crumpled the letter in his hand and walked to the fire, and then cursed longer and with increasing profanity as he realised he could not make himself burn it. Instead, he gritted his teeth and snatched up a clean sheet of paper. Inigo dipped his pen into the ink well and wrote with almost feverish determination, despite his promise to himself not to reply. She'd get a reply. She'd also get the shock of her life when he spelled things out for her. No doubt she'd swoon or cry, or have a fit of the vapours or whatever these society women were prone to. Either way, she'd realise how wrong she'd been about him and leave him be. After the first paragraph, his pen hovered over the page, something disturbingly like regret making his chest feel odd and empty.

No.

He must be rid of her. She was affecting his work, and that was intolerable. With renewed determination, he finished the letter and read it through, a bitter smile curving his lips. Let her find the romance in that if she could.

Miss Butler,

> *You have the invitation you sought. If you have any care for your reputation or your future happiness, I beg you will leave it at that. I am certain that your friend, the Countess St Clair, is quite capable of guiding you if you have any further need of reading material or wish to continue your studies.*
>
> *In short, Miss Butler, leave me be. If you do not, you may find that things take a turn you are not prepared for. My heart is in no danger, I assure you. I do not believe in love. I do not believe in marriage or even monogamy. I believe men and women are equal and ought to take their pleasure as and when they desire, without the need to tie each other together for life. As a man I can afford*

such opinions. You cannot. Please do not continue to deceive yourself and persist with these romantic delusions. Whatever you believe, believe this: I am perfectly willing to take my own pleasure and move on without a backward glance or a shred of guilt.

I can only hope you keep this in mind.

De Beauvoir.

***

Minerva stared down at the letter her mouth curved into a little 'o' of shock. Well, she'd certainly rattled his cage this time. It was hardly surprising. She'd been deliberately provoking the poor man for some weeks now. If she was honest, she'd been surprised he'd lasted this long. The words of the letter were certainly blunt and to the point, yet they seemed to reveal a great deal he might not have meant to let her know. Firstly, she was delighted and intrigued by his assertion that men and women were equal. Although Minerva had no great opinion of her own intelligence, she had surprised herself of late by discovering she was not the ninny she'd believed herself to be, and she knew some brilliant women. Those women were far more intelligent and capable than most men she knew. It seemed reasonable to suppose that there were clever and stupid women and clever and stupid men too. It was just that the men had all the power and kept things so that even the most intelligent of women had little or no control over their lives. To discover a man who believed that to be wrong was… fascinating.

She reread the letter again, pausing over the bit where he said he didn't believe in love, marriage, or monogamy. Well. That was…. Actually that was rather tragic. Life was hard enough, but to go through it with no hope of falling in love and finding someone to love you in return… her heart filled with compassion for him. How lonely he must be, and how could such a clever man be so utterly stupid? Minerva shook her head in wonder. Although she had elevated herself above ninny and peahen, she knew Mr de Beauvoir's mind to be far superior. Some said he was the most brilliant mind of their generation. So, how could he be so blind, so wilfully ignorant of everything about him?

Minerva paused as a movement outside the window caught her eye, and she saw her cousin Prue and her husband walking in the garden. The swell of Prue's stomach was just visible now, and Minerva could not keep the smile from her lips as Robert laid his hand there, such a look in his eyes that Minerva felt her throat tighten. He leaned in to kiss his wife and Minerva turned away, not wanting to play the voyeur but unable to deny the ache in her heart. How she wanted that. She wanted to be loved with such devotion, and to love with a passion. More than anything, she wanted to teach Mr de Beauvoir that he might be a brilliant natural philosopher, but that there was a thing or two he might learn from her, if only he'd listen. His letter suggested that to try such a thing was to invite disaster but, just as his science might obsess him, she had become obsessed with the idea that he needed someone. Each time she saw him he looked more of a fright. He'd lost weight, that much was obvious. He was a big man, but his clothes hung off him, and often buttons hung off the clothes by a thread. The last time she'd seen him, he appeared to have slept in them. His hair was too long, and he was pale and drawn with dark circles under his eyes. She shivered as she remembered his eyes. Green and grey and so very compelling, as though there were a spark glittering somewhere inside him, looking for something to ignite. It was obvious he'd not bothered to replace the housekeeper he'd frightened off, the poor woman terrified by one of his experiments. Well, Minerva should remind him that needed doing, otherwise he'd starve, or make himself ill.

With a sigh, she folded the letter and hid it with his other correspondence in the false bottom of her jewellery box. If her mother ever found out she'd been corresponding with an unmarried man, she'd have an apoplexy. If she ever caught sight of that last letter, she'd likely turn up her toes on the spot with the horror of it. Dear Mama was still of the opinion that Minerva could catch herself a title, if only she put her mind to it. Minerva hadn't the heart to tell the woman that she'd decided she didn't want a title, so she certainly wasn't about to admit to an infatuation with an impoverished natural philosopher. Poor Mama would be so disappointed.

Speaking of which, Minerva had to go home. Darling Prue was such a dear and invited her to stay often, knowing Minerva needed a respite from her mother's matchmaking and gossiping from time to time or she'd go mad. So she'd stayed for a few days, but now her things had been packed and she was ready to return home. She sighed. Still, she was taking tea with Matilda this afternoon. That, at least, was something to look forward to.

***

"Minerva, darling, how lovely to see you, and what a dashing outfit. I declare you look more enchanting every time I see you."

Minerva laughed and did a little twirl for Matilda. "Thank you, Tilda. Coming from you, I take that as the greatest compliment, for we are all copying you unashamedly, as I'm sure you know."

"Flattery will get you nowhere, darling," Matilda said, taking Minerva's arm once she'd dispensed with her hat and coat. "Actually, that's a lie. Don't stop."

Minerva grinned at her. "Is Jemima still staying with you?"

For a moment Matilda's smile faltered. "She is," she said, her blonde brows drawing together. "But she's not here. It seems she's been left a generous bequest by her aunt and she's forever off doing things. I believe she's gone to the country for a few days to find a place to live."

"By herself?" Minerva asked, a little shocked, now understanding why Matilda looked troubled.

"Not exactly. She's employed a companion, and I believe she will have a maidservant."

"Oh, well, that's all right, then." Minerva let out a breath. Though she thought Mr de Beauvoir's assertion that men and women were equal fascinating, and agreed wholeheartedly, he was also correct that there was one rule for men, and another for women. A woman living by herself would be open to all manner of speculation and gossip, none of it pleasant.

"Yes," Matilda said, nodding, though there was still a glimmer of anxiety in her eyes. "Yes, that's all right, then. Now, I have the most decadent selection of cream cakes for you, and I hope that you will be an absolute glutton, so that I may join you. Don't let me down."

"You can rely on me," Minerva said staunchly, following her friend into the parlour.

Once a staggering amount of cream cakes had been disposed of, and three cups of tea apiece, Minerva steered the conversation around to the point of her visit, for Inigo's letter hadn't been the only one she'd received of late.

"I'm so sorry I couldn't come sooner," she said, setting down her teacup. "I've been staying with Prue and Robert, but in your letter, you said you urgently needed a confidante and that you'd done... you'd done something—"

"Remarkably stupid," Matilda supplied for her with a wry smile. "Yes. I remember."

"Oh, dear." Minerva twisted her fingers together, having a fair idea of what, or rather who, her friend had been stupid with. "Montagu?"

Matilda's blush was startling and vivid, but she held Minerva's gaze and gave a taut nod.

"Oh, dear," Minerva said again, knowing that was not the least bit helpful. She took a breath and straightened her spine, keeping her tone brisk. "Well, it appears whatever happened, no one knows about it, so there's no harm done."

Matilda groaned and put her head in her hands.

"Oh my, did... did someone see...?"

"No." Matilda shook her head and peered at Minerva through her fingers. "No one saw, but I cannot agree that no harm was done."

Minerva bristled with fury. "Did he…? Oh, my word, Matilda, did that terrible man—?"

"No!" Matilda exclaimed, going a deeper shade of scarlet, but shaking her head with vigour. "No, he did nothing wrong. Well, he steered me into a room where we could be alone, which he ought never to have done, but we were about to leave—at my request—when someone came in and we had no choice but to hide ourselves."

"Oh, I see."

"No," Matilda replied, wretched now. "You don't see. The circumstances were somewhat *fraught,* and our hiding place was tiny. We were forced into very close proximity and… and…."

"Oh, and he took advantage of that fact I suppose?"

Minerva's eyebrows went up as Matilda shook her head once more. "No, not exactly," she said, clearly mortified. "Well perhaps a little but… but when I told him stop, he did. No… it… it was me."

"Matilda!" Minerva exclaimed, though more with delight than shock. "What did you do? What happened?"

With burning cheeks and a deal of stammering, Matilda outlined what had happened with Montagu. By the time she was finished, the poor woman looked ready weep with shame.

"Oh, Matilda." Minerva got up and went to sit beside her, taking her hands. "Montagu is a very handsome man, there's no denying it, and he's been pursuing you for months now. It's hardly surprising you should have desired him, you're only human."

"Yes, but he isn't," Matilda objected, swiping away a tear. "He's… he's cold and manipulative and I must be the greatest fool alive to want such a man. It's like falling in love with a serpent."

Minerva sighed and leaned into her. "If you're a fool, I'm no better. I wrote to Mr de Beauvoir again, and he replied this morning. It… It was rather to the point."

Discovering it was her turn to blush, Minerva gave Matilda a brief summary of the letter.

"What is wrong with us?" Matilda demanded, throwing up her hands. "Why can't we fall in love with nice, ordinary men?"

Minerva shrugged. "Where's the fun in that?"

Matilda gave a bark of laughter, though it sounded a tad hysterical.

"What will you do about Montagu?"

"I don't know. Try to avoid him?" Matilda replied, though she sounded half-hearted about the idea. "What about you? You will be careful, Min, dear? It sounds as if he's only too willing to seduce you and cast you aside if you pursue him."

Minerva nodded. "I know, that's why I have to be the one in charge of the seducing."

"What?" Matilda exclaimed, horrified.

"Oh, not like that," Minerva said, laughing a little. "Not exactly like that, anyway. No, I will seduce him into falling in love."

Chapter 2

Tonight I am to speak at Joseph Banks' conversazioni. It is just another lecture, the same as any other. I am not the least bit troubled by it and will not even notice one extra female among those assembled. It will be over, and we will be done.

—Excerpt of an entry by Mr Inigo de Beauvoir to his journal.

22nd December 1814. Joseph Banks conversazioni, Soho Square, London.

"Thank heavens for that."

Minerva turned at the sound of Helena's voice, feeling as though she was a sleepwalker woken in a strange place as the sound of chatter rose around her and people got to their feet. She gave Helena a sympathetic smile.

"You didn't enjoy it?"

Helena returned a quizzical expression. "And you did? Good Lord, he may as well have been speaking Russian for all I got from it. When he started talking about diamonds, my hopes rose, but it went swiftly downhill. How could he say diamonds are the same as a piece of charcoal? Surely that's heresy, and when he spoke of burning a diamond… My dear, I almost swooned."

Minerva laughed and shook her head. "The bit about diamonds was fascinating, if rather depressing. Does it take the romance away from them, do you think, knowing what they are made of?"

"I should say it does," Helena grumbled, regarding the diamond bracelet she wore and wrinkling her nose. She turned her wrist back and forth, and gave a sigh as the stones sparkled like tiny rainbows. "A fellow like that might just give you a sack of coal and have done with it."

Minerva giggled as she imagined the look on Helena's face if any of her beaus tried such a thing, and Helena's eyes flashed with amusement.

"I don't understand it, you know," she said, lowering her voice. "The allure this fellow holds for you."

"I'm not sure I do either," Minerva admitted. "I just… I love to hear him talk, to know all that knowledge is stored inside him. How amazing to understand such things, to prove the way things work or what they are made of." She shook her head in wonder. "I think he's fascinating."

Helena rolled her eyes, exasperated.

"Well, you have your Mr Knight," Minerva objected, indignant on de Beauvoir's account. "I don't understand the attraction to him, either. He looks frightfully fearsome and bad-tempered."

"*Your* Mr de Beauvoir isn't exactly a *hail-fellow-well-met*," Helena retorted. "I could feel his eyes burning into us every time he looked our way, which was far too often. I was only glad you were the focus of his attention and not me. He's terribly intense."

"I know." Minerva gave a wistful sigh and Helena threw up her hands. "You know, I understood a fair bit of his lecture." Minerva added, a tad defensively.

"Good heavens!" Helena pressed her gloved fingers to her breast and adopted a look of scandalised horror. "Min, darling, you're surely not… an *intellectual*?"

Trying and failing to subdue a snort of laughter, Minerva blushed and got to her feet as the elderly gentleman beside her sent a reproving glance her way.

"Come along," she urged, taking Helena's hand and guiding her away from the chairs, and into the throngs of people now clustering around de Beauvoir. She looked at them all with dismay. "I'll never get to speak to him at this rate."

Helena drew her away. "It's never a good idea to look too keen. Come and eat. Look, there are some delicious little treats here. Oh, and champagne," she added, clapping her hands with delight. "It was almost worth coming."

Minerva sighed but allowed her friend to steer her towards the refreshments table. Helena seemed delighted by the food and the champagne, though Minerva was too nervous to eat a bite. While the little knot of people around Mr de Beauvoir thinned a little, it didn't dissipate entirely, and Minerva wondered if she would be able to speak with him at all. She sighed, dejected and unequal to elbowing her way through an intimidating wall of intellectual and scientifically minded men.

Helena had seen someone she knew and wandered off to greet them, so Minerva turned back to the refreshments table, wondering if perhaps she should eat something. Despite having dressed more soberly than usual, in a gown of deep plum velvet, and despite there being several women present, she felt rather out of place. As least she could look less like a misplaced item if she was busy with the food. She lifted a small pastry and put it on a plate, more for something do to than with any desire to eat it. With a resigned expression she picked it up and was about to bite into it when a shadow fell over her.

Minerva turned and looked up, and her breath caught.

Those unusual grey-green eyes stared down at her, enigmatic and every bit as intense as Helena had stated, and Minerva could do nothing but stare back. It was irritating to realise all the clever little things she'd thought of saying on seeing him again had vanished from her mind, and she could do nothing, say nothing, only gaze back at him. In her defence, he seemed to be equally at a loss, and the moment stretched on between them.

Minerva felt colour rise to her cheeks and cursed herself, fighting for something—*anything*—to say.

"You should eat," she said, inwardly rolling her eyes, but at least it was better than silence. "Here, let me prepare you a plate."

Relieved to have something to do for a moment while she took herself in hand, she set about arranging a tempting variety of bite-sized morsels on a plate before turning back to him.

"Here," she said, smiling as his dark brows drew together a little and he stared her offering as if it was a platter of beetles. "It's food. You eat it. I know a brilliant man like you must have little time for such inconsequential bodily needs, but you must look after yourself. I think you've lost weight again."

The frown became a scowl. "I do not need treating like a child."

Minerva raised her eyebrows. "No, but at the very least you need a housekeeper to feed you and sew your buttons on. Having your clothes pressed properly would be a good idea, too. Did you sleep in that coat? It looks like you may have."

He stiffened and Minerva sighed. "Oh, dear. I beg your pardon. We've gotten off on the wrong foot. I so hoped we wouldn't. Only, do please eat something. I can't bear the thought of you working all hours on an empty stomach."

Minerva received the kind of look he likely reserved for puzzling residues left in the bottom of a boiling tube after one of his experiments, but then he gave a huff, and took the plate. She watched, pleased, as he devoured it in short order. He even appeared surprised to discover it had all gone. Beaming at him, she took the plate and refilled it before handing it back to him.

"When was the last time you had a proper meal?"

He huffed, evidently impatient, and she had to wait until he'd finished chewing to hear the answer. "I eat."

"Yes," she said, deadpan. "About as much as you sleep, I imagine."

"And do you spend a deal of time imagining me sleeping, Miss Butler?"

There was challenge in his eyes and she held his gaze, though with difficulty, determined not to be frightened off.

"Not just sleeping."

To her astonishment, it was his cheeks that pinked in response to her words, his eyes suddenly dark.

"Did you not receive my last letter?" he demanded, shaking off whatever had sent colour to his face and returning to the belligerent scowl. "Do you still not understand what you are doing?"

Minerva nodded. "I received it, and yes, I think I understand. I risk ruin, and you risk falling in love. It seems a fair wager."

His expression of astonished outrage was so fierce that she almost laughed.

"I risk nothing, you little fool," he muttered, glaring at her.

He was angry at her for putting herself at risk. She understood that and appreciated it, so she smiled at him.

"Then you have nothing to lose by accepting my wager. Or perhaps I should appeal to the natural philosopher in you and in fact suggest an experiment?" Minerva tilted her head, interested to see how he took this.

"An experiment?" he repeated, a glimmer of interest in his eyes. "What do you mean? What kind of experiment?"

"To prove the existence of love."

He made a sound of exasperation. "To prove the absurdity of the notion, perhaps."

"Fine," Minerva said, nodding her approval. "Fine, prove it doesn't exist if that suits you better. I have every intention of proving otherwise. You are doomed to failure."

He stared at her and she warmed under his scrutiny, remembering how she'd wondered what it would feel like to be the focus of his undivided attention. Marvellous, she decided. She could not read his expression with any certainty, though there was curiosity there.

"You will not trap me into marriage, Miss Butler."

She gave a little laugh. "I should not want to, Mr de Beauvoir. Either you want to marry me because you love me, and to be without me would cause you pain, or I should not wish to be your wife. I have no desire to trap an unwilling husband."

He let out a breath, looking every bit as exasperated with her as Helena had done earlier. "Miss Butler, what you are suggesting—"

"Is an experiment," she said, before he could make it sound tawdry.

"Is an affair," he amended, his expression hard.

Her heart gave an uncertain little kick in her chest, making unease roll through her. He was right of course, and she knew what she was risking. "No," she said, carefully. "I am suggesting a series of…tests. We shall spend some time together, getting to know each other, and… and I will allow you one kiss after every meeting. Then we will gauge how you feel about me."

She thought that sounded reasonable—reasonably mad, possibly—but would not give him the idea she was about to hand over her maidenhead, for she wasn't. She was prepared to take risks, but not be a complete fool.

He'd grown very still, and she could hear her heart beating in her ears.

"You're serious?" He looked as if he doubted her sanity, let alone her sincerity.

"Quite serious."

"Minerva, darling, do introduce me to your friend."

Minerva jolted in surprise as Helena appeared, giving Me de Beauvoir a cool assessing glance. She gathered herself as best she could, hoping her friend had not overheard the conversation. "Mr de Beauvoir, may I present Lady Helena Adolphus."

De Beauvoir gave a stiff bow. "Lady Helena. I believe I have corresponded with your brother."

Helena nodded. "Bedwin has an interest in the sciences. In fact, he asked me to invite you to dine with us if I had the opportunity to speak with you. Something about elements," she added with a dismissive wave of her hand. "I believe your work interests him."

"I should be honoured," he replied, looking a little surprised.

There was a stilted silence and Minerva pinched Helena's arm, willing her to leave them alone.

"Well, we ought to be on our way, Minerva," Helena said, ignoring her. "It's getting late."

Minerva glared and Helena's lips twitched.

"Good evening, Mr de Beauvoir. I will send an invitation to dine with us after Christmas."

"Lady Helena, Miss Butler. Good evening to you," de Beauvoir said politely, before taking his leave and walking away.

"Helena!" Minerva stared at her in outrage once they were alone. "Why did you do that? I was actually getting somewhere."

"That much was obvious," Helena retorted, her expression grim as she escorted Minerva to the foyer to retrieve their pelisses. "And not only to me. For heaven's sake, Min, have a care. Whatever were you talking about? He was looking at you like you were one of Gunter's ices on a hot day."

Minerva flushed, taken aback by both Helena's words and the subsequent images they produced.

"N-Never you mind," she replied, putting her nose in the air.

"Well, I do mind," Helena retorted. "And if you want an invitation to dine the same night as him, you'd best tell me everything."

"Oh, Helena!" Minerva squealed and grabbed hold of her hand. "Truly?"

"Yes, truly," she said, tutting. "Though I'm not at all certain I'm doing you any favours. You will be careful, won't you, Min?"

Minerva saw the anxiety in her eyes and nodded, patting her hand. "I promise. I am in no rush to be ruined and shall take every precaution, though… I may need some help."

Helena snorted. "Oh, I just knew that was coming. Well, I suppose I'd better get Robert to invite you to stay again, though if you tell Prue I had a hand in any of this I shall never speak to you again. She's quite terrifying when she's in a temper."

"I swear I won't, and I promise to help you with your Mr Knight," Minerva agreed at once.

They had to hold their tongues whilst they donned their pelisses and made their goodbyes, but once safely in the carriage they were free to talk again.

"Well, as you and your mama are with us for Christmas, it will be easy enough to ask for you to stay on. Oh, does that mean your mother will want to stay too?" Helena said, aghast at the idea. "That would put a wrinkle in the plans."

Minerva shook her head, delighted. "No, she's going back to Bath in the new year. In fact, she wanted to drag me with her, and she knows I don't want to go. This will be perfect."

"Hmmm," Helena replied doubtfully. "That remains to be seen. So then, Miss Butler, out with it. What nefarious plan have you cooked up? I'm all ears."

"Ah," Minerva said, biting her lip with anxiety, and wondered just how to make the planned experiments sound anything but mad and scandalous.

Chapter 3

I was sorry that we could not complete our fascinating conversation last night, however, I'm sure it will thrill you to know that I am staying with Lady Helena for Christmas and for some time into the new year. So I shall be present at the dinner you have been invited to. Perhaps we may speak privately then?

I do hope that you enjoy a Merry Christmas, Mr de Beauvoir, though I cannot help but worry that you won't pay the holiday any mind. Do at least try to eat something, for my sake. I worry for your health.

I hope you like the little gift. I embroidered it myself.

—Excerpt of a letter from Miss Minerva Butler to Mr Inigo de Beauvoir.

25th December 1814. Church Street, Isleworth, London.

Inigo flung his papers aside with a curse of frustration.

"Concentrate, damn you!" he exploded, smacking his head with the palm of his hand as if he could beat his brain into doing as he wished. The bloody thing seemed to resist any other method, so it was worth a try. He groaned and let his head fall to the bench, banging his forehead against the wood several times to see if that helped. "Stop thinking of her. Stop it, stop it, stop it."

His brain wasn't listening. His brain was an idiot.

He sat there for a long moment, his head pressed to the bench, staring at the blur of dark wood. A sigh escaped him, and his stomach growled.

"Ugh."

He'd best eat something. No, *not* because Miss Minerva Butler had told him to. Not because she worried about his health and got that little anxious expression that made her blonde brows furrow together and made her look like a troubled kitten.

"Argh!"

Thoroughly nauseated with himself, Inigo stalked to the pantry and rifled through the shelves and cupboards, only to discover there was nothing to be had. Damn. Perhaps he ought to think about hiring another housekeeper. Only they were so bloody bothersome. They fussed and interfered, wanting to tidy his lab and his study and disturbing his papers, shrieking about unexpected noises and foul smells, and complaining if he left the food they made untouched. No, he was better off without one, especially if Miss Butler was intent on ruining herself. The last thing he needed was some housekeeper sticking her nose in and gossiping about them.

Not that Miss Butler would go through with it, he assured himself. She would come to her senses eventually. No gently bred young lady was that lost to propriety to suggest… to even consider…

Hunger of another kind gnawed at him.

She would let him kiss her.

She would come here, alone, and spend time with him, and she would let him put his hands on her and….

"Stop it."

The words rang out in the silence of his home. He would not do this. She was a foolish young woman, dreaming of romance where there was nothing but sex and scandal. Whilst he did not believe in the notion of sin, society at large did not agree. He might believe it to be her right to share her body when and with whom she pleased because it pleased her, but that did not mean that she would be any less ruined for it.

It didn't make any difference if she presented it as an experiment. If anyone discovered them, that would not save her from salacious gossip and condemnation. He imagined submitting a paper on the subject to the Royal Society Journal and gave a snort of laughter.

She would let him kiss her.

No matter how hard he tried to keep the images at bay, he remembered the day at Holbrooke House, when she had kissed him. He had never been so shocked in his life. It had angered him, made him furious. That this beautiful society miss should believe he could be so easily wrapped around her thumb, that she could crook her little finger and he would fall to his knees in gratitude for her condescension in noticing one so lowly....

He'd simmered over that for weeks.

Only, he'd realised that hadn't been her intention at all. It was worse than that. She didn't just want him to love her, she wanted to love him in return. It wouldn't be love, of course, it would be obsession. Inigo was familiar with obsession. It was what gave him the focus to work for hours and days and weeks with barely a moment spared to eat or sleep. It was what had taken him from impoverished orphan to a man of science, respected and sought out for his opinion. The suspicion that Miss Butler could inspire an obsession, the like of which he'd never before encountered, made him feel hot and anxious. An uneasy voice in his head suggested it had already begun, but he silenced it.

No woman would destroy his life, his plans, his work. She would play her little game and he would find it amusing. He would enjoy the liberties she offered, and he would say goodbye and send her on her way, a little bruised and with her eyes wide open to reality. No foolish young slip of a girl would get their hooks in him and march him down the aisle. He laughed, shaking his head, imagining her expression when she realised that love was an illusion, and then felt an odd, uncomfortable sensation in his chest as he discovered the image did not please him as it ought.

He reached into his waistcoat pocket and withdrew the gift she'd sent him. It was a handkerchief and the strange creature had painstakingly embroidered the border with the symbols for the elements and their compounds. The scent of her lingered on the fabric, vanilla and jasmine, and he lifted it to his nose and inhaled. God, she was intoxicating. If he didn't know better, he'd think she was a blasted witch. He stared at the delicate embroidery. In the corner were his initials, IdB, in dark blue, the colour of her eyes. Inigo traced a finger over the silken threads, wondering how long she'd spent over the tiny stitches, how long she'd spent thinking of him. Hell. With a curse, he stuffed it away again.

"Oh, damn you, you bloody fool. Get back to work," he muttered, before stalking out of the kitchen and doing his best to ignore the hunger gnawing at his belly and the strange, aching sensation in his chest.

***

29th December 1814. Beverwyck, London.

"You're not serious?" Helena stared at the book Minerva had put in her lap with as much enthusiasm as if it had been a dead rat. "You know, when given the opportunity to dine with the man who has captured their interest, most women put on their best gown, spend hours on their hair, and douse themselves with perfume."

"I'm not most women," Minerva retorted, folding her arms.

Helena snorted. "No, you want to waste a perfectly agreeable morning learning…" She peered at the book as if it really were a dead rat. "*Wollaston's Synoptic Scale of Chemical Equivalents*? Really, Minerva!"

"What? It's interesting."

"You should have gone and stayed with Harriet," Helena muttered, putting her own novel aside with a huff. "What's wrong with *Childe Harold*?"

"Nothing," Minerva said with a shrug. "And if Harriet hadn't buried herself at Holbrooke with her handsome husband, I *would* stay with her."

"La! I see, this is merely cupboard love," Helena exclaimed dramatically. "You only want my friendship for my proximity to your strange natural philosopher."

"Well, naturally," Minerva replied with a placid smile.

"Wretch!"

She ducked, laughing, as Helena lanced a cushion at her head.

"You are a despicable person," Helena lamented, staring down at *Wollaston's Synoptic Scale* with resignation.

"Of course I am, and so are you. It's why we get on so well."

Helena stuck her tongue out and the two of them dissolved into laughter.

"Oh, very well then, Min, but you owe me dearly."

Minerva beamed at her and settled down to test her knowledge.

***

Minerva turned this way and that in front of Helena's full length looking glass. She was wearing a new gown, one she'd saved for the occasion. It was a rich blue and the neckline, whilst not scandalous, was deep cut and showed a pleasing swell of bosom. Helena had lent her a sapphire pendant which nestled invitingly at her décolletage and drew the eye. Her hair was arranged on top of her head in a negligent tumble of blonde curls, one of which trailed suggestively over one shoulder.

"Well?" she asked, frowning at her image.

Helena snorted. "The poor man doesn't stand a chance. You look like Athena, goddess of wisdom, minus the owl."

"Oh! Thank you, Helena, what a lovely compliment."

Helena laughed and moved towards her, her own emerald green gown swishing as she moved to take Minerva's hands. "Darling, have you thought this through? He's not even a gentleman. I mean, what do you know about him, really? He doesn't look able to support himself, let alone a wife."

Minerva rolled her eyes, but Helena interrupted her before she could speak.

"Do not give me any nonsense about not caring about money, for we both know that isn't true. You hated being poor, and don't deny it. Your life changed when Prue married my brother and I, for one, do not blame you for enjoying your change in fortunes. Surely you don't wish to return to those days?"

"Of course not!" Minerva retorted, a little irritated. She loved Helena dearly but sometimes her forthright nature could be hard to take. "I have no desire to be poor, but I will marry for love not money. I do not need a fortune or a title to make me happy. Besides which, a brilliant man like Mr de Beauvoir ought to be a good deal wealthier than he is. The trouble is, I don't think he cares a fig about such things, or at least he cannot be bothered to deal with them. He's so absorbed with his work he barely remembers to eat, let alone troubling himself with financial issues. Which is why he needs a woman like me to take him in hand. He is a fellow of the Royal Society, he's already a huge success, he just needs someone to manage such tedious details as financial rewards for his work."

Helena stared at her, clearly taken aback, and Minerva snorted.

"I may be infatuated, Helena, but I am not a complete ninny. I admit it's taken me most of my life to realise this myself, however, so I shall forgive you for overlooking it."

"Well," Helena said. "That's told me."

Minerva laughed and took her arm. "Good, so stop fretting. Matilda has taken the role of a mother hen, I don't need you clucking and ruffling your feathers too, thank you very much."

"Fine," Helena said, giving a blithe wave of her hand. "Go off and dally with de Beauvoir, ruin yourself, see if I care."

Minerva huffed, knowing that Helena was not nearly so brittle as she made out. Although she was every bit as reckless as Minerva, she worried because Minerva was not an heiress and the daughter of a duke, and far more likely to get herself into a fix there was no getting out of.

"I will be discreet, I promise you. I am in no hurry to create a scandal."

"Hmph," said Helena, clearly unconvinced.

"Ah, at last," Robert said, smiling at them when he saw them enter the parlour. "Mr de Beauvoir, you have met my sister, Lady Helena, and I believe you are acquainted with my wife's cousin, Miss Butler."

Mr de Beauvoir's back was to them, and Minerva saw his shoulders stiffen as the duke spoke her name. She watched as he turned and felt a little surge of triumph at the look in his eyes when he saw her. She thought perhaps he drew in a sharp breath, though it was difficult to tell, and he soon had himself in hand, the cool, unreadable mask back in place as he bowed to them, stiff and polite.

"A pleasure as always, Lady Helena, Miss Butler."

She looked him over, pleased to see he'd made quite an effort. His evening blacks were neatly pressed, he'd made a creditable attempt with his cravat, and—wonder of wonders! —he'd had his hair cut. Warmth bloomed inside her. He'd done that for her, she was certain of it. Though he was dining with a duke, which would give most people cause to appear at their best, but... No, she decided, determined to take the credit. It was for her sake.

"Ah, our final guest," Robert said, moving to greet Harriet's brother, Henry Stanhope as he arrived.

"Your grace. Evening all," Henry said, beaming at the assembled company. "I say, it was awfully good of you to invite me. I was facing an evening of whist with my aunt and her cronies. Not an enticing prospect," he added with a shudder.

"You're very welcome. I'm glad we could save you from such a fate," Robert said, grinning and slapping him on the back. "De Beauvoir, this is Henry Stanhope."

"We've met," Mr de Beauvoir said, his tone rather dry as the assembled company all remembered he'd been engaged to Henry's sister Harriet. "How is your sister, Mr Stanhope? I hope she is well?"

"Merry as grig," Henry said with a rueful smile. "Couldn't bear it at Holbrooke a moment longer. Astonishing how in a place that size you're still constantly tripping over the lovebirds. It was quite nauseating. I had to get away." He turned then to greet Lady Helena, before grinning at Minerva. "Hello, Minerva, how are you?"

"All the better for seeing you," Minerva replied, meaning it. Henry was great fun and always seemed in good spirits.

"Let's go through," Prue said, getting to her feet. "I'm famished."

Robert laughed and took her arm, his expression one of affectionate amusement. "You're always famished, love."

Prue snorted. "Blame your son. I shall be the size of a house before too much longer if he has any say in the matter."

"My daughter," Robert corrected, raising her hand to his lips and kissing her knuckles tenderly.

Minerva glanced at de Beauvoir, curious to see his reaction to this open display of affection, which spoke volumes of Robert and Prue's relationship. She caught her breath as she discovered he was not looking at them at all, but at her. Minerva did not turn away but held his gaze and smiled, moving closer.

"I believe I must ask you to escort me into dinner, Mr de Beauvoir," she said, watching his face.

His expression didn't change, but he held out his arm to her. Minerva took her time, hanging back to allow the others to get ahead of them.

"Am I correct that you live on Church Street?" she said, lowering her voice.

His head snapped about and his eyes on her were intent, the muscle under her gloved hand growing taut. He was surprisingly strong, going on what lay beneath her fingers, and she wondered how long it would take her to feed him up, so his clothes fit him as they once had.

"Don't tell me you are still intent on this farcical idea?" he muttered, though there was something about the way he said it suggested he was not as indifferent to the idea as he made out.

"Experiment," she corrected. "And yes, I am. Tomorrow afternoon?"

He halted, staring down at her. "You'd come to my home, alone? You damn fool. You have no idea what kind of man I am, Miss Butler. For all you know I will force my attentions on you, and there would not be a thing you could do to stop me."

Minerva stared up at him, struck by the heat of words. "Would you do that? Would you deliberately hurt me?"

He glowered at her and she could almost see the battle behind his eyes, the desire to shock her and scare her off, but he only let out an exasperated breath.

"No," he admitted, though it was begrudging. "But if anyone discovers you —"

"I know," she said, smoothing a hand over his lapel, soothing him like a restless horse. "I'll be careful, don't worry for me."

"I'm not worried for you," he ground out. "The last thing I need is some sordid scandal attached to my name. I live near to Spring Grove and, if you think I want the President of the Royal Society to become aware of a dalliance with some foolish miss who's no better than she ought to be, you may think again."

Minerva gazed up at him, wondering if perhaps she had misjudged. She waited for his gaze to return to hers, studying him.

"Do you not wish me to come?" she asked softly.

His jaw clenched and once again she sensed the battle going on inside him. He looked away from her, scanning the empty room and then turned back, grasping her chin with his hand and tilting it up. The kiss was brief, barely more than a second, but it scorched her and left her lips tingling, her blood fizzing in her veins like champagne.

He said nothing more, simply walked off with her on his arm, hurrying to catch up with the others before they were missed. Minerva bit her lip and struggled to hold back a little yip of triumph.

Dinner was a lively affair, though Robert and Mr de Beauvoir played little part in the general conversation, as both seemed engrossed in speaking of some experiment Humphry Davy had recently published. Minerva did not attempt to gain his attention again. Robert could be crucial in his future success if he were to have enough interest in his work. Instead she simmered with pleasure as she remembered his kiss, and enjoyed the company of her cousin Prue, and Helena and Henry.

Henry was in fine form this evening and kept them all laughing and entertained with anecdotes, many which were entirely at his expense.

"I believe she said you were incapable of chaperoning a sponge cake," Minerva said, recalling something Harriet had repeated more than once.

"Oh," Henry exclaimed, flattening his hand over his heart as though he'd been pierced by an arrow. "You wound me, Miss Butler. How can someone so lovely be so heartless as to take anything my wretched sister says of me seriously?"

"Ah, but loveliness does not always equal kindness, Mr Stanhope," Helena parried. "She may have the face and form of Athena, but there is a calculating heart beating in her breast, I assure you."

Minerva narrowed her eyes at Helena, whose eyes twinkled mischievously.

"No," Henry said, gallant as ever. "That I cannot believe. She is as lovely as she is kind, and has been led astray by my wicked sibling."

***

Inigo allowed his mind to wander, an easy enough thing while the duke tried to wrap his brain around the explanation he'd just been given about Humphry Davy's experiments with fluoric compounds. Mr Stanhope, Harriet's brother, was beaming at Miss Butler with the fresh faced enthusiasm of a schoolboy, or possibly a puppy. Charming and exuberant, the young man was full of *bonhomie* and obviously taken with her. Inigo experienced a sudden and unwelcome shaft of something unpleasant which he refused to dignify by naming. The boy irritated him, that was all, a fribble with nothing between his ears but fluff. As if Miss Butler would be taken with such a creature. Yet she was laughing merrily, her beautiful eyes glittering, her cheeks flushed with pleasure, and he could not drag his unwilling gaze away from her. He remembered the moments alone with her in the parlour, more specifically the moment he'd pressed his mouth to hers. When he'd withdrawn, her skin had been flushed like that, her mouth rosy and soft, and her eyes, those impossibly blue eyes had grown darker.

Prussian blue. Just as dangerous as that tantalising colour he suspected. There was cyanide in Prussian blue, just as there was something destructive in the temptation she offered him. Though he assured himself it was she alone who took the risk, there was a darker voice that whispered that was a lie, and one he'd do well not to ignore.

The sensation of someone's eyes upon him made him look away from her to discover Lady Helena watching him, her expression impassive. Did she know, he wondered? If she did, and had not done all in her power to stop her friend from the dangerous path she was contemplating, she was doing Miss Butler no kindness.

After dinner, and rather to Inigo's surprise, the men were not left alone with their port, but joined the ladies in the parlour where he continued his conversation with the duke and endeavoured to ignore Miss Butler.

"Robert."

Everyone turned as the Duchess of Bedwin called her husband. She looked pale and rather unwell.

"Prue, darling, what is it?"

"I'm a little fatigued is all," she assured them all with a smile, which appeared rather forced. "I believe I shall retire for the evening, but please carry on in my absence."

Amid various well wishes the duchess left the room, and Inigo and Henry stood as the duke insisted on escorting his wife upstairs. Lady Helena at once took over the role of hostess and enlisted Henry's help in selecting some music to play on the pianoforte, leaving Inigo alone with Miss Butler.

"Shall we say midday?" She gave him an enquiring glance, carrying on that same maddening conversation as if there had been no interval. "I'll bring lunch. At least that way I'll know you've eaten something."

Inigo stared at her, perplexed. Why did she care? Why him? With her astonishing beauty and her connection to the duke, not to mention the handsome dowry the man had given her, she could have anyone she wanted. Why was she not angling for a title, or a wealthy husband? The gown she wore this evening likely cost as much as he earned in a month, more for all he could tell, having no idea about ladies' fashion. He knew only that she looked glorious in it, that the colour only highlighted her lovely eyes, and that his gaze kept returning to the blue pendant sapphire that nestled between her breasts. Desire surged in his blood as he imagined pressing his mouth to that satin skin, trailing his tongue along that tantalising valley.

Christ.

"What game are you playing, Miss Butler?" he demanded, unnerved to hear the hoarse quality of his voice.

"It's no game, it's—"

"An experiment," he said with a snort. "Yes, I know. Why, though? Why me?"

She gave him an odd look, her head tilted to one side, puzzled. "Why not you?"

"I was born in the slums of St Giles."

He said it in the same way he might say he took sugar in his tea, with no inflection, no emotion, and he waited for her to rear back in horror, for her lip to curl in disgust as she realised what that meant. He'd been born into abject poverty. She paled, her eyes growing wide, but he had not counted on the odd creature she was. Unlike most ladies of her ilk, she did not swoon or move away from him. Miss Butler moved closer.

She got up and sat beside him, laying a hand on his sleeve, such an instinctive gesture of comfort that he froze, not knowing what to make of it.

"You surely cannot think this can do anything but increase my admiration for all you have achieved?" she asked, her voice soft.

He muttered an oath and looked away from her. Thinking perhaps she'd not taken his meaning, he thought he'd best press the point home.

"My parents died when I was two, and I was raised in the Foundling Hospital. I am no gentleman, Miss Butler. You'd do well to remember that. So I'll ask again, why me?"

She gave a little huff of laughter and shook her head. "Oh, I've met plenty of gentlemen who are far less deserving of the title, I assure you, Mr de Beauvoir."

He frowned, unsettled by the wave of anger that her words provoked, that any man might have treated her with disrespect.

She continued, perhaps misinterpreting his frown. "When you are at the fringes of society, clinging on by your fingertips, men seem to believe that desperation overrides pride or good sense. Happily, I was never quite desperate enough to prove them correct."

"Who?" he demanded, his heart thudding with the desire to seek retribution from anyone who had dishonoured her with such lewd suggestions.

She smiled at him, and the effect was so overwhelming to his senses that it was like being hit in the head. There was an odd lurching sensation in his chest, and he felt dazed and stupid. He saw such warmth and admiration in her eyes, gratitude too and it made him unaccountably happy.

"There, I was right. You are more of a gentleman than you realised, Mr de Beauvoir. But, to answer your question, I don't entirely understand why it is you. I only know that, from the moment we met in the bookshop, I had to see you again, and that every time we meet my certainty about you only grows."

"You could marry anyone," he said, still under the spell of that smile, unable to tear his eyes away from that impossible blue.

She laughed, sending a joyous thrill of delight through him that made him want to hear it again, to say something else that would make her laugh.

"You sound like my mother," she said, her tone rueful. "But I'm afraid you are both wrong, and besides which you both refuse to acknowledge the truth. I don't want a duke or an earl, or even a lowly baron. I want *you*."

She whispered those last words, but they seemed to ring in his ears so loudly that he felt dizzy. The desire he'd tried to quash moments earlier returned with force, and he found himself holding onto sanity by the most tenuous thread. It would be so easy to pull her into his arms and kiss her, to put his hands on her, his mouth on her skin. His gaze travelled to the other side of the room, to where Lady Helena was bantering with Mr Stanhope over the choice of music. Inigo took a deep, if somewhat uneven, breath.

"Tomorrow," he said, knowing he was being a fool, that he was inviting trouble into his life and probably condemning this foolish female to a fate she did not understand.

"Tomorrow," she agreed, sounding as breathless as he was.

God help them both.

Chapter 4

Dear Bonnie,

I hope you enjoyed a lovely Christmas and send you all good wishes for the new year. Gordy also sends his best and hopes you are not causing your poor husband too much distress – his words, not mine.

Christmas at Wildsyde was lovely. Though I feel rather guilty admitting it as it is the first I have spent away from my parents, it was without a doubt the happiest I have ever known. We had a superb meal thanks to Mrs MacLeod, who did a marvellous job, and we had music and dancing and a great deal of laughter. I hope you and Mr Cadogan will come and visit us one day soon. Gordy has promised to be on his best behaviour.

—*Excerpt of a letter from Mrs Ruth Anderson to Mrs Bonnie Cadogan.*

30th December 1814. Church Street, Isleworth, London.

Inigo took a deep breath and stared at the sheet of paper with his latest calculations on to no avail. Despite promising himself he would not look, his fingers searched for and found his pocket watch, only for him to discover it was precisely six minutes since he had last looked at it. This was hopeless. He might as well write off the entire day as a disaster. Hardly professional, in light of the work he'd been contracted to do. Paid work. The kind that supported his own by allowing him to pay his bills and eat... when he remembered.

The government had commissioned him to inspect selected pharmacies in the West End of London. Several wealthy clients had been taken ill and the common denominator had proven to be a brand of skin cream. Allegations of the cream being contaminated by arsenic had caused an uproar and, as the victims were important members of society, the government had acted quickly and asked Inigo to investigate. It was a fascinating subject and Inigo had been immersed in his work, until Miss Butler had suggested her experiment and deprived him of sleep, sense, and any possibility of rational thought.

Worse was the ridiculous desire to tidy his home, which was admittedly not at its best since his housekeeper had run away. It was a fine building, in his opinion, and had been a source of great pride to a man who had grown up unable to lay claim to even the clothes on his back. Spread over three storeys, it was a handsome red brick townhouse sporting a dark green painted front door with a fanlight window over the top. It was neither large nor grand but had excellent light, especially in the biggest room at the back, which Inigo had made into his laboratory. He'd done little else except put a bed in the bedroom and oddities of furniture here and there. It was spartan and currently dusty and shabby, too. He had lit the fires, which he didn't always manage, so that was something.

He stared at his papers for a while longer, until the writing blurred before his eyes, and sighed with frustration. Once he'd put them back in a neat pile, he looked about for something else to occupy his mind, and almost jumped out of his skin when there was a knock at the door. All at once his heart was thudding in his chest as anticipation made his breath come fast.

"Pack it in, you bloody half-wit," he muttered to himself, wiping sweaty palms on his clothes as he hurried to open the door.

There she was, bold as brass on his doorstep. He could only stare as the pale afternoon sunlight glinted on her golden hair. The cold weather had made roses bloom in her cheeks and he was suddenly tongue-tied in the face of such astonishing beauty.

"Let me in!" she said in a harsh whisper, as he remembered too late that she ought not be seen here, and he was just staring at her like some lovesick mooncalf.

"Oh!" he exclaimed, and stood back, allowing her to enter and closing the door behind her.

"I'm sorry," she said sheepishly, looking up at him from under her lashes. "I'm afraid I'm a little early, but… but I was so excited to see you."

Inigo blinked at her, too dumbstruck to say anything to that. His tongue seemed to have been nailed down and his brain had tied itself into some manner of Gordian knot. Belatedly, he noticed she was carrying a basket.

"Here, let me take that," he said, sounding gruff and not very pleased to see her, too overwrought to manage much else.

He was rather afraid he might begin spouting poetry or fall at her feet and plead for her to kiss him. To his profound relief, she didn't seem notice his turmoil as she stared about his home with interest.

"It's a lovely house," she said as he led her through the gloomy corridor.

Inigo grunted, fighting not to feel embarrassed for how mean and tattered everything appeared in her presence. As usual, she looked as if she'd stepped out of some society fashion plate. Irritated he told himself he was being idiotic. He'd always been proud of his home. It was a lovely house and the finest thing he'd ever owned. A place of his own had been everything he'd dreamed of as he'd worked all hours, scrimping and saving. His own space, his own laboratory. No one to bother him and interfere. So much for that. The problem was he'd never had time to furnish the place properly, at least nothing past absolute essentials. Ah, well, it wasn't like she was going to come back again. He went through to the kitchen, relieved to discover it was at least warm, and then scowled as he set the basket on the table and noticed his cuffs were frayed. Inigo thrust his hands behind his back, feeling ridiculous, ill at ease and a long way out of his depth. Why had she come? This was absurd.

"I brought lunch," she said, as bright as ever and paying his unwelcoming demeanour no mind at all as she moved to the basket. "There's a lovely chicken and ham pie, and potato salad, bread and cheese and fruit, oh, and cake too, and…." She rummaged about, taking out the items as she spoke, and then withdrew a bottle with a little triumphant grin. "And wine!" She beamed at him. Inigo's stomach growled. Minerva tutted. "Just as I thought. Come and sit down."

She drew out a chair and patted the seat invitingly. Inigo sighed and rolled his eyes but decided he may as well humour her; he was hungry. At least if he ate, he didn't have to talk to her and risk humiliating himself.

"There now, you open the wine and I'll find…." She stared about the kitchen, and her nose wrinkled as she saw a stack of dirty dishes. "Plates," she finished, rallying and moving about. She bustled into the scullery and onto the pantry and back again. "Mr de Beauvoir," she said, shaking her head with impatience. "There's barely enough food in this house to feed a mouse. In fact," she added, crouching down to inspect something on the floor. "I think you are feeding the mice. You need a housekeeper, and a cat. At once."

"What I need is to be left in peace by interfering women," he muttered, folding his arms and looking mutinous.

Miss Butler laughed, peering into a glass and turning it this way and that before deeming it clean enough and placing it on the table. Plates, knives and forks were duly arranged for two.

"Yes, I don't doubt," she said. "But your life and your work would go a deal smoother if your house was properly organised. Just think how nice it would be to find a hot meal waiting for you when you finish work, rather than having to go to the bother of hunting about and finding nothing but stale bread and mouldy cheese."

She gave a delicate shudder of revulsion.

"I manage perfectly well."

At this moment, his stomach made a loud and voluble protest, and Miss Butler snorted. Inigo huffed but couldn't deny that the pie she'd brought looked delicious. She cut a large slice and put it on his plate with a variety of other delectable looking items and set it before him.

"Tuck in," she said cheerfully, before helping herself.

They ate in silence for a while and Inigo felt his clamouring stomach relax. The food was marvellous. As his hunger abated, however, his attention once again became riveted on the young woman beside him, on the delicate slope of her nose and her elegant neck, on the soft, pink lips he'd only had the barest taste of and yet were never far from his thoughts.

She turned to look at him and he hurriedly redirected his gaze to his food.

"I don't know how you can work when you're so famished," she said, cutting him another slice of pie and putting it on his plate. "I'm intolerable when I'm hungry. Bad-tempered and snappy." She shook her head. "I can't abide it."

Inigo made an amused sound and she glanced back at him.

"What?"

He hesitated before replying. "I cannot imagine you in a temper. It must be like watching a kitten having a tantrum," he added, his lips curling upwards.

She gave a disgusted sniff. "Just you wait," she said darkly, putting bread and cheese on a side plate for him. "Thwart me and you'll discover this kitten has claws."

"That doesn't sound so bad," he murmured, staring at her.

Miss Butler blushed, recognising the tone of his voice and Inigo knew he ought to behave but... damn it, she'd come here, knowing full well what she was doing. She'd offered to let him kiss her, hadn't she?

"Finish your lunch," she said, setting the smaller plate at his elbow and putting her chin up. "There's cake and fruit yet."

Inigo did as he was told, eating everything she put in front of him and enjoying the excellent wine, which she'd no doubt pilfered from the duke. She chattered away as he ate, not appearing to need any help from him with the conversation and it was oddly... relaxing.

It was so unusual to have company at all, let alone company like Miss Butler, and it was refreshing and surprisingly easy. There was something domestic and homely about it, the two of them sharing a meal together in the warmth of the kitchen. Despite the bare store cupboards and the distinct possibility of furry invaders, it was cosy and intimate.

Miss Butler beamed at him as he took a second slice of cake, in spite of feeling fit to burst, but she was so pleased every time he accepted her hospitality he found it difficult to deny her. The smiles she gave away with such ease seemed to brighten the room and make everything seem so much sunnier. Inigo groaned inwardly, nauseated by the thought. She was turning him into a regular sapskull. Well, it was time to do something about that.

He watched her as she packed the food away and put it in the pantry, extracting a promise from him that he would eat it. Once everything was tidy, she turned back to him and her smile faltered, colour rising to her cheeks as she noticed the look in his eyes.

Inigo moved his chair, so it was side on to the table, and allowed a smile to curve over his mouth at the rapid rise and fall of her chest.

"Cold feet, Miss Butler?"

"Not at all, Mr de Beauvoir," she said, putting up her chin in what he suspected was to become a familiar gesture. "I am only a… a little nervous. I'm sure that's to be expected."

He snorted at that. "Last chance, Miss Butler. Leave now, while you still have your reputation, *and everything else*, intact."

She stared at him for a long moment and Inigo was aware of his heart in a way he'd never been before she'd entered his life. It was beating so hard it reverberated through him and he wondered if perhaps she could hear it too.

"No."

Thank God. Thank God. Oh God he was in deep trouble.

Inigo watched, aware of his own heartbeat, of the quickening of his breath and the rustle of her skirts as she moved closer to him.

"Here?" she demanded, her voice a little higher pitched than usual.

She sounded breathless, and her cheeks blazed with colour. At least he wasn't the only one in a fever over this ridiculous arrangement.

"Here," he agreed, hardly able to get the word out, staring up at her, daring her to make good on her promise.

He still didn't believe she'd stay. Watching her now, she seemed to be on the verge of bolting, which was likely for the best. She lifted a trembling hand to tuck a stray yellow curl behind her ear, and longing pierced him. It was such an intimate gesture and he imagined seeing her in his bed, with her hair all undone, tucking one heavy coil behind her ear like that.

Oh, please… please….

Yes. She'd run, he was sure of it. She wanted love, he wanted sex, sooner or later she would recognise the difference. He was neither that lucky nor an appealing enough prospect for her to throw herself away on, not when she could have anyone she wanted and marriage in the bargain. A woman like her could crook her little finger and have men come running. He felt indignation burn as he remembered he'd said he'd never do it, never fall at her pretty feet. How the mighty had fallen. He was so desperate to touch her that begging seemed not only likely but inevitable. *Leave,* he prayed, hoping to keep his dignity intact. *Stay,* he begged, aching to put his hands on her. It was only desire though, a normal male response to an attractive female. If she wanted to ruin herself, why should he care? Why should he worry for her reputation? He wanted to kiss her, put his hands on her and do a great deal more she likely hadn't the faintest idea was even possible. He watched, intent as she licked her lips, still hesitating. She'd balk any moment now and run for the door and....

His breath caught as she moved, sitting herself down on his lap in a feminine rustle of expensive fabric. The scent of vanilla and jasmine teased his senses, scattering what remained of his wits.

"There," she said, giving him a defiant look which Inigo was too dazed to appreciate.

She wriggled a little, shifting her plump behind until she was comfortable and sending jolts of desire like electric shocks, singing through him. He bit back a moan, instantly hard and aching as the yearning to do unspeakable things burned through him, as though she'd set a match to gunpowder. *Oh. Good. Lord.*

"How shall we do this?" she asked, making him wonder just how innocent she was. Before he could form a reply she added, "I mean, should we use a scale, like from one to ten?"

"What?" he croaked.

He sounded dazed even to his own ear, though it was hardly surprising. He couldn't think of anything past the fact she was sitting in his lap, that her lush bottom was too close to his arousal and yet a million miles away. He need only shift her a little to be able to press his aching member against her softness and find some measure of relief. Her subtle perfume coiled about him, invading his senses: sweet and tantalising, warm, and entirely female.

"Well, on a scale of one to ten," she began her expression serious. "How much do you love me?"

"I don't love you," he replied at once, wishing his heart would slow down as he was feeling lightheaded.

She sighed and gave a shrug. "Well, it was worth a try. For my own feelings, hmmm, let me see… I shall give you a five."

"A *five*?" he demanded, a little stung.

The blasted woman had been pursuing him for weeks and he only merited a five?

He held his breath as she touched his face, delicate fingers trailing over his cheek and sending shivers racing over his flesh. "Don't be cross. I haven't the least doubt I shall be head over ears in love with you and it will be at ten soon enough, but I can't tell you I love you until I know you better. You might have some dreadful habit that will make me change my mind."

How absurd he was. He didn't want her to love him, yet her words unsettled him and made him anxious. "How very reasonable you are, Miss Butler."

She smiled at him, the corners of her beautiful mouth twitching up into something that looked just a little smug. "You *are* cross."

Inigo huffed with impatience. "I am not. You do not love me, Miss Butler, not even a pitiful five. You don't know me at all."

"Hmmm, I think I do," she murmured, and her voice was like a caress, making longing surge through his blood. It was the hardest thing not to put his hands on her and get this ridiculous nonsense over with. He clutched the sides of the chair with white knuckles just to be sure. "Anyway, moving on, if we use the same method, on a scale of one to ten, how much do you desire me?"

She turned to stare down at him, and it was too much. His eyes dropped to her mouth and he couldn't take any more.

"Ten," he rasped, and pulled her to him, one hand sliding into the warm silk of her hair, urging her head down, and pressing his lips against hers.

There wasn't the least resistance, just a breathy gasp. God, she was sweet, so soft, her lush curves willing and pliant in his arms. Beautiful and eager too, it was a heady combination. Though his body was hard and desperate he found he didn't want to rush. It would be sacrilege, like gulping down a fine wine instead of savouring the flavours. So he took his time, brushing their lips together, teasing at the seam of her mouth with his tongue and experiencing a shock of pure lust as she tentatively met it with her own.

Inigo groaned, pulling her closer still, until her body pressed hard against him. Oh, she felt good, so warm and feminine. *His*. The thought stole through his brain and he pushed it away. Nonsense. That was ridiculous. She belonged to herself. There was no way one person could possess another. It was morally wrong, unnatural, like marriage. It was some throwback to living in caves and dragging your woman about by the hair. Yet as she kissed him, her mouth firming against his, surer as she learned the way of it, he experienced that possessive heat burning inside of him and it *wanted*. It wanted so badly he felt himself unravelling, the edges of his mind coming undone and threatening retribution if he didn't make her his. It wanted to know he was the only one, that she was his alone. The hand he'd settled upon her tiny waist travelled up her side until his thumb was close enough to stroke the underside of her breast. Her breath caught on a gasp at his touch and Inigo deepened the kiss, the hand he'd tangled in her hair angling her head so he could take more, and more and she didn't so much as murmur a protest.

In a daze he realised she'd slid her arms about his neck, and it was his turn to gasp as one hand tugged at his cravat. She cast it aside, and Inigo shivered with pleasure as her slender fingers insinuated themselves under his shirt, her fingers trailing teasing patterns on his skin. He watched as she drew back, eyes dark with desire, her lips swollen and red from his kisses. She was so beautiful, so warm and vibrant and alive, and he wanted to carry her up to his bed and show her just where this was leading.

"Well," she said, sounding rather unsteady. "T-That seems like a good start, but I… I think perhaps we should leave it there."

No. The word was on his lips, but he bit it back. This was madness. It would end in disaster. His body hurt, the ache of unsatisfied desire making him fractious and unreasonable. A sudden rush of anger burned through him as he realised, he'd never be allowed this. Not really. Why had she come here to torment him? She'd been teasing him from the start, believing she'd only need bat her lashes at him and he'd fall to his knees in gratitude at being noticed. Fear slithered under his skin as he wondered just how close to the truth she'd been. Taking his hands from her was like parting opposing magnets, the two forces fighting to remain joined.

He watched in silence as she got to her feet, smoothing her skirts and deftly rearranging her hair. It irritated him, seeing her put back to rights when he'd been swept up in a hurricane and left in bewildering disorder.

"I suppose I ought to go," she said, turning to smile at him and looking a little uncertain.

"Yes, now that you've had what you came for," he sneered, wishing he wasn't so damned angry.

He folded his arms, fighting to appear indifferent. Let her go, what did he care? She'd laugh with her friends about how daring she'd been, no doubt, and he'd never see her again. Well, so much the better.

He glanced at her, despite his best intentions, and found her expression soften.

"I'm sorry," she said, moving back to him. "I don't want to go, I promise. It would be much nicer to stay with you but… but I will be missed, and it probably isn't wise. I shall come back again soon though, if… if I may?"

She reached out a tentative hand and put it to his cheek. Before Inigo could think better of it, could think at all, he'd turned into it like a cat seeking a caress.

If he had any sense, he'd warn her to run while she could and never come back. For this was going in one direction only and he wouldn't be the one to stop it happening. As it was, he closed his eyes, determined to sound unconcerned even though he would count the minutes until she returned to him.

"Do as you please, Miss Butler," he said. "I think we both know where this will end. I've made my opinion of love and marriage clear. I don't believe in either, I have no room in my life for either. If you find pleasure with me, however, I'm more than willing to continue."

She dropped her hand, something in her eyes that looked remarkably like pity.

"Goodbye, Inigo," she whispered, and bent to kiss his cheek.

It was only several seconds later that he realised he hadn't seen her to the door, and that she'd used his Christian name.

Chapter 5

Dear Matilda,

I hope you and the Peculiar Ladies are well. I had a very welcome visit from Bonnie last week with her new husband. What a handful they are! The ton must quake in their satin slippers wondering what the dreadful creatures will get up to next. It was lovely to see them both so happy.

I, for my part, feel I am ready to be put out to grass. It is almost six months now and I am the size of a house. I'm always hungry and nap more than the ginger cat Nate has recently adopted. It delivered six kittens this morning and looks dreadfully smug. Not that I can blame it. Do write and tell me what everyone is up to. Life is rather idyllic, but I still miss you all and long for news of all your adventures.

How has Minerva got on with her dare, and when are you going to take yours?

—Excerpt of a letter from Mrs Alice Hunt to Miss Matilda Hunt.

30th December 1814. Beverwyck, London.

"Well?"

Minerva blushed as she discovered Helena lying in wait for her when she returned to Beverwyck. She was almost bouncing on the spot, the beautiful russet colour dress she wore catching what remained of the grey December light as she moved.

"Hush," Minerva said, glaring at her as she handed over her hat and coat to a footman. Helena grabbed her by the hand and dragged her up the stairs, not stopping until they were in the privacy of her bedroom, where she slammed the door and leapt onto the bed with a most unladylike squeal.

"Tell me," she demanded. "I can't believe you completed your dare and it's not the most scandalous thing you've done today! Tell me everything. Don't leave out a single detail."

Minerva bit her lip and then laughed, covering her mouth with her hand.

"Oh, Helena," she said, staring at her friend and not knowing where on earth to begin. "Oh, my word."

"Good Lord, you did it," Helena said, eyes wide with a mixture of outrage and admiration. "You kissed him."

Minerva nodded, though to say *she kissed him*, hardly seemed an adequate description. It was like saying the sun was *quite warm* when confronted with the fiery ball of flame.

"I did."

"What was it like?"

Minerva let out a shaky breath and went to sit beside her friend on the bed. She collapsed against the pillows with a sigh. "It was...."

"Yes?" Helena demanded impatiently when the answer didn't come.

She laughed, shaking her head. "Well, I can understand how easily a woman can lose her virtue, put it that way. Oh, my, Helena."

Helena lay on her side, her head resting on her hand, regarding Minerva with troubled green eyes. "This is dangerous, Min, you do know that?"

"I do," she said, meeting Helena's gaze. "If I was in any doubt of that fact today has banished any misconceptions, I assure you. I didn't want to leave him. I can't think of anything but seeing him again."

"And him?" Helena asked. "What did he have to say?"

Minerva smiled, remembering his indignation at being given a five out of ten, the sneering way he'd spoken when she'd ended the kiss, and the way he'd closed his eyes and turned into her hand when she'd caressed his cheek. He might not believe in love, but he needed it, more than anyone she'd ever met before.

"He thinks I'm deranged," she said happily.

Helena snorted. "I'm uncertain I can disagree with that. You're risking ruin for a penniless natural philosopher who's not even a gentleman. Your mother will never allow you to marry him, even supposing you can get him to the altar. Assuming that's what you want?" Helena stared at her, narrowing her gaze. "*Is* it what you want?"

Minerva pondered this. "I don't know. Mr de Beauvoir does not believe in love or marriage. He believes men and women are equal and ought to take their pleasure as and when they desire."

"Good heavens," Helena said in alarm, one slender hand pressed to her heart. "He's a radical."

"I don't think so," she said, smiling. "Or at least it's a very personal revolution. I don't believe he has the slightest interest in politics. His work is his passion."

Not his only passion, she thought, smiling as she remembered the feel of his mouth on hers, the urgency of his kisses. He wanted her. He wanted her very badly. She might not know a great deal about men, or passion, but she wasn't a fool. If he wasn't such a gentleman, things might have gone a deal farther than they had.

"I'm not sure I should help you again."

Minerva stiffened at Helena's words, seeing the worry in her friend's eyes. "Oh, Helena, you promised!"

Helena sat up, the rich skirts of her dress rustling as she moved. She was uncharacteristically serious, plucking at the counterpane on the bed with nervous fingers. "I know I did, but I'm frightened, Min. What if you're discovered? What if he ruins you and won't marry you?"

Minerva pondered this. She knew it was a very real risk, but she also knew it didn't change a thing. She wanted to see him again. The desire to be close to him was so much worse now. Before it had been a wistful ache, but now… now she *needed* to see him or she felt she might run mad. She could not consider forgetting it, pretending it had never happened, the thought of never being in his arms again, of never kissing him again, made panic rise in her chest.

"I'm going back to him, Helena. Whether or not you help me," she said, giving an apologetic shrug. "I'm sorry, but I must."

Helena blew out a breath, folding her arms over her chest. "Somehow, I just knew you would say that," she muttered, obviously frustrated.

"Sorry."

Helena laughed, a slightly despairing sound as she shook her head. "I'm wondering if I should steer clear of Mr Knight. If this is the state I will end up in, he's best avoided."

Minerva grinned and flopped back on the pillows. "I'll remind you of that after the first time he kisses you. Ooof!" The world went white and blurry as a Helena hit her with a pillow. "Oh, you'll pay for that," she said, snatching up her own weapon and whacking Helena about the head with it.

Helena's elegant coiffure sagged to one side and Minerva gave a bark of laughter until Helena retaliated. A moment later, they were shrieking and screaming, and the air was full of feathers.

"What the devil is going on in there?"

Helena covered her mouth with her hand as her brother's voice sounded from behind the door.

"Nothing," Helena replied through her fingers, her voice quavering.

The door opened a crack and Robert peered around the corner. "Aren't you a bit old for pillow fights?" he asked, his expression mild.

Helena stuck his tongue out at him. Robert sighed.

"Hoydens," he remarked sadly, shaking his head. "I'm surrounded by hoydens."

"Well, you married one, your grace," Helena shot back.

The duke grinned at them.

"So I did," he said. "Carry on."

They watched as the door closed, and then collapsed on the bed in fits.

***

7th January 1815. Hatchard's Bookshop, Piccadilly, London.

Jemima stared at the rows of books in front of her and wished she could focus on anything but the fact she was too hot, extremely flustered, and more than a little lightheaded. She gave up trying to read the titles and concentrated instead on counting them. Perhaps if she did that, she'd calm herself down, perhaps she'd wake up and discover this was all some terrible dream. Her aunt wasn't dead, she wasn't penniless, she wasn't so very desperate that she'd agreed to meet a man here; a man she didn't know, a man who….

"Miss Fernside?"

Jemima jolted in alarm, staggering backwards in shock and knocking into the arm of an elderly man. The book he held shot up into the air and she watched, helpless, numb with embarrassment, until a gloved hand snatched the book up before it could thud to the floor.

"I beg your pardon, sir," the man before her said smoothly to the disgruntled customer. "Entirely my fault."

The old man huffed but grabbed the book and moved away, glaring a little at Jemima as he went.

"Oh, my goodness. I'm so sorry," Jemima said, cheeks blazing. She'd been overheated to begin with; now she felt ready to set light to her bonnet. "I'm not usually so clumsy."

"Nonsense. I startled you. Quite understandable."

Jemima stared up at the man before her, taken aback by the brisk, imperturbable words. He was tall and broad, with brown hair, though brown did not seem to adequately describe tones that ranged from gold to mahogany. His eyes were darker than the darkest shade and rather intense as they scrutinised her, a slight frown drawing his eyebrows together.

"You are Miss Fernside?"

Jemima nodded.

"Right," he said, nodding in return. He thudded the floor with the cane he held in one hand, though whether from impatience or uncertainty she could not tell. He looked around the book shop, which was mercifully empty, save for the old man whom Jemima had almost upended. Typical, barely one other person in the wretched place to bump into, and she'd found him.

"Have you chosen a book?" he asked, frowning at her empty hands with suspicion.

Jemima shook her head, unable to form words though she knew she must look like a complete ninny. Yet all she could do was stare at him and think *I will go to bed with this man*. The urge to laugh, albeit hysterically, was so strong she could do nothing but clamp her mouth shut. At least he was handsome. Oh, lord, was he handsome. He looked as if he'd been chiselled from granite. She'd known he'd been a soldier, but she had not been prepared for the force of his presence, the obvious military bearing. There was nothing soft about him, every inch of him hard planes and uncompromising angles.

"Are you going to?" he pressed, and there was a touch of impatience there now.

Jemima racked her brain, trying to recall the question. Oh, a book. Was she buying a book? She shook her head again, aware she was on the edge of panic and did her utmost to stop breathing as if she'd been running uphill. He gave her a quizzical look, his eyes narrowed with suspicion.

"I thought Mr Briggs had settled everything with you. If you're having second thoughts—"

"No!" Jemima exclaimed, forcing the word out and shaking her head to make certain he clearly understood her answer. "No, Lord Rothborn. I have n-not changed my mind."

He nodded, still frowning a little.

"Good," he said, as if they'd discovered it would be sunny that afternoon, and not as if she'd just agreed to be his mistress. "That's good," he said again, his commanding voice rather too loud in the quiet book shop.

Jemima swallowed down a bubble of hysterical laughter.

Thump, thump, thump, went the cane on the floor.

Silence.

Jemima willed the man to say something, *anything*, for she appeared to have used up her entire supply of words. Apparently, they were being rationed today.

"Well, I... er... I understand we are to take a walk. It's a pleasant enough afternoon, though chilly. Are you...?"

He looked over her pelisse and half boots with rather too much attention and a deal of misgiving.

"I'm quite warm, thank you," she managed, thinking that was a remarkable understatement as she felt ready to combust with a combination of mortification and unease. "I should be grateful for some fresh air."

"Right. Good."

He held out his arm to her and Jemima hesitated eliciting another frown.

"I arranged the woman for you, the er... *chaperone*?"

Jemima bit back a tart comment and only nodded. "She's waiting over there," she said, gesturing closer to the door.

Her chaperone, Mrs Attwood, was nothing of the sort. A woman of a certain age, she'd been employed by the baron to give Jemima the outward appearance of respectability, though she knew exactly what Jemima was up to. They'd only met for the first time earlier today and that had been the most excruciating moment of Jemima's life... well, since the day she'd agreed to this shameful arrangement with Mr Briggs, the lawyer who worked on the baron's behalf.

Until now.

"Excellent." He gave her a look which seemed to expect action and so she forced herself to reach out and place her hand on his sleeve. The baron walked her to the door, and she realised his gait was a little uneven as they moved through the shop. So the cane was not merely for show.

Mrs Attwood, hurried forwards and curtseyed to the baron before falling in behind them as they headed outside. The air was blessedly cold, and Jemima drew in a deep breath, relishing the chill against her overheated skin.

They walked, in no hurry, towards The Green Park and Jemima wondered if he'd slowed to accommodate her or if whatever injury he'd sustained to his leg bothered him. Mr Briggs had mentioned a bad war. She assumed this was a war wound, then, but she wasn't about to ask on such a brief acquaintance, though she supposed she'd know him intimately enough soon. Pushing that unnerving thought aside, she glanced up at him, at the uncompromising line of his jaw and the square cut of his chin. There was a hard, ruthless edge to him that was extremely daunting.

Oh, Jemima, what have you done?

The day was bright, a vivid blue sky overhead and patches of frost still visible in the places the sun had not yet touched. A chill wind gusted, lifting the curls that framed her face beneath the bonnet and Jemima shivered.

"You're cold, Miss Fernside. That coat is not warm enough for such cold weather."

The words were barked, and Jemima jumped. She had no problem whatsoever imagining this man shouting orders as soldiers leapt to obey him.

"I'm fine, my lord. The wind is a little chilly, that's all. The coat is quite snug, I assure you."

"Hmph." He glowered down at her looking unconvinced.

They walked on in silence until they got to the large ornamental pond. In fine weather there was a pretty fountain, but today the water was quiet and still, glittering under the blue sky. Jemima wondered if they were just going to walk in a circle and then he'd deposit her back at Hatchard's without saying another word. This was supposed to be an initial meeting to break the ice and see if they suited each other. What if he didn't like her? The idea made panic rise in her chest. Images of the workhouse beckoned, and she repressed a shudder lest he should feel the need to scold her for being cold again. Fighting to find some small crumb of courage, she made herself speak to him.

"I understand Mitcham Priory in Sussex is your home, my lord."

"It is," he replied, turning to look at her. "Do you know it?"

"Oh, no, but my friends visited while they were staying with Lord St Clair during the summer. I hear it is very fine."

"I remember. I wasn't there myself. I believe my housekeeper gave them a tour. You know St Clair?" he asked, frowning.

Jemima shook her head. "I cannot claim an acquaintance, no. Though he has recently married a friend of mine, so I expect...."

She trailed off as she realised there was little likelihood of the earl wanting to befriend her, or of wanting his wife to know her at all, once this arrangement became public. There was only so long a secret of this kind could be kept.

"You expect?" he pressed.

"So I expect I shall hear a great deal of him," she finished, smiling as convincingly as she could manage. The expression felt stiff and unnatural on her freezing cheeks. "My friends thought the priory a wonderful place, though. Charming and romantic, I believe they said."

He snorted at that. "Cold and draughty, and devilish expensive to upkeep, more like."

Jemima sighed inwardly and tried again.

"Is it very old?"

"Thirteenth century."

"Good heavens! Are there ghosts?" she exclaimed, too astonished by how very ancient the house was to guard her tongue.

"I don't believe in ghosts."

Of course he didn't.

"I don't suppose you do," Jemima said, her tone rueful. "I imagine there are stories, though, in such an old place?"

He sighed and appeared to be resigning himself to the inevitable. "There are supposed to be eight ghosts in all."

"Eight!" she squeaked, unconsciously squeezing his arm tighter.

His dark brows drew together, and he covered her hand with his own. "My dear young woman. There is no such thing as ghosts, at least not the kind to rattle chains and wail. I've lived there all my life and never seen a thing."

"But others have," she insisted. "How can you dismiss the idea if people see the same thing as each other? They have, haven't they?"

He let out a frustrated breath. "Hysteria. The story gets about, and the highly strung can convince themselves of anything."

"Oh, dear. How unromantic you are," she said with a despondent sigh.

He stopped in his tracks, turning to give her a stern stare. "Miss Fernside. I do hope that Mr Briggs has not given you any... *unrealistic* expectations of what I am looking for from our arrangement?"

Jemima felt the blush scald her cheeks and chase away any lingering chills the fierce north wind had given her. "No. Indeed, he has not."

"Good," he said, still staring at her. "I am only looking for someone to share an occasional meal with, to converse with and… and to…."

"Yes," Jemima said in a rush, not wishing to delve any further into his requirements for the moment. "Mr Briggs explained everything, and I do understand, I assure you. I have no… no *romantic* expectations, I promise."

Those dark eyes bore into hers a moment longer before he nodded and looked away. They walked on again and Jemima glanced over her shoulder, noting with relief that Mrs Attwood had maintained a discreet distance.

"You've visited the cottage?"

"I have," Jemima agreed, smiling for real now. It was the one truly bright spot in all of this, perfect and charming and all hers, so long as she held to their agreement. Still, if she could manage it for the full five years, she'd be financially independent. "It's wonderful, thank you."

"It's hardly that," he said, brusque as ever. "But I'm seeing to the work. It should be ready for you by the end of the month. I will arrange a carriage to collect your things, and yourself, as soon as it is."

It was Jemima's turn to stop now, heart thudding as she stared up at him. "You've decided, then? You think that we... that *I* should... s-suit you?"

He looked puzzled, staring at her as though she'd said something extraordinary.

"Whyever not?" he asked. "You are more than I could ever have hoped for."

"Oh." Stupidly, Jemima felt utterly disarmed by that, and some of the tension in her relaxed a little. "Thank you."

He shrugged. "I have no illusions, Miss Fernside. I know you would not be here if you were not desperate. If I were a better man, I would not take advantage of that fact but I'm afraid I'm too tired of my own company. I begin to fear I might run mad if I spend too much more time alone, yet I detest dinners and parties, and the usual social interaction most people seem so enamoured of. I have no patience for people and idle chatter. I am afraid you'll find little joy in my company, but you will at least have nothing to fear, either from me or from your circumstances."

"That is no small thing, my lord."

"Believe me, I know that," he said, his expression grim. He glanced at her again. "You need not fear me."

The words were gentler this time, less abrupt, and Jemima believed him.

"I know what women want and I'm afraid I can no longer provide such… such warm feelings as you may prefer, but I would never hurt you, certainly not physically. I know my manner can be abrupt, though, but you'll just have to get used to that."

Jemima knew she ought to be appalled by such plain speaking, but she was oddly touched. In his own way, this man was as desperate as she was, not financially, but desperate for some human contact and unable to reach for it in the usual way.

"I will," she promised. "And I'm sure we'll deal admirably together."

Chapter 6

Dear Alice,

I hope you are not considering presenting your husband with six babies! The cat may look smug, but I don't recommend copying her. One pink bundle of either variety will be quite perfect enough.

I will proceed to update you on all the latest gossip, but I just wished to make one thing clear. I at no time agreed to take a dare and will not be doing so. It has been my joy and privilege to see all the Peculiar Ladies go through this appropriately peculiar rite, but I am too perilously close to scandal to risk anything further. As self-appointed mother hen I have and will continue to watch over you all and take vicarious pleasure in all your adventures. I hope you will forgive me for disappointing you.

—Excerpt of a letter from Miss Matilda Hunt to Mrs Alice Hunt.

7th January 1815. Church Street, Isleworth, London.

Minerva smoothed her gloved hand over the thick velvet of her coat and drew in a deep breath, trying her best to calm herself, to quiet her fluttering heart and stop breathing as though she'd just run from monsters.

It had been over a week since her first visit to Mr de Beauvoir—*Inigo*—and there had not been another chance to visit him. Today she had snatched at an unexpected opportunity and taken fate into her own hands. The only problem being, he wasn't expecting her.

It will be fine. It will be fine.

She repeated the words like a mantra, though they didn't seem to help a great deal. *What if he has company?* That idea struck her too late as the carriage turned into his road. *What if he's with a woman?* Although this seemed unlikely, the surge of jealousy that rose in her chest unsettled her so badly her breath caught. So much for trying to keep calm. Well, she'd soon find out.

Lifting the heavy basket she'd stuffed full of food for him, and ensuring her hood was pulled up well over her head to hide her blonde curls, she looked furtively up and down the street before stepping down from the carriage.

"Wait until I enter and then return for me at four o'clock, please," she instructed the driver.

It was much longer than she'd stayed last time, but she didn't know when she'd be able to come again, and she intended to make the most of it. She strode to the door and lifted the knocker, rapping once and waiting, knowing she was holding her breath but unable to stop herself.

A moment later the door was flung back, and she started, a little shocked to see him, even though she'd been anticipating this moment all week. He was in his shirtsleeves, unshaven, and dark circles lurked beneath his eyes. Those eyes widened with alarm at the sight of her.

"Christ!" he exclaimed, before grasping her arm and hauling her inside, slamming the door behind her. "Are you insane?"

"It's lovely to see you too," she said, feeling all the anxiety slide away now she was with him.

That was probably odd, as he appeared none too pleased, but she wasn't about to analyse it.

He raked a hand through his thick, dark hair, which had already looked tangled and mussed, and now stood out at all angles. He looked wild and dishevelled and everything inside her coiled into a tight knot of anticipation.

"I'm working," he said, crossing his arms over his chest, so tightly her eyes were drawn to where the sleeves stretched over his biceps.

Not so skinny as she'd imagined.

"Well, you still need to eat," she said, giving him a bright smile and hefting the basket. "Besides which, the carriage won't return for me until four, so you're stuck with me."

He let out a groan and Minerva blew him a kiss. "Don't be grumpy," she coaxed, looking at him from under her lashes. "I brought cold chicken and potato salad, pickles and some bread and cheese, oh, and wine, of course."

He glowered a little, his dark brows drawn down. "Cake?" he asked, and she bit back a smile of triumph at the hopeful note in the question.

"Well, obviously I brought cake," she said, shaking her head at him. "What do you take me for?"

Pleased to discover that he had a sweet tooth, Minerva filed that away under useful information and headed to the kitchen.

The room was freezing and in a worse state than last time she'd been here. Tutting under her breath, she set the basket down on the table.

"I wasn't expecting company." He was standing in the doorway, arms folded again, a defensive air vibrating from him as he glowered into the darkened room.

"That's all right," Minerva said, not the least bit daunted.

She knew he was unused to visitors, to being cared for, and it was only natural he should be ungracious when he didn't know how to act. Besides, she had landed on his doorstep without so much as a by your leave. He was entitled to be irritated, though she couldn't help but feel that, beneath the bluster, he was pleased she'd come.

"You go and wash up, and I'll prepare the lunch. Come back when you're ready."

He harrumphed and left her to it.

Minerva moved through into the scullery, where she found what must have been his last housekeeper's apron. She'd probably run away screaming and forgotten to pack it in her haste. Minerva hung up her pelisse and bonnet, put the apron on and tied it about her waist before she set to in the kitchen. She lit the lamps first and then the fire, pleased at how much better the place seemed at once with a brighter light to illuminate the… well perhaps not the grubby bits, but still. Undaunted, she cleaned the surfaces, swept the floor, washed the dirty dishes and then laid the table for two. With chagrin, she realised her mother would have a fit of the vapours if she saw her doing such menial work.

She was just putting the food out when Inigo reappeared. He was still in his shirtsleeves, but his hair was tidy, and he'd shaved. Her heart felt funny and gave a peculiar little flip flop sensation in her chest.

"Perfect timing," she said, pulling out a chair for him.

He scowled at her, looking around the kitchen. "You're not my skivvy, Miss Butler, there was no need—"

"Oh, fiddlesticks." Minerva rolled her eyes at him. "I know that, and I promise you I shan't make a habit of it, but a friend can give another a helping hand when one is required, don't you think? I was happy to do it, I assure you."

"Friends?" he repeated, giving her an odd look.

"Yes, of course we're friends." She smiled and shook her head at him. "Do come and sit down. I don't suppose you've eaten all day, have you?"

He frowned and made his way to the table. "I ate."

"What did you eat?"

"Bread and jam," he shot back, so defensive she almost laughed.

Instead, she clicked her tongue at him.

"If you are referring to the rock I found, that *bread* was stale two days ago, besides which, bread and jam is not enough for a man of your size to eat in a day, and don't pretend you were having something else for lunch. There isn't anything. Bread and jam," she muttered under her breath. "That's a fine meal for a grown man. Now come along and eat some real food. How you expect to think straight when you're half-starved is beyond me."

He allowed her to hustle him into the chair. Minerva helped him to fill his plate and then sat back to eat her own meal, content to see him eating properly. Though she did her best not to stare, she watched him covertly, taking in every detail to remember later, when she was alone. He had the most extraordinarily long eyelashes, thick and black and straight, which made her smile. He'd unrolled his sleeves and fastened them, which was a pity as he had lovely arms, but she noticed now that his cuffs were frayed, and her heart did that funny little flip in her chest again. Why this man brought her every maternal instinct screaming to the surface she did not know, but she had the strongest urge to protect him from the world, to look after him and make sure he was fed and warm and getting enough rest. For all his prickly exterior, he seemed desperately in need of looking after, protecting. Which was ridiculous, she reflected. He'd started from nothing and become one of the most respected men of science in the world. His success was astonishing, by anyone's standards, and yet still she felt he was lonely and unhappy and she wanted to make it better for him.

Good heavens, how appalled he'd be if he had the slightest inkling of how she felt.

"How is your work coming along?" she asked, curious to know what he'd been studying. "Is it interesting?"

He reached for his wine and took a sip, sliding a glance at her as he set the glass down, as if he wasn't certain she was really interested.

"Perplexing," he said, picking up his knife and fork again.

"How so?"

He cut into a piece of chicken and speared it with his fork, but didn't eat it, just sat staring at it. Minerva waited, realising he was thinking.

"Usually, if you heat zinc carbonate to red hot, it will convert to oxide, which is white," he began, sounding as though he was still working on the problem as he spoke. "This batch is yellow, almost orange. That would suggest it's been contaminated with lead or iron, but I can find no evidence of either."

"How curious," she said, delighted that he was discussing his work with her. "So, what will you do?"

"Continue studying it until I understand what the cause is. I have been analysing the yellow oxide to discover why it is different. I believe I may have found something new, a metallic oxide."

"A discovery?" she demanded, beaming at him. "How exciting."

He looked at her sharply, perhaps suspecting she was teasing him, but relaxed as he realised she meant it. He smiled at her then, a genuine, proper smile that made her breath catch.

"It *is* exciting," he admitted, looking adorably pleased with himself. "I may have discovered a new element."

"That's important," she said, setting down her knife and fork.

She wasn't about to pretend she had anything but a very basic understanding of his work, but a breakthrough like that would be hugely important to the scientific world. Minerva stared at him in wonder, rather awed to be with him now, a little overwhelmed by how frighteningly intelligent he was.

"I mean… it's a great discovery, isn't it?"

He gave her a disarmingly sheepish expression before turning back to his dinner.

"One must not count one's chickens, Miss Butler. I need to do more tests before I am certain, but… yes," he admitted. "It would give me a place in history, to have discovered such a thing."

"Oh, Inigo!" Quite unable to stop herself she leapt to her feet and threw her arms about his neck, kissing his cheek. "I'm so very proud of you."

To her surprise he blushed, and she thought she saw pleasure in his eyes, but suddenly they darkened, the pupils blown wide. His chair shifted back with a screech against the tiled floor and his hands grasped her waist, pulling her into his lap. Minerva didn't so much as squeak a protest, being only too happy to comply. She put her arms around him as his mouth sought hers, kissing her hard. One large hand cupped her face whilst the other slid up her side, resting beneath her breast. Anticipation thrilled under her skin, a mixture of fear and desire, willing him to go further, afraid that he would.

He drew back, staring at her as she gazed into his eyes. This close, she could see the pattern of colours clearly, the green a bright blaze circling the pupil like rays around the sun, set against a dark grey background.

"You have the most extraordinary eyes," she said, reaching a hand up to stroke his cheek, the skin smooth now he'd shaved. She rather regretted that. She'd wanted to touch the prickle of his beard, to see how it felt. "It was one of the first things that struck me about you. They are beautiful."

He let out a breath, somewhere between irritation and despair. "You ought not have come, Miss Butler."

"Minerva," she corrected, trailing her fingers over his jaw, to his mouth. "I think we are past such formality, don't you?"

There was a snort of amusement, but he didn't disagree.

She got up and went back to her seat, smiling at him as he sighed and returned his attention to his food.

Once they'd eaten and Minerva had put the leftovers in the pantry, she took off the apron and found he'd left the kitchen. Pleased to be given the chance to see more of the house, she went in search of him.

"Inigo?" she called, once back out in the hallway.

"Here."

She followed his voice towards and opened a door onto a large, bright room. It had windows on three sides and a high ceiling, and was like no other she'd seen before. There was a huge table in the middle with weighing scales in various sizes, there were bell jars and books, dozens of peculiar odd brass instruments she had no name for and large copper pots. All around the room, wherever there was wall space, he'd crammed it with shelves filled with glass jars of every size, from no larger than her little finger to others she doubted she could lift. Some were empty, others full of powders or liquids, most with labels she could hardly pronounce let alone recognise. There were huge copper vats and strange shaped glass vials, pestles and mortars, and crucibles, and an odd scent lingered in the air. It was smoky and astringent, somewhat metallic and, she assumed, caused by the combination of chemicals and whatever experiments he'd been working on.

Minerva moved cautiously into the room, afraid to jostle anything for fear of ruining some crucial part of the procedure.

She discovered Inigo watching her, as though some wild creature had crept into his laboratory and he wasn't quite sure what to do about it.

"Fascinating," she said, aware that he must see the excitement in her eyes. She felt flushed with it, with the honour she knew was being extended to her, to allow her here of all places.

He ran a hand through his hair, leaving it as messy as when she'd first arrived and she smiled, finding him more charming than ever when he was dishevelled.

"So, this is where the great man works."

"Hmmm," he said, darting a look at her before turning his attention to putting a stopper back into a bottle of white powder.

"Will you show me the experiment you are working on?"

"No."

Minerva sighed. "You think I won't understand it, I suppose?"

"No. I think you are a pain in the neck and I want you to go home."

"I could help you, act as your assistant. I'm good at following instructions."

He turned and glared at her. "Like when I told you to go away and leave me alone?"

"Instructions I *want* to follow," she clarified with a smile.

"Hmph."

Minerva sighed, sensing she was not going to get anywhere today. She wanted to understand him, his work, to help even—if he would allow her. Cleary she was pushing too hard to expect that.

"Do you always work alone? You don't have assistants?"

"Sometimes," he said, hefting the jar back on the shelf. "When I can afford them."

"You ought to be paid more for your work," she said, frowning. It was wrong that this brilliant man struggled to make ends meet when he was making discoveries that would help shape the history of science. "You need a sponsor. Artists have them, so I don't see why you ought not. I'm sure Bedwin would be interested if you approached him."

He frowned, turning to look at her. "I'm unlikely to get another chance to speak with him and…." His brow furrowed, a troubled glint in his eyes. "No," he shook his head. "I couldn't…."

"No, but I could," she said, laughing at his shocked expression. "Oh, don't look so scandalised. I can do it discreetly. It's not like I'd ask outright, just… put the idea in his head."

Inigo's eyes narrowed. "I begin to fear you're more calculating than even I imagined."

"Calculating?" Minerva's placing her hand on her heart. "*Moi*? As if. That's a very cruel accusation."

"You deny it?" he asked, amused now, watching her as she manoeuvred around the room towards him. "You beguiled me into giving you my card by pretending you were afraid you were not clever enough to understand the book you had, and then you plagued me to death with questions and flirtation until I was browbeaten into inviting you to my lecture to avoid the prospect of you making a terrible scene."

"Don't forget the kiss," she said, moving closer to him, looking at him from under her lashes. "I kissed you when you were wounded and unable to defend yourself."

"So you did," he murmured, his voice pitched low, intimate. "You are a wicked, dreadful creature."

Minerva tilted her head to one side. "But you said women and men were equal, that you don't believe in love or marriage. Why is it terrible of me to pursue you if I want you? It's what a man would do, isn't it?"

His breath caught, his eyes growing dark.

"You really want me that badly?" he said, looking so perplexed by the idea that she laughed a little.

"I really do."

He moved towards her and put his hands to her waist, lifting her and setting her down on the edge of the table. Minerva squeaked and looked behind her.

"Don't let me knock anything over," she said in alarm, clutching at his arms, panicked by all the scientific equipment around her.

"Let me worry about that."

She let out a breath and stared up at him, finding him staring back down at her, so close, such heat and desire in his eyes. Minerva licked her lips, a little nervous now, and her heart beat harder as his gaze fell to her mouth, tracking the movement.

"Do you want to go home now?" he asked.

Minerva shook her head.

"I will take whatever you offer," he warned her, and she understood it *was* a warning.

"I know," she whispered, reaching up to press her lips to the corner of his mouth.

She moved her mouth over his in small, slow increments until he lost patience and tipped her head back with one large hand, taking the kiss he wanted. Strong fingers tangled in her hair, tugging a little though it was not unpleasant. His other hand grasped her waist, his palm burning through her gown as it slid up her side to linger once more beneath her breast. Minerva melted into him, surrendering to his will, beguiled by the slick slide of his tongue against hers until she was breathless, almost panting. He released her, trailing his lips over her jaw, down her neck while the hand which had stilled beneath her breast moved higher, cupping and squeezing as Minerva gave a shocked little cry. His thumb rubbed against the material, across the peaked nub of skin beneath and she jerked, surprised by the jolt of pleasure, torn between bolting and begging for more as she saw the raw look in his eyes.

"Still want to stay?"

"Yes."

Inigo kissed her again, harder and deeper and she leaned into his touch, seeking more. He gave it, a gentle pinch of her nipple with thumb and forefinger that made her gasp. Inigo gave a soft grunt of satisfaction, releasing her mouth once more. This time his hands rose to the pearl buttons that fastened the bodice and Minerva could do nothing but sit, still and obedient, waiting for what came next. She was dazed, her blood fizzing in her veins like champagne, more alive than ever in her life before as she watched him, her eyes fixed on his face as he concentrated on the buttons. She wondered if this was how he looked when he was working, so intent, as though nothing else in the world mattered. Her breath caught as he parted the open neck of her gown, tugging it down over her shoulders.

Belatedly, she glanced at the windows surrounding them, relieved to see they were not overlooked, as a high wall bordered the garden beyond and trees made it secluded and private. She turned back to him, struck by the look in his eyes. He seemed just as stunned as she felt.

"On a scale of one to ten, how much do you love me?" she demanded, even though she knew the answer.

"I don't love you, Miss Butler."

"Minerva."

"Minerva," he murmured, breathless now, his gaze fixed upon her breasts, covered only by her thin chemise and the short corset which pushed them up, as though offering them to him.

"Oh, come now," she coaxed, determined to have him give something, or he'd keep returning the same answer no matter if it were true or not. "You cannot tell me you have no feelings at all. Let us say zero is indifference, which I do not believe. One is an appreciation of someone's better qualities, like you feel for someone you've just met and think you might be friends with. Two is a friend, three a very good friend, and so on...."

"Fine. One," he said, tracing a fingertip over the curve of her breast, flirting with the edge of the chemise, teasing her. His touch was distracting, making her shiver but she fought to concentrate.

"I thought we were already friends."

"You said, that, not me." His voice was rough now, his gaze fixed to the place where his fingers trailed back and forth over her skin. "So soft," he murmured, and she wondered if he realised he'd said it aloud. The words were so reverent.

She stared at him, captivated by the look in his eyes. He was breathing hard. "How much do you desire me?" she asked, her voice low.

He made a sound which might have been a laugh but sounded a little too desperate, a little too ragged to be amused. "Too much."

He cupped her breasts with both hands, kneading them gently before ducking his head and kissing one rounded swell. Minerva let out a shaky breath and sank her fingers into his dark hair as he blazed a fiery trail of damp kisses over her skin, dipping his tongue into her cleavage. This made her shiver so hard he chuckled and did it again. He drew back and gave her corset a hard tug down before pulling at the bow on the neckline of her chemise, loosening it.

Minerva could hardly breathe now. Helena had warned her this was dangerous, not that she'd needed anyone else to tell her. Inigo had told her what would happen. She had lost her wits over this man, she knew she had, but couldn't bring herself to care. She wanted his hands on her, wanted to touch him in return.

To Experiment with Desire

Cool air fluttered over her skin and she gasped as he exposed her breasts to his hungry gaze, and he did look hungry: famished, as if he would eat her alive. He didn't move for a long moment, just stared at her, transfixed.

"Why are you here?" he asked, his voice scratchy and uneven. "God, you're so beautiful. Why are you here with me, throwing yourself away…?"

"Because I want you," she said, meaning it, "Because I want to know you, understand you. Because I can't not come to you." She leaned towards him and kissed him. "Seven," she whispered against his mouth and he gave a soft bark of laughter.

"You're insane," he murmured against her lips. "Beautiful and insane and deadly. You'll drive me distracted yet, Minerva. Goddess of wisdom and one mad fool."

He pressed his mouth to the tender spot beneath her ear, licking and biting his way down, down, until his lips closed over her breast and Minerva cried out, clutching at him, holding his head against her as he suckled and nipped at the hard bud of flesh under his tongue. The sensation was intoxicating, making her ache and moan and want more, so much more.

"Inigo," she gasped as her head fell back. She was on fire, molten and beyond knowing what exactly it was she wanted but knowing she had to have it. "Oh, please…."

His lifted his head, trailing kisses back up her neck to her mouth, kissing her, devouring her as he filled his hands with her breasts. He moaned, the sound so thrilling that Minerva wanted to laugh with the joy of it, but then he moved away. It was an oddly fierce movement, snatching his hands away from her body like she'd scalded him.

Minerva watched him, perplexed as he put distance between them, his hands going up to clutch at his hair.

"Christ," he murmured, his chest rising and falling as though he too had run from monsters. "I can't...." He took a deep breath and let it out again, slowly. "You need to go, Miss Butler."

Oh, they were back to Miss Butler again.

"Why?"

He gave a laugh which sounded just a little hysterical. "Do you want a scandal? Is that it? Do you think the attention will be exciting? I promise you, it won't be. You'll feel ashamed, your friends will shun you, and men will proposition you because they'll think you a whore."

The words were hard and angry, and Minerva blushed, tugging her chemise back over her breasts.

"Is that what you think?" she asked softly. "Do you think me a whore?"

The rigid line of his jaw softened, and he shook his head. "You know I don't. Women feel desire the same way men do. To believe otherwise is just wilful ignorance. If the world were another place, we could take our pleasure and enjoy it and move on, but the world is cruel and judgmental and full of consequences, and it is you who will endure them, not me."

Minerva stared at him, wishing she knew him well enough to read him, to know what was going on in that brilliant mind. "Is that all you want, Inigo? To enjoy me physically and then move on and forget me?"

"Of course," he said at once, and Minerva wondered if perhaps he'd been a bit too ready with the answer. He'd looked away from her, though, so she had no way of learning anything from his expression. "I've made no secret of it, Miss Butler."

"Minerva," she said again, though his words had made her confidence falter. Why, she didn't know. She'd told herself she had no illusions. He'd been explicit in his desires and what he would or would not give from the start and it had changed nothing. "So, you don't want me to come back again?"

"It... would be best if you did not."

"That's not what I asked."

He made a sound of frustration, turning to glare at her. "I want you to come back so I can take you to bed. You're a beautiful woman with a warm, willing body and I'm a man. Two plus two will always equal four, you little fool."

Minerva swallowed. "And that's all. You... You don't like me at all. You won't miss my company or... or wish to see me for any other reason?"

There was a taut silence before he replied. "No."

She didn't believe him, couldn't believe him, but her stupid heart hurt, which was ridiculous. Even if it were true, she'd steeled herself against his indifference, or at least she'd thought she had. He'd turned away from her, staring out the window at the garden beyond. The sun, which had been so bright and cheerful all morning, had been lost behind a bank of thick grey cloud and she felt cold suddenly. With fingers that were not entirely steady, she fastened the ribbon on her chemise, tugged her corset back into place and did up her buttons.

He didn't turn around.

"My carriage won't return for another twenty minutes yet, but I'll wait in the kitchen. You needn't see me out."

Silence.

Minerva swallowed down the ache in her throat.

"I'm staying with Bedwin for the next few weeks if... if you wanted to write to me. If you change your mind. I won't forget to speak to him for you, either." He still said nothing, keeping his back to her, his arms folded. "I'd like to see you again and... and I'll come if you ask me to, but... but I shan't come again like this, without an invitation, so you need not worry. I'm sorry if I disturbed your work. I do hope… I hope you find what you are looking for."

She stared at him for a moment longer, wishing he'd at least say goodbye to her, but she felt foolish now, so she turned and left the room, closing the door quietly behind her.

Chapter 7

Dear Prue,

How are you feeling? I hope the dreadful sickness has passed now. I know just how you feel. If it makes you feel better, I'm waddling like a duck and can barely see my toes. How lovely it will be to see our children playing together, though. I can't wait.

I wanted to ask you if you've seen Matilda of late. Did you know she's determined not to take a dare? She says her reputation is too damaged already to take any risks and I do understand that but Prue, all of ours changed us for the better. Do you not think she needs to do this? I feel like she's standing on the edge of something, as though she's too frightened to decide which way to go, but if she does nothing, she'll end up with nothing. I'm sorry, I'm not sure this makes the slightest bit of sense and it's likely I'm being over emotional. Do you know I burst into tears at the sight of Nate holding a kitten yesterday? I mean, it was an adorable sight, but still, hardly something to bawl over.

Babies have a great deal to answer for.

—Excerpt of a letter from Mrs Alice Hunt to Her Grace, Prunella Adolphus, Duchess of Bedwin.

7th January 1815. Church Street, Isleworth, London.

Inigo didn't dare move until he heard the front door close. He let out a breath that was not at all steady. His hands were clenched into fists and his fingers ached from being held so tightly for so long. It wasn't the only part of him aching.

Oh, God.

Oh, God, oh, God, oh, God.

He raked a hand through his hair, trying to rid himself of the sight of Minerva sat on the work bench in his laboratory, her lips swollen from his kisses, her beautiful breasts exposed to him. Something proprietary and possessive burned inside him, and he cursed himself for a fool. She didn't belong to him, he didn't even believe in that kind of ownership, and she was way beyond his touch. A lady. Not for him. Oh, but the taste of her, the feel of her under his hands, his mouth. She was so unbelievably soft, so sweet, and he wanted her so very badly.

He'd known she was trouble from the first. Not because she was beautiful, not because she belonged to that class of women who usually ignored him as though he were furniture, because he was beneath their notice. No, it was because of the curiosity in her eyes, the desire to know him, to figure him out like a puzzle. She wanted to know how he worked, what he felt and why and, in some strange way, he understood that. The problem was he was afraid she could do it, she could unravel him and figure him out and, soon enough, she'd see it hadn't been complex at all, it had been easier than she could have imagined. Then she would grow bored and move on to someone more interesting.

It wouldn't be like that for him.

Inigo knew himself. He knew the way his mind worked, knew the single-minded devotion and passion that took him up and held him captive. All well and good when your passion was your work. Not so when it was a woman. He'd been too busy with his work to let anyone close, but he knew he risked his sanity if he allowed himself to become captivated by her. He'd meant everything he'd said. He didn't believe in love, but he understood obsession, he knew the signs of his mind grasping hold of an idea, a desire to know something, *everything.* Never had such feelings been provoked by a woman, though. Not that he'd ever met one so thoroughly provoking as Minerva. He could feel it already, the wanting, the need to have her near him, to know everything about her. Sleep had eluded him since the last time she'd been here. If he allowed his brain to do anything but work, it immediately returned to her, and keeping his attention on his work had been no easy task.

He was losing his mind, and today he knew she'd taken an even bigger slice of his sanity, alongside a generous helping of his peace of mind. *Work, go back to work*, he chided himself, moving further into the room, trying to find something he could concentrate on. Except he found himself in front of the place where she'd sat, and he was certain he could detect the scent of her still. He closed his eyes and inhaled, wanting to cry with frustration. Why had she come into his life? She would wreck everything, wreck *him.* If he didn't break this now, he'd do something stupid and destructive. He'd have to have her near him, with him, just to keep himself sane, and he wouldn't be able to do that. It would ruin her. So, he'd be forced to marry her, and then he'd be saddled with a wife.

Inigo gave a bitter laugh. He'd once told Harriet he couldn't have an ordinary marriage, because it wouldn't be fair on his wife to be constantly ignored for his work. He'd been quite honest in that. Marriage to Harriet would have been simple. She would have kept his life in order, and he could have offered her the security and support to pursue her own work in a world where women could not do such things with ease. They'd liked each other well enough, too, respected each other's work and intellect, but most importantly he didn't desire her beyond reason, didn't want to figure out every hidden part of her, to know her thoughts, to know everything about her.

Then he'd met Minerva.

Why in the name of God had he given her his card that day? He never did that. He barely gave colleagues his card, not wanting to be interrupted by social calls when he was working. He didn't like society, and he certainly didn't want a conventional marriage. He didn't want one based on obsession, either. How would he work with Minerva in the house, when he could touch her, taste her, whenever he wanted to? The idea was tantalising. *It's physical*, he reminded himself, *nothing more*. Perhaps he should marry her, get her out of his system, and get someone to keep his life in order at the same time. That was hardly fair to her, though, and what if he never got her out of his system? What if he wed her and the obsession only grew? No, he assured himself with a bitter laugh, once Bedwin found out he'd put an end to any plans for marriage. Even Minerva had admitted her mother wanted her to hunt down a title, so Inigo couldn't believe the duke would want anything less for his wife's cousin.

No, they'd not let them marry. She'd be sent away, and he'd go quietly insane.

Rubbish. Pull yourself together, de Beauvoir. You're just ripe for a tumble, that's all. Easy enough to fix.

In usual circumstances he had no qualms with making use of the many convenient houses where a man could satisfy his desires for a few coins. He knew places where the girls were clean, and there was one he visited from time to time as the fancy took him. The girls, and especially Rachel, were straightforward, and he respected their good natured crudeness as to what he wanted and what was expected of each of them. There was nothing complicated about it. There was nothing particularly satisfying about it, either. It filled a physical desire which he needed filled, nothing more than that. He knew it would not be the same with Minerva. Even thinking about taking her to bed made him tremble with desire. He clutched the edge of the workbench, leaning onto it, trying to steady his breathing, trying and trying not to remember the feel of her, the moment he'd taken her breast into his mouth and sucked, the little cry of pleasure she'd given.

Oh, God.

Stop it, stop it, stop it.

No, he'd done the right thing. He'd sent her away and that was for the best. He was protecting her, protecting them both. His gut twisted with remorse as he remembered the hurt in her voice when he'd said he'd bed her if she came back, but that he no other interest in her.

And that's all. You… You don't like me at all. You won't miss my company, or… or wish to see me for any other reason?

Inigo scrubbed his hands over his face, willing himself to forget it, but there was an odd aching sensation in his chest, and it was hard to breathe. *Unfulfilled desire*, he assured himself. It wasn't the only part of him aching, after all. It would pass. He would go back to work and it would pass. It would.

***

21st January 1815. Church Street, Isleworth, London.

It didn't pass.

Two weeks went by—*crawled* by—and every day was worse. Three times he'd given in, sitting down and writing letters inviting her to visit, letters that ranged from terse commands to damn near begging. Each time he'd crumpled them up and thrown them in the fire before he did something stupid, such as put them in the post.

The only bright point in his miserable existence was that he was certain he'd discovered a new element. Yet even that triumph seemed diminished somehow, for he couldn't share it with her. He kept remembering the delight in her eyes when he'd told her about his discovery. She'd looked so pleased, so proud of him. No one had ever been proud of him before. He'd had no one to *be* proud before.

Inigo had never been sentimental about his past. Growing up in an orphanage was hardly a recipe for an idyllic childhood, but he'd been one of the lucky ones. The Foundling Hospital in

Bloomsbury had been good to him. They'd fed and clothed him and given him an education. When they discovered he was above average intelligence, they had found him an apprenticeship working as an assistant in an apothecary shop. The bottles and jars and the precise order of it all had fascinated him. He'd loved weighing out exact measurements and mixing the various tinctures and elixirs; he'd even improved many of them once he'd realised the potential uses of each ingredient. In his every spare hour he read anything he could get his hands on, but especially any scientific texts. They were hard to get hold of but, for a boy willing to sell his soul to gain more insight into a world he wanted a part of, he always found something.

They had allowed him to sleep in the shop, on a lumpy tick mattress in a storeroom. He'd been glad of it, thrilled to have a space of his own where he didn't have put up with the other boys and their rough housing, teasing and bantering, mocking each other and fighting. Inigo had never fit in, never been a fighter, and had never understood the banter. The other boys thought him aloof and so picked on him for not being one of them, and for his cleverness. Thank God he'd been big enough not to be bullied by any but the oldest boys, though that had been bad enough. He'd been only too pleased to escape.

He'd worked long and hard to get where he was. The day he'd bought this house had been one of the proudest of his life. It was his, his home, his house, his laboratory, all the things he'd ever wanted enclosed behind walls of brick and mortar. Safe from the world, cocooned in his lab with his science and an insatiable desire to learn *everything*. He'd been at peace, content, and then Minerva Butler had kissed him, and his world had crumbled at the edges. Now the house he'd worked so hard for, the laboratory that had been the pinnacle of his every desire—even the enormity of this new discovery—felt empty, hollowed out and meaningless, because he could not see the pride in her eyes at his achievement.

God, he was pathetic.

To Experiment with Desire

***

Minerva stared at the book before her in mute frustration before throwing it to one side. *An Essay on Heat, Light, and the Combinations of Light* by Humphry Davy had stretched her brain farther than it was willing to go. She didn't understand the wretched thing at all. It might as well have been written in Russian or hieroglyphics for all the sense she could make of it. She was stupid to persevere. What was the point? What good would it do her, even if she could understand it? If ever she married, she'd likely only have to hide the fact she had something approaching a brain. God forbid her husband ever discovered she'd had an original thought in her head. *Men don't like clever women, Minerva,* was a common complaint her mother threw at her. To begin with, Minerva had been compelled to point out that her cousin Prue was far cleverer than she, and Prue had caught a duke. Her mother seemed to wilfully ignore this evidence, however, dismissing it as a fluke. Prue had just been lucky and in the right place at the right time, and it could have been Minerva if only she'd tried harder.

Ugh.

She looked up, hearing voices outside the door. A moment later, Helena bustled in with the post.

"Two for you," she said with a bright smile, handing Minerva two letters.

Minerva smiled at the familiar extravagant loops on the first letter. Kitty. She put it aside to read later, picked up the second, and her heart skipped. The writing was a near illegible scrawl and suddenly her heart was thudding in her chest. She turned it over, sliding a trembling finger beneath the seal to break it.

The British Museum. 21stJan. 11am.

IdB

Minerva let out a shaky breath and allowed a smile to break over her mouth. Arrogant devil. For all he knew, she had plans.

Trust him to arrange something last moment and expect her to drop everything. Except then she wondered if he *did* expect that. Perhaps he believed she'd not come, and that would be proof that he'd been right, and she wasn't serious. She frowned, wishing she knew which it was. Was the fear she sensed in him real, that aching vulnerability, or was it because she was foolish and sentimental, and she wanted to believe it? Was he as cold and hard and emotionless as he wanted her to believe?

She traced her hand back and forth over the scrawled words. He hadn't invited her back to his house. If he'd done that, she'd have been clearer about what he wanted. It would have been unambiguous. A public place, though? If she had a chaperone, that gave her security, and him no chance to have his wicked way with her. If all he wanted from her was physical, why would he suggest such a thing? Her smile widened.

"Why do you look like the cat that got the cream?" Helena demanded, green eyes cool and suspicious.

Minerva bit her lip. "Helena, how to you fancy a trip to the British Museum this afternoon?"

Chapter 8

Dear Bonnie,

I don't know if I'm doing the right thing. Minerva has begun an affair with Mr de Beauvoir and there's no talking her out of it. You were there when Minerva met him, what do you think? What should I do? She's a grown woman and I am so tired of the restrictions upon us it seems I should be the last person to object. Yet I am afraid she will get into real trouble. I don't know what his intentions are towards her, but I know her mother will do all in her power to stop it if he tries to marry her.

Oh, but Bonnie, what if he doesn't?

—Excerpt of a letter from Lady Helena Adolphus to Mrs Bonnie Cadogan.

21st January 1815. The British Museum. London.

"My brother will lock me in my room and throw away the key," Helena muttered. "And then your mother will set fire to it."

"Oh, hush. No one will even know." Minerva glanced behind her towards Helena's maid. "At least, not if Tilly is as loyal as you say she is."

"Oh, she is," Helena replied, smiling fondly at the young woman trailing behind them. "She's a darling. Would walk through fire if I asked her to. You don't come across such loyalty often. I'd not part with her for the world."

Minerva nodded, pleased to see Helena returned the loyalty. It was easy to believe the beautiful heiress was just what she seemed: spoiled, wilful, and demanding. It took time to see beneath the hard exterior, and she didn't let many people get a glimpse.

"Oh," Minerva said. Her breath left her all in a rush at the sight of the tall, severe figure lingering in the shadows of the room. "There he is."

At that moment, Inigo turned and saw her too, and she saw him stiffen like a hound catching the scent of fox. Why she'd thought that she didn't know, but it seemed apt, even if the hound was reluctant to give chase and the fox was hellbent on destruction.

Minerva lifted a hand to her hair, unaccountably nervous in the circumstances. He'd seen her bare breasts, for heaven's sake! He'd touched them, kissed them. That thought sent desire pooling low in her belly and heat rushing to her cheeks.

Helena gave Minerva a long hard look, stared at Inigo, and then back to Minerva.

"You two had better stay away from naked flames," she said, shaking her head. "He's very intense, isn't he? He looks ready to eat you in two bites."

It didn't help Minerva's blush any, and Helena looked increasingly concerned.

"And you look like you'd let him. Honestly, Min, have a care."

"I will, I will," Minerva said, nodding, not meaning it.

She wanted to be the flame, to set him alight, to be the focus of his attention.

"Miss Butler, Lady Helena." His bow was stiff and formal, and Minerva could tell he was all on edge. No doubt he was already regretting being here.

"I've booked a tour," he said, nodding at a slender, scholarly looking man in his thirties who was hurrying towards them. He wore small spectacles and his face was narrow and serious. "Mr Crick is the under librarian for the museum. You'll find him very knowledgeable about the collection."

Mr Crick beamed at Inigo. "Mr de Beauvoir, such an honour to meet you, sir. I attended one of your lectures in the spring of last year. Standing room only, but worth it. Fascinating, Fascinating."

Inigo looked a little ill at ease beneath such praise, but nodded his thanks. "Lady Helena, Miss Butler, may I introduce our guide, Mr Crick."

Mr Crick's eyes went wide, and colour stained his face as he took in the picture than was Lady Helena Adolphus. "M-My lady," he stammered, bowing as though she were a duchess, and not just the daughter of one.

"A pleasure to meet you, Mr Crick. We have so been looking forward to the tour."

Mr Crick barely spared Minerva a glance, which was fine by her. Helena, bless her, gave Minerva a wry smile, and bore Mr Crick off ahead of them with Tilly trailing behind, leaving her with Inigo to follow at their own pace.

Inigo offered her his arm. "Miss Butler."

Minerva looked up at him. "Minerva," she said.

He sighed, glancing around the huge room and then back at her, dark eyes wary.

"Minerva," he said softly.

Minerva beamed at him, and he grunted with amusement.

"Why did you invite me?"

The question had been burning to get out ever since she'd received his note. She'd meant to wait, not to tease him over it so quickly, but she couldn't. Of all the curiosities that might be on display here, he was the only one she found truly fascinating.

He didn't answer, perusing a specimen tray filled with different rocks and minerals.

"Inigo."

He lifted his gaze from the tray, focusing on her. She shivered, wanting his attention so badly she might have purred if she could.

"I don't know," he said.

"Liar."

He glowered and straightened, following the guide and ignoring the rest of the exhibits in this room.

"Inigo. Why?"

No answer.

She let it go for a moment, past old bones and ancient stones, the quiet murmur of Mr Crick's voice up ahead, looking dazed in Helena's presence, trying to impress his duchess.

"It's lovely to see you," she said, pressing against his arm a little tighter.

The muscles beneath her palm tensed as her body brushed his and he glanced down at her, then back and forth around the room. It was quiet today. If there were other tours, they were far ahead of them.

Inigo turned and backed her into a secluded corner made by tall glass-fronted cabinets. Mr Crick was still talking, a low burble of sound not too far off, but they were out of sight. Minerva lifted her hands to his chest at the same moment he reached for her, pulling her closer, finding her mouth with his own like true north. He kissed her hard, almost angrily, knocking her bonnet off so the ribbons tugged at her throat as he held her in an iron grip. It lasted seconds, fierce and blinding, a bright flare of lit magnesium, and then he sighed, all the tension leaving him in a rush. He rested his forehead against hers and she stayed still, not wanting to disturb whatever battle he was fighting, or tempt him back to anger again. His hand came up, stroking her face and he tilted her chin, kissing her again, but tenderly now, soft, butterfly kisses, his mouth caressing hers as if they had all the time in the world.

Sadly they didn't, and she regretted the moment he realised it too.

He straightened, giving her a critical one over and replaced her bonnet, retying the ribbons with deft fingers.

"How much do you love me?" she asked.

He gave her an impatient look and she smiled, pressing a gloved finger to his lips.

"More than one, or else you'd not be here." She didn't let her finger up, sealing his mouth shut. "Not two either, don't tell fibs."

"Why don't you answer for me, then?" he said, raising one dark eyebrow.

"Hmmm, let's say three, for now. I don't want to scare you off."

He snorted at that. "I tried running away. You chased me."

Minerva flashed him a grin. "Sorry. Are you terribly vexed?"

"You're not the least bit sorry, and yes, I am. Extremely vexed."

She sighed and leaned her head against his shoulder.

"Poor Inigo," she soothed. "But you're right, I'm not the least bit sorry. So, three it is. A very good friend."

He snorted and she looked up at him.

"What? You have friends, don't you?"

He didn't look at her and she felt anxiety stir in her belly.

"You *do* have friends?" She watched as he examined one of the cabinets: bits of pottery, odd shapes, bits left behind from other people's lives, long gone. He wasn't that interested in them, she was certain. He was just avoiding the question. "Inigo."

"Yes," he said, too quickly this time. "I have friends."

She frowned at him and he made an exasperated face at her.

"What do you care?"

"I care, Inigo," she said, hoping he could hear the truth of it. "Everyone needs friends. You can't be friends with bell jars and elements."

He said nothing.

"Name one. Name one friend."

"Oh, honestly," he protested.

"One friend. Not me," she added before he could answer.

"Solo Rothborn."

"Baron Rothborn?" she queried, frowning a little. "I thought he was a recluse."

Inigo gave a low chuckle and his smile was lopsided. "He is. I'm one of the few people he can tolerate. In small doses."

Minerva couldn't help but laugh at that. "A matching pair."

"Yes," he agreed.

She sighed. She wanted to make him smile, to make sure he ate properly and didn't work too hard, that his work was appreciated and that he didn't have to worry about paying bills and the ordinary grind of life that took the shine from his brilliance and dulled his passion. Nothing should dull his passion, that spark inside him that seemed to burn him up, burning him out too fast with no one there to keep the blaze under control.

He stared down at her, his face inscrutable, and then he leaned down and kissed her again, hard, before tugging her back into the room. They hurried to catch up with the guide, ignoring the exhibits. Once they had Mr Crick and Helena in sight again, Inigo slowed. Helena turned and sent a narrow-eyed glare at Minerva, which Minerva returned with a bland smile and a shrug.

"How old are you?"

She looked back at him, a little shocked by the question. Not that he'd asked it and that men ought never do so; she'd never supposed Inigo would play by polite society's rules, if he even knew them, he'd likely not care. It shocked her because it was personal, because he wanted to know.

"One and twenty. My birthday is in July."

His mouth firmed into a hard line and she couldn't help but chuckle, guessing at the route his mind had taken.

"Tut, tut, Mr de Beauvoir, what are you about, debauching a woman ten years your junior in a public place?"

He ran a hand through his hair, and it stuck up all over, making him look increasingly anxious. "It's not funny. Christ, I… I ought to be horsewhipped."

Minerva slid her hand down his arm, tangling their fingers together. "It was just a kiss, and you're hardly a wicked old man hell bent on seduction. I'm chasing *you*, remember."

Her heart ached at seeing the unhappy glower on his face. She wanted to smooth the creases from his brow and make him smile. It was strange how she had this sense of being so much older than him when he was by far her senior. She couldn't account for the protectiveness she felt for him.

"I ought to know better than to let you," he said, his frustration evident. "And it wasn't *just* a bloody kiss, and now you made me curse in front of you, damn you… you make me act like a madman."

"My mad natural philosopher, all brilliance and irritation. I must have provoked you badly, to make you drag yourself away from your laboratory."

"You have," he said, his voice low. "I didn't want to come here, but I didn't know where else to suggest."

"I would have come to you."

He closed his eyes, an expression close to pain flitting over his harsh features. "Don't."

"Why not? You know you only had to—"

"*Don't!*" he said again, his voice a harsh whisper. "You don't know."

There was something wild and dark in his eyes now and Minerva responded to it at once, wanting to push him until it spilled over and made him do it, whatever it was he was afraid of doing.

"Then tell me."

She stared at him, outwardly calm though her pulse was thundering beneath her skin.

"Perhaps I *should* tell you," he said, that angry note in his voice now, the same anger she'd tasted when he'd kissed her. "Perhaps if I told you all the depraved things I want from you, you'd have the sense to run away."

Excitement simmered in her belly. Minerva knew he was doing it to save himself, to force her to run from him, to shock her into sense, but she knew he wasn't lying either. She had seen enough of men to understand the heat in his eyes, even if she'd little experience of what it promised.

"Perhaps," she said, pursing her lips. "But doubtful."

Inigo made a low sound of desperation and turned away from her.

"Do you like chestnuts?"

"What?" he sounded irritable and snappy now, the change in subject making him glower at her suspiciously.

"I do. Roasted chestnuts. I always burn myself, though, every winter. No matter how many times I'm warned to let them cool down, I can't wait. I burn my fingers and my tongue, too eager to taste the sweetness inside." She stared at him, holding his gaze. "I'm rash and stubborn and sometimes I get burned. It's my own fault. I just won't learn my lesson."

He swallowed and the tension seemed to prickle between them. *It's him,* she thought, *I'm all he's thinking of in this moment and it's like being struck by lightning, to be in the glare of his attention.*

"Then perhaps someone should teach you more thoroughly, so you won't forget."

"Perhaps," she said with a shrug, which she doubted looked the least bit nonchalant, she was too alive, too aware of him to look indifferent. "But no one's managed it yet."

He walked away from her, leaving her side to stare at a vast collection of Roman coins. Minerva glanced ahead to where Helena's dark head was bent over a cabinet, Mr Crick beside her flushed and animated as he explained something to her. Minerva followed Inigo, standing close beside him, not touching him. Waiting.

"I want you."

It was raw and honest, and she could still hear the anger behind his words, the evidence that he didn't want to want her. There was resignation, too. He was done fighting, for now at least, and he was giving her fair warning. Noted. For all the good it would do.

"I want you too," she said, sounding remarkably calm, but then they couldn't both have an attack of the vapours, and he seemed to live on his nerves and sensibilities far more than Minerva did.

He huffed out a breath and glared at her, a furious glint in his eyes.

"Well, there's not much point in pretending otherwise now, is there?" she said, thinking that both obvious and reasonable.

"Do you have no sense of self-preservation?" he demanded.

"Apparently not where you are concerned, no."

He leaned his forehead against the cabinet, eyes closed. She thought perhaps he was counting to ten, or perhaps a thousand. It was hard to tell.

"What do we do now?" she asked.

One eye opened, squinting at her in outrage. "So eager to be ruined?"

"Oh, really, don't be so dramatic. I just want to see you again." Minerva shook her head and walked off, but he caught hold of her arm.

"Haven't you been listening?" he demanded. "It's the same thing."

Oh.

"Well, a public place then, if you're so untrustworthy." She threw the words back at him, her own patience wearing thin now.

"I never have been before, but you make me insane!" He threw up his hands and then sank them into his hair, disarranging it all. She could see he was angry now, or perhaps that was merely frustration at not wanting to be responsible for her ruination. "You never say no when you should, and I can't trust you to look after yourself. I want to bed you, I'm a man, flesh and blood. I just don't want to deal with the tears and hysteria that will come when you regret it. I don't much want Bedwin to call me out for it either."

Minerva tapped her foot, just as frustrated as he was. It wasn't fair. She wanted to be alone with him.

"I'm not courting you," he said, pointing a finger at her to underscore the point, as if he hadn't made that abundantly clear. "So we can't keep being seen in each other's company without tongues wagging."

"Fine. Then I'll come to you. Friday. I'll bring lunch."

There, decision made. Her stomach tied itself into a great big knot. She turned to stare at him, daring him to quibble.

"Your funeral." He bit the words out, his fists clenched.

Minerva sighed.

"Inigo," she said, her voice soft and she lay her hand on one rigid arm. "Would you hurt me?"

An appalled expression made his lip curl with revulsion. "Good God, what do you take me for?"

"It's not me that's thinking the worst, it's you," she said, shaking her head. "You're not a bad man, Inigo, we both know this. So, if I tell you no, you'll stop. Yes?"

"Yes, of course," he said, frowning.

"Well, then, I promise to say it if you go too far." She smiled at him. "Friday it is."

She walked away to join Helena, wracking her brain to think of anything she would be likely to say *no* to.

Chapter 9

She's a big girl. We all must take our chances for happiness, to live and love as we see fit. It may be her only chance to be with the man she loves, or it may be the worst mistake of her life. All we can do is try to keep her safe and pick up the pieces if things go badly. If you interfere and she decides a course of action because you persuaded her to and come to regret it, she'll never forgive you. If it's her decision and you stick by her, no matter what, you're a good friend.

—Excerpt of a letter from Mrs Bonnie Cadogan to Lady Helena Adolphus.

22nd January 1815. Meeting of the Peculiar Ladies. South Audley Street, London.

"Well, Ruth certainly sounds happy," Matilda said with a satisfied smile as she folded the letter she'd just read out.

Minerva looked towards Helena, who sighed wistfully.

"Hmmm, a remote castle with a great big Highlander to keep her warm. I should say she's happy."

Minerva made a muffled snorting sound, and Bonnie a bark of laughter before reaching for her second cream cake as Jemima passed the plate around. "I can't wait to visit her and see Gordon bloody Anderson eating out of her hand like a little lamb," Bonnie said, smirking. "Oh, that man will tie himself in knots, having to keep a civil tongue in his head with me."

Prue snorted and shook her head. "You're wicked through and through, Bonnie. When are you thinking of going?"

"Oh, not until the summer. If you think I'm going to the Highlands in February, you have another think coming. That damn castle is freezing, even in August. I don't doubt it's a sight better than it was, but I'll still wait until August. Then I know I'll only have to take my winter clothes to survive."

"And here we were thinking you were a hardy Highlander yourself," Matilda said, lips quirking.

Bonnie put her nose in the air. "I'll have you know I'm as delicate as a rose petal."

Helena choked on her tea so hard that Prue had to take the cup and saucer away from her before she spilt it in her lap.

"I had a letter from Kitty," Minerva said, as Jemima waved the delicious selection of cream cakes at her. "Wicked creature," she murmured to Jemima before sighing and taking one. "And she arranged for Harriet to send me the hat and the remaining dares, which arrived this morning. Harriet has buried herself at Holbrooke."

"I hardly think we can blame her for that," Helena said, fanning herself with her napkin. "If I was married to St Clair, I'd never leave the house either."

"I thought you wanted a Highlander?" Matilda retorted.

"I thought you wanted a *knight* in shining armour," Minerva murmured, earning herself a warning glare from Helena.

"The hat, Minerva," Helena said, *sotto voce*.

"Ah, yes, the hat," Minerva said, grinning as Jemima shifted nervously and Matilda grew very still.

"But you and Helena haven't completed your dares yet," Matilda objected.

"I have!" Minerva said, and then felt a furious blush stain her cheeks as she wondered what the others would think of her for having done so.

Would they think her no better than she ought to be?

"Oh?" Everyone but Helena and Bonnie gazed at her.

Suddenly, Minerva realised Helena must have spoken to Bonnie about her. It took her a moment to decide whether or not she was annoyed, but only a moment. Helena and Bonnie were very close, and she knew Helena was worried about her part in helping Minerva cover up her visits to Inigo. She could hardly blame her for confiding in her best friend.

"Yes, I... I called on Mr de Beauvoir."

"Alone?" Matilda said, eyes wide with horror. "Oh, Minerva."

"No one saw me," Minerva said in a rush, seeing at once all of Matilda's protective instincts rush to the surface. "I'm fine, and he treated me very well... once he got over the shock," she added with a smirk.

"I'll just bet he did," Helena muttered.

It was Minerva's turn to glare. "So, Helena to go," she said, loud enough to hope the attention would turn away from her.

"I can't do mine until Robert goes away, and he's delayed his trip because Prue wasn't well," Helena returned, smug devil.

"I'm fine now," Prue said, holding up one hand whilst the other covered the slight bump beneath her dress. She looked like a beautiful Madonna, all rosy cheeked and serene. "He's just fussing. I'm trying to get him to rearrange it, I swear," she said to Helena apologetically, before her gaze settled on Minerva, making her blush.

"I know, it's fine." Helena grinned and patted Prue's hand. "My new niece or nephew is far more important than a silly dare."

"But what happened with Mr de Beauvoir?" Matilda pressed, as Minerva groaned inwardly.

So much for distracting her attention, and now Prue was going to be after her blood too.

Minerva shrugged. "I took him lunch. The poor man never eats. He doesn't have a housekeeper since he did an experiment that blew up in his laboratory—on purpose—but she accused him of being a devil worshiper or something ridiculous, and ran screaming."

Bonnie snorted. "You're quite certain she wasn't onto something?"

"Quite certain," Minerva retorted. "He's a brilliant natural philosopher. It just breaks my heart to see him scratching about in that empty house because he's too devoted to his work to light the fires or find anyone to feed him."

"Well, then, we should get him a housekeeper," Matilda said firmly. "Then you can stop worrying and putting your reputation at risk. I'll not have you ruining your life out of… of pity."

Minerva stared at Matilda in surprise. She always worried about all of them, but she was never quite so… strident. It was only the quaver in her voice that gave away how very frightened she was. Minerva looked at her, holding her gaze steadily.

"I have thought of doing just that, Matilda, and I will, but I don't want anyone there spying on us when I visit. So, until I know how I stand with him, I'll leave things as they are."

"You're going back?" Matilda demanded, looking as though she might cast up her accounts there and then, she was so pale. "You're not serious? You must not, Minerva, it's—"

"I *am* serious," Minerva said, interrupting, but keeping her voice calm. "And it's not for you to tell me who I may and may not see, but I do appreciate your concern. I truly do, and I swear to be careful."

Matilda made a disparaging sound, her eyes glittering too brightly. "No, you won't. You'll be foolish and put your heart on the line, and he'll take everything you offer him and then, when he's had all he wants, you'll be put aside, all in bits and with no other options."

Minerva felt the words like a stab to the heart. She knew it was a possible outcome of her actions—there was no point in not having her eyes open to the risk she was running—but to hear Matilda spell it out so baldly, her tone so hard it was almost cruel, still hurt.

"He's not Montagu," she replied before she could think it through, seeing the words strike Matilda just as hard.

The room had grown very still, no one daring to breathe.

"Damn Montagu," Matilda said, putting her chin up. "I can't stop you from being a little fool, but I will not end up in bits. I shall marry Mr Burton."

There was a collective gasp around her, though Minerva was too shocked to even draw a breath. She was certain Matilda had just decided, at that very moment, perhaps to set an example of what a sensible woman did in a difficult situation.

"You don't love him," she said, watching Matilda, who was so pale her skin seemed translucent, blue veins visible beneath the porcelain complexion. "I'm not convinced you even like him."

"I'm not convinced he even likes me," Matilda retorted. "He wants me the same way he wants a pretty picture or a nice house in the right part of town. So what? He gets me on his arm, and I get a home, security, a family. I'm sure we'll be content enough with each other, and those are not things I can ignore. If you had an ounce of sense in that silly head of yours, you'd see it too."

Anger sparked in Minerva's heart at being called silly. Matilda, of all people, knew how hard she was trying to be anything but silly, and the accusation rankled.

"And what about Montagu?" Minerva pressed, knowing she was crossing a line but too irritated to consider it. "What about the fact you're in love with him?"

The silence was so profound Minerva's ears rang with it. Matilda looked as if she'd been slapped, two high spots of colour burning against the snow white pallor of her cheeks. She got to her feet.

"If you'll excuse me, ladies. I'm sure you can find your own way out."

Minerva watched, heart thudding and stomach clenching with regret as Matilda turned for the door.

"Mat—" Minerva began, but Helena reached out and clasped her arm, holding tight and shaking her head.

Everyone watched her go, and Minerva put her head in her hands. "I should not have said that."

"I'm glad one of us finally got up the nerve to and, selfishly, I'm glad it was you and not me," Prue said with a sigh.

Minerva stared at her in shock. She'd expected Prue to be furious with her. Going on the glint in her eyes, she was not entirely wrong.

"We will be having words about your visits to Mr de Beauvoir, Min," she said, her voice stern. Prue had always seen her as her foolish baby cousin, though she was only five years older than Minerva.

Minerva had believed that had changed, but the tone of Prue's voice made her doubt it.

"You won't tell Mama?" Minerva said in a rush, feeling as though she might cry, her eyes burning. If her mother found out, she'd be sent away and never see Inigo again.

"Minerva Butler!" her cousin said in outrage. "Whatever do you take me for? I'll not tell her, nor Robert, for its none of their business, but for heaven's sake, Matilda is right. You are playing with fire."

Minerva nodded, unable to deny it. "I k-know," she said, her voice breaking. "But I-I'm in love with him."

A collective murmur whispered around the group, a mixture of wistful longing and resignation.

"Does he love you?" Prue asked, gentle now.

"I don't know yet. He doesn't want to love me, I know that. I think he's afraid to, but… but I think he could, if he let himself." She wiped her eyes, looking around at the faces of the surrounding women, her dearest friends, the people she trusted most in the world. "He says he doesn't believe in love."

"Idiot," Bonnie said with her usual candour.

Minerva choked back a laugh. "I know. He's the stupidest genius I ever met." She looked around as Helena's hand slid into hers, holding on tight.

"You're really in love with him?" Helena's eyes were grave, more serious than Minerva had ever seen them.

"I am."

"Well, then. We have to figure out how the two of them can be together with no one finding out." This from Bonnie, who'd never shied away from a scandal in her whole life.

Minerva could have kissed her. Instead, she just sent a grateful smile in her direction.

"I've done far more stupid things for love, Min," she said. "I promise you, you have a lot of catching up to do."

"Yes, and there's absolutely no requirement to do so," Prue chipped in, giving Bonnie an impatient glare. "You're happily married now. Minerva has a way to go before we can all breathe easy."

"I should apologise to Matilda," Minerva said, staring at the door with a sick sensation churning in her stomach.

"There's plenty of time for that. Matilda won't hold a grudge, and it's not like we didn't all want to say it. She's been playing with fire far longer than you and, as much as I wish marrying Mr Burton was the answer, I'm just uncertain that it is." Prue sighed and sat back, smoothing her palm over her belly. "She's so afraid of being alone, and she's quite right, he offers her security."

"Unlike Montagu, who will chew her up and spit her out," Jemima said, her expression bleak. "And *he's* the man she falls head over heels for. Life is so bloody unfair."

All of them started in surprise. Jemima rarely spoke up, so hearing her swear was nothing short of extraordinary.

"Well, is it?" she demanded as they all stared at her in shock.

"No, it bloody isn't," Helena replied, succinctly and with such force they all laughed.

The laughter rose until there were tears in their eyes and they were leaning into each other, relieved to let go of the tension that had been holding all of them in its grip.

Friends, thought Minerva, looking around the room and feeling her heart swell with affection and pride. The best friends in the world.

***

24th January 1815. Church Street, Isleworth, London.

Inigo sat at his work bench in the laboratory, leaning on his elbows and ignoring the slide he'd just put under the microscope in favour of staring out of the window. It was a grimy day, grey and cold, a steady drizzle of rain plastering itself against the windows as the wind gusted towards the back of the house. A draught of cold air snaked around the ill-fitting glass, making him shiver and reminding himself he'd not lit the fires. Usually he was too wrapped up in his work to notice such things until it hit freezing, but today his home seemed grim and empty. Loneliness curled in the pit of his belly like an old dog, a familiar companion settling down for a long nap.

She was coming today, he reminded himself, and he hated the flutter of anticipation in his chest, the way hope chased away the grey clouds and made everything lighter. *Stop it. Stop it,* he told himself. Hope was dangerous, and he'd learned to distrust it a long time ago. He'd once had a friend at the foundling hospital. Timothy Brown had arrived in the summer Inigo turned eight and they'd become fast friends. Inigo, inured to the hard life of an orphan, had protected Tim, who'd been lost and vulnerable, susceptible to bullying. He'd been the sweetest little boy, with white blond curls and big blue eyes, the face of an angel. He was also sturdily built and healthy. So when a respectable childless couple came to the hospital looking to take a boy into their family, to help them on their farm, sure enough it was Timothy they took.

"Don't worry," Tim had said, hugging him tightly before he left. "When I'm settled, I'll make them come back for you. Two hands are better than one."

Inigo had believed him. He'd waited days, weeks, wondering how long it would take Tim to settle in. When one of the wardens had caught him staring out the window for the fiftieth time, he'd asked what Inigo was doing.

"Waiting for Tim, sir," he'd replied. "He's been adopted, and he said he'll ask the family to take me too. He promised to come back for me."

Inigo could still see the careworn face of the warden. He'd been one of the decent ones, not so handy with his fists as some of the others. "Give it up, lad," he'd said, gruff though not unkind. "They don't want boys like you. 'Tis only the pretty and the strong what get taken in and you ain't neither, 'sides which, it ain't up to Tim who gets adopted. They ain't never comin' back. Best you get used to the idea."

"No," Inigo had cried, shaking his head, hot tears coursing down his face. "*No,* it ain't true. He promised. He promised me…."

He'd hit the warden in his fury and been sent to bed with no supper, but as the days went by, it became clear the man had spoken true. That truth had hurt more than anything Inigo had ever known, which seemed ridiculous, for he'd lost nothing. Nothing had changed for he'd had nothing to lose, but he'd hoped, and losing hope had killed something inside him for good. Or so he'd thought. Yet here he was again, with that dangerous emotion stalking about in his head, distracting him from his work, from what mattered, to stare out of windows and dream of things he could never have.

Only the pretty and the strong, the warden had said. Well, that had changed, at least. Now it was the wealthy, well-bred gentlemen of the *ton* who had the right to take what he wanted. He didn't want it, he reminded himself. Yes, he'd wanted a wife, someone to organise his life, so he didn't spend all his days in a house with no fire lit and no food in the cupboards. *Liar.* It hadn't been only for that. It was because he was tired of being alone. Harriet had been his friend and he'd thought it would be nice to have a friend with him. It would be good to have someone to talk to about his work, to share a meal with, to have someone bring him a cup of tea and ask how he was getting on and had he remembered to eat his lunch, someone who might remember he existed and worry for him.

Inigo pressed the heels of his hands against his eyes and drew in a deep breath. It would have been enough, it would, if he hadn't met Minerva. He'd never thought he'd feel possessive of a woman, would ever want one woman over all others. He'd never understood those feelings. If he'd found a woman who enjoyed him physically but wanted no commitment, no marriage, he'd always believed that would suit him. Yet when the scandalous Mrs Tate had offered just that some months back, he'd run a mile. Why? Why Minerva Butler of all people? Why on earth was this one woman getting under his skin and making him question everything he'd ever believed about himself, about what he wanted? Damn her! Now his guts were in a knot and he couldn't sleep, and too often he could swear he caught the delicate scent of her, like a phantom haunting his home, his heart. He let the breath out, steadying himself, refusing to look at his watch. She wouldn't come. She'd warned him she might struggle to get away but that she'd do her best. She wouldn't come. Now she knew what would happen if she did, and she'd come to her senses, and....

A knock sounded at the front door and Inigo scrambled to his feet, almost knocking the stool over in his haste. Cursing, he looked down at his crumpled shirt and regretted not having dressed properly. He tugged the sleeves down at least, though he had no idea where he'd left his cufflinks. He ran a hand through his hair, trying to smooth it down, relieved that he'd shaved as he hurried to the door and pulled it open.

Inigo stared in shock, taking a step back as he was confronted with a veritable wall of femininity.

"Good day, Mr de Beauvoir," said the Duchess of Bedwin, giving him a taut smile as she looked him over and made him feel every bit the ragged orphan boy he'd been as she took in the creased shirt and the fact he wore no waistcoat or cravat.

That they must know he'd been waiting for Minerva and hadn't at least dressed properly made heat crawl up the back of his neck. He searched what seemed to be a crowd of women, to discover Minerva staring at him, looking equally mortified.

"Sorry," she mouthed, eyes wide with anxiety.

"We've come to see your laboratory," piped up one of the women, a curvy, dark-haired girl with a faint Scottish accent. He thought she looked vaguely familiar. "Don't worry, we won't stay long."

She shot him a mischievous look, giving him a once over and grinning.

Now his ears were burning as well as his neck.

"May we come in then, Mr de Beauvoir, or shall we stand on the doorstep in the rain for the next twenty minutes?" the duchess demanded coolly.

Inigo took another step back, too dumbstruck to do anything else.

The women filed in, one after another. It felt as if there were dozens of them, skirts rustling and pretty, delicate perfumes scenting the air. Suddenly the dim hallway was full of impossibly bright colours and frills, as if a flock of exotic birds had flown in through the window to escape the rain. He was outnumbered and had no idea what to do next.

"The laboratory is through there," Minerva instructed.

The duchess nodded and the women followed her out, leaving Inigo alone with Minerva.

"I'm so sorry," she said, wringing her hands. "When they discovered I've been visiting you they got all protective. They'll go in a minute, leaving me, and then come back again when Prue pretends to have left her umbrella. That way no one will notice I'm here."

Inigo fought to find words to react to this preposterous scheme, but found he could do nothing but stare at her.

"Are you angry?" she asked, her lovely face clouding as he just glared at her in outrage. "Please don't be. I know it's ridiculous and I have no idea what they'll do next time. I shall have to escape without them knowing, but they are only looking out for me."

Inigo swallowed. "I'm... not angry," he said, realising he meant it.

These women were her friends; they were trying to protect the foolish creature from herself. Admittedly it would have been better if they'd just locked her in her room, but still.

Minerva let out a breath, her relief palpable. "Oh, I'm glad. I've been so looking forward to seeing you."

She put one hand on his shoulder and lifted onto her toes, pressing a soft kiss to the corner of his mouth. Inigo closed his eyes as her lips touched his, reminding himself sternly to breathe.

"Come," she said, taking his hand. "I've been working on Prue to ask Bedwin to sponsor your work."

Utterly dazed, Inigo followed her through to his laboratory, pausing on the way to shrug on a coat and tie a haphazard cravat, and tried not to get hysterical at the sight of his sanctuary filled to the rafters with women. In fact, there were only five of them including Minerva. It felt like an invasion.

"We swear we won't touch anything," the duchess remarked, amusement glinting in her sharp gaze as she noticed his panicked expression. "Minerva tells us you believe you have made a significant discovery. A new element?"

Inigo nodded. "I'm writing a paper at the moment," he said, wryly acknowledging to himself at least that the paper currently consisted of about five lines, as his mind had been elsewhere.

"Bedwin is fascinated by such things," the duchess said, casting a curious glance over the shelves and work surfaces. "You must come to dinner once your paper is written, before you publish it. I'm certain he would find it interesting. He's a keen sponsor of the arts and sciences."

Inigo blinked, stunned, only coming to his senses as Minerva's gloved fingers curled around his.

"I... I should be honoured to, your grace. Thank you," he managed.

The duchess nodded before chivvying the rest of the women up and herding them back towards the door. Her hazel eyes settled on him for a moment, considering. "I admire anyone who makes a success of their life, especially those who have struggled against adversity. I, for one, do not believe the act of being a gentleman is something one comes to by birth. I expect you to be a gentleman, Mr de Beauvoir. Do I make myself clear?"

"Prue!" Minerva exclaimed, glaring at her cousin in exasperation.

"It needs saying, Min," Prue replied, perfectly calm and never taking her attention from Inigo.

For his part, he felt like a scolded toddler. She was remarkably intimidating for such a slender young woman. Inigo squared his shoulders, scowling a little.

"I've warned her she ought not come, she ought not be here with me," he said, every bit as belligerent and irritated as he sounded.

"And how is that working out for you?" Prue replied with the faint lift of one eyebrow.

Inigo huffed and folded his arms.

"Precisely," she replied, clipped and cool, though her lips quirked a little. That ghost of a smile faded, and she took a step closer, lowering her voice. "Being married to a duke has certain advantages, Mr de Beauvoir. It gives me the power to do you a good turn, but hurt my cousin and I'll hurt you where you'll feel it most."

Inigo hadn't been threatened since he was a boy, at the hands of those bigger and stronger than he was. It still felt the same. He was vaguely aware of Minerva groaning and putting her head in her hands. The duchess stepped back and gave them a broad smile.

"Have a lovely afternoon. Min, we'll collect you at four as arranged. Goodbye, darling."

The duchess swept out with a rustle of expensive fabric, leaving them alone. They heard the front door bang shut. Inigo sat on the edge of the workbench, uncertain what had just happened.

Chapter 10

I think it's the right thing to do. I mean, you married a man you didn't know at all, one that wasn't even very nice to you, and look how that turned out. I know Mr Burton isn't what I've dreamed of, but how many of us get to live our dreams? I don't believe he would hurt me, and I'd have a lovely home, a family. The sensible thing is just to accept his offer when it comes and be grateful that he asked, and so that is what I shall do.

Don't you think it's for the best?

—Excerpt of a letter from Miss Matilda Hunt to Mrs Ruth Anderson.

Still the 21st January 1815. Church Street, Isleworth, London.

"Inigo?"

Minerva set the basket she was carrying down and move towards him. Inigo didn't move, leaning his weight back on the workbench and watching her warily as she approached. She stepped between his open thighs, sliding her hands around his neck.

"It's all right," she said, her voice soft.

Inigo looked at her, indignant at her assurance when it was clearly nothing of the sort.

"In what way is it all right? I'm being blackmailed by the Duchess of Bedwin. I'm just not certain what it is I'm supposed to do. I am to propose now?"

There was a bitter note to his words which he didn't entirely feel and regretted at once as Minerva withdrew her hands from his neck and stepped away.

"Of course not," she said, and there was something wistful in her eyes that made him want to cut out his tongue. "I'm so sorry, Inigo, truly. I... I couldn't stop them, stop *her*. Prue is very headstrong and... and she's protective of me. It's a wonder she didn't just lock me up or send me away. She's not sneaky though, she won't trick you into marrying me. She knows I'm pursuing you and that you are not to blame. I told her everything I'd done. It's a mark of her trust that she's let me stay here with you."

Inigo stared at her, uncertain of what he felt and with no idea of what to say. She was here and, no matter what else, he couldn't find anything to regret in that fact.

Her face fell as he continued to watch her in silence. "I'll put the lunch things out."

She picked up the basket and left him feeling as uneasy and wrong-footed as her visits always did. After a moment, he stirred himself. There was little point in pretending he didn't want to see her, didn't want this time with her, so he'd best make the most of it. He went to the parlour, seeing it through Minerva's eyes and grimacing. There was a threadbare rug in front of the fire, two mismatched chairs—one of which was losing the stuffing from a rip in the cushion—and not a great deal else. Well, it wasn't as if he'd pretended to be a rich man. He'd told her he'd been born in the slums, orphaned and dragged up among the desperate. This house had always seemed a palace to him, a mark of his success; he was damned if he'd feel ashamed of it now. Yet an uneasy sense of inadequacy set him all on edge.

Inigo went to the hearth and lit the fire, sweeping up the ash and making sure it was burning merrily. There was no point in pretending he would ignore her presence and go back to work after lunch. They could sit in here and… and what? Make polite conversation? Drink tea? He knew what he wanted to do, and he knew that Prue's warning had not been an idle threat. She'd cut off his balls if he overstepped the mark. The trouble was, he did not know where the mark was. What were they expecting of him? Surely the duchess wasn't condoning a marriage between them. So was she just allowing Minerva to enjoy a love affair before she settled down to marriage with a suitable choice? Some chinless nobleman with pots of money, no doubt.

He told himself that was fine, that it was the perfect arrangement. He got what he wanted with no strings attached, no guilt. Yet jealousy simmered beneath his skin, much as he tried to pretend it was nothing of the sort. You couldn't own another human being. You could not have a hold on another person or keep them all to yourself. Everyone belonged to themselves alone, and should live their lives as they saw fit with minimal interference from anyone else. What people did in the privacy of their beds, with whom, how many times, or with how many lovers was their own affair. He told himself that, told himself he had no claim to Minerva, and she had none on him, but the sick churning sensation in his gut strongly disagreed.

"Here you are."

His head jerked up as he discovered he was kneeling in the dust, still staring at the flames.

Minerva came in, smiling at him. "What a charming room," she said, looking about her.

Inigo frowned, wondering if she was being polite or facetious but it appeared she meant it.

"It must be cosy in here when the fire gets going."

"I like it," he admitted, a little grudgingly but realising it was true.

Despite his misgivings about what she might think of it, besides his laboratory, it was his favourite room in the house.

"Will you come and eat now?" she asked, holding out her hands to him. There was a glimmer of uncertainty in her eyes which he realised he didn't like.

"Did you bring cake?" he asked, knowing she would have.

"Of course I did," she said. She reached out and stroked his hair from his face, carding it through her fingers as if she was stroking a cat.

Inigo closed his eyes and restrained the urge to purr.

"You look tired," she said, as her hand moved down, cupping his cheek.

Inigo covered it with his own hand, turning into it and kissing the palm as relief surged through him. Oh, God, yes, this. Her hands on him, her touch… he'd been longing for it, aching for it, and yet he'd not known how much until this moment.

He heard her breath catch, and he chased the sound by tracing a circle on her palm with his tongue, wanting it again. She obliged, the little gasp increasingly breathless as his lips moved to her wrist. He could feel her pulse against his mouth, beating madly, like a tiny trapped bird beneath her skin. It was exhilarating.

"Come and eat first," she said.

He looked up at her, knowing his eyes must be dark with wanting, but holding onto the most important part of the sentence… *first.* Before. Anticipation would not kill him, he supposed, though in this moment that didn't seem a certainty.

Inigo stood, staring down at Minerva as she returned his gaze, too trusting, too certain of his ability to behave as he ought. Foolish girl. He was halfway mad with wanting her. Nonetheless he followed her back to the kitchen, meek as a lamb. She'd lit the stove and a lamp burned on the table, giving a warm glow that illuminated the room against the grim, leaden sky outside. Strange how the place had seemed so barren when he'd come foraging for breakfast this morning. He'd managed tea, at least, and found some biscuits. It occurred to him then it wasn't the lit stove or the lamp that changed how his house felt around him, it was her. He ought to be nauseated by that idea, but that reckless, dangerous feeling rose inside him again. Hope.

Fool.

"Sit down," she said, smiling at him and pulling out a chair.

"Isn't that my job?" He ignored her, pulling out her chair instead, wishing his chest didn't react so oddly every time she smiled at him, chipping away at the armour he'd built to protect himself from wanting things he couldn't have.

She sat down and Inigo fought the proprietary sensation it gave him to see her seated at his table.

"I heated some soup," she said, lifting the lid on a large pot as Inigo noted the delicious scent curling about the room. No wonder that basket had looked so heavy. "And there are fresh rolls and butter, and I asked Cook to put in some of the game pie she made, as you enjoyed the chicken and ham one so much."

"Thank you," he said, watching her ladle soup into a bowl.

She handed him the bowl before serving herself, and he was aware of the way she watched him, the weight of her gaze on him like a caress. It made his body grow tight, desire simmering beneath his skin.

"Is it good?"

He nodded, too unsettled to speak, worried he'd say something he ought not. They ate in silence, as though she felt it too, this uncertainty, this anticipation, this terror of wanting something that he knew he wouldn't be allowed to keep. All the while reminding himself he didn't want it at all. Temporary, it was only temporary. She was playing with him, enjoying herself and indulging her own desires before she married to please her family.

No.

The force with which his emotions rebelled at the idea shocked him. No. Not temporary.

His.

You cannot own her. You cannot keep her. She is not yours.

Inigo ate because it pleased her, even though it wasted time, took it away from the moment he could put his hands on her, touch her, kiss her. He couldn't deny her because of the way her eyes lit up with pleasure. She seemed to enjoy taking care of him and that was a novel experience.

'I'm glad you liked it," she said, looking far too pleased with herself.

"I feel like a Christmas turkey," he grumbled, not meaning it.

"Well, you've got a way to go," she said, laughing as she stood and then giving him a critical once over. "Though I think perhaps you have put on a little weight already." Her gaze travelled across his shoulders, his chest, making him hot and restless. "I keep thinking I ought to arrange a housekeeper for you, but I'm too selfish."

Her words faded as she walked away and took the leftovers to his pantry, storing them for him.

"Selfish?" he queried once she returned.

"Yes," she said, giving him a quizzical look as she collected the dirty plates and utensils. "I don't want anyone else here. I want to have you all to myself."

Oh, God.

"Leave that," he commanded, getting to his feet and taking hold of her wrist.

The knives and forks she'd been holding clattered onto the table and he tugged her, forcing her to follow him back to the parlour. He slammed the door shut and hauled her into his arms, kissing her like he'd been starved and would devour her. Her cousin's threats rang in his ears, but he was deaf to them, out of control, and she did nothing to dissuade him, nothing to tell him no, to halt his assault on her mouth, though she damn well ought to.

Somehow, he forced himself to break the kiss, aware he was trembling. They both were. Minerva stared up at him, dark eyed, her lips red and swollen and oh, god, he wanted her.

"You ought not let me," he said, his voice all scratchy and odd. "You're supposed to say no, remember?"

She gave a shaky laugh. "I will, if I want you to stop."

Inigo groaned. They were both doomed. The duchess would have him chopped up and dropped in the Thames, and Minerva would be ruined. It was inevitable.

"Stop looking so anguished."

He looked back to Minerva to see such an expression of bemused affection in her eyes that his throat grew inexplicably tight. Sighing, he moved away from her and sat down in the chair by the fire. She dropped into his lap a moment later, like a ripe peach, as if it were the most natural thing in the world, as if she belonged there. Oh, yes, she belonged there.

"Your cousin will have me castrated if you don't go home in the same state you arrived," he stated, too aware of her soft behind pressed against his arousal.

She shifted a little in his lap and he bit back a groan.

"Prue isn't a fool. She knows I will kiss you, that I want to be with you for a reason."

He did groan this time, closing his eyes and resting his head against the chair back. He stilled, hardly daring to breathe as nimble fingers undid his cravat and tugged it free. A warm hand slid inside his shirt and he gasped in concert with Minerva as her hand moved over his bare chest.

"You're so hot," she marvelled. "Silky, too. I think your skin is softer than mine."

She smirked as Inigo grunted, too aroused to do anything but let her explore. She found the coarse hair on his chest and raked her fingers back and forth through it, making him shiver.

"Take off your shirt," she whispered. "I want to see you."

Inigo stared at her, wondering if he'd imagined her words, but she tugged at the offending item impatiently, making her desires plain enough.

"Let me up." His voice was gruff, betraying his urgency as she stood and then stole his place in the seat, watching him intently while he stripped off his coat and hauled the shirt over his head.

The way her breath caught, the heated look in her eyes, made him feel unhinged, teetering on the edge of what he knew to be acceptable. Though how he could know what was acceptable in this situation, he couldn't fathom. She wasn't some lightskirt he could pay for a quick tumble. She had no experience at all, and he ought not be the one to give it to her, that was for her husband to do. That thought got pushed away fast. She wanted him, wanted this, and he was going to meet that desire. He didn't think there were rules for this though, like there were for choosing the right fork or spoon.

Inigo knelt before her, fighting to keep his breathing under control as she reached to touch him. Her cheeks were flushed, her eyes fever bright as she put her hands to his skin. He did his best not to react but still jolted liked he'd been shocked as her soft palms smoothed down his chest. Her fingers traced along the lines of muscle and sinew and he shivered with pleasure, so hard for her that she had to be aware of his arousal, pressing as it was against the confines of his clothes, desperate for her touch to shift lower. He held her gaze as he curled his hands around her ankles, watching her lips part, hearing her breath hitch as his hands slid up, lingering over her calves, pushing up the froth of skirts and petticoats as she went.

"Come closer," he said, his voice dark with want.

She inched towards the edge of the chair and he leaned in, kissing her softly. His hands found the tender flesh at the top of her stockings, stroking back and forth with his fingertips, enjoying the way she trembled against him.

"You definitely have softer skin than I do," he murmured against her mouth. "And I've not even found the softest places of all yet. Shall I find them?"

She was breathing hard as he drew back to study her, but she nodded her agreement, allowing him to slide his palms higher, his thumbs to dip into the silky crease at the juncture of each thigh.

"Like satin," he murmured, wondering how he'd ever find his way back to sanity, back to a place where his mind could focus on anything but this, the feel of her beneath his hands, the warm, feminine scent of her arousal intoxicating him.

He was desperate, holding on by a thread to keep from frightening her away when he wanted to taste her, devour her, make her his in every way. It was a ridiculous urge, primitive and possessive, but as much as he told himself he wasn't a bloody caveman, he couldn't reason away the need to make her his, to mark her in some way that showed the world she belonged to him and him alone. Madness. It was madness, but he couldn't pretend he wanted sanity ever again when this was so sweet.

He leaned into her, kissing her again as his thumbs stroked up and down the satiny path, tantalisingly close to where he wanted to be as he deepened the kiss, pushing her to lay back in the chair.

"Show me," he demanded, staring at the buttons that closed the demure neckline of her gown.

Her fingers trembled as she reached for them, fumbling and taking an agonising amount of time as she slipped each one free to expose her chemise and the corset that held her breasts high and plump.

Inigo held his breath as she pulled the ribbon that tied the chemise.

"Show me," he said again, with more force, sounding demented and out of control, which was all too true.

She tugged at the corset, forcing it down before peeling back the chemise to expose her breasts to him. He groaned, the sound ripped from him as he lowered his mouth to her, covering the ample curves with kisses as her hands sank into his hair, holding him to her.

"Minerva," he said, speaking her name like a promise of devotion. "Oh, God, Minerva."

She made a soft sound, a sigh of pleasure and it made him want to weep with gratitude, to worship her for everything she gave him. One hand slid from the coaxing path he teased up her thigh, his fingers sifting through the velvet curls between her legs as she stilled and gasped, a little anxious now.

"I want to touch you," he said, aware it sounded like pleading but unable to stop himself. "Please, love, let me touch you."

She nodded, her eyes dark and glassy with desire. That she looked that way for him seemed impossible, but she'd come to him, chosen him when she might have had anyone.

"I won't hurt you," he promised. "I'd never hurt you."

"I know," she said, her smile so sweet, so trusting, that his chest ached with the enormity of it.

He buried his face against her neck, breathing in the scent of her, so familiar now and yet still so enthralling as his fingers slid between her thighs. A sound was torn from him as he sought and found the place where she burned for him, found her wet and so hot. His body throbbed so insistently he had to grit his teeth to keep from shattering. Inigo caressed her with slow, gentle strokes, reminding himself it was her he wanted to please. He wanted to give her a taste of what could be between them. Just a taste, he promised himself. He would not take everything, would not ruin her wholly, and not just because her cousin would ruin him if he did.

Minerva sighed, restless under his touch, guiding his mouth back to her breasts. Inigo was only too happy to oblige her. He was enslaved, a prisoner to her will, but then he had been from the start, no matter how much it terrified him. No matter how hard he fought it, he had no strength to resist. When she opened her legs, allowing him more, he almost sobbed, his desire to be inside her was so great. Instead he moved back, pushing her skirts up to her hips, his breath catching at the sight of the soft, dark blonde curls between her thighs.

"I-Inigo," she said, her expression uncertain as he tore his gaze away to meet her eyes.

"I… I need…." he began, trying to find the words when anything resembling a coherent thought had been burned from his brain. "Taste you… I want to taste…."

Minerva's mouth dropped open in shock and he feared he'd pushed too far, feared she would deny him.

"You… you *want* to…?"

She looked so puzzled by the idea it might have been amusing if he wasn't so desperate.

"Yes," he said, the word rough with desire. "Yes, please. Oh, God, please, Minerva."

"It… it will feel… nice?" she asked, her cheeks scarlet.

Inigo could not help the wolfish smile that curved over his mouth.

"Oh, yes," he said, his voice grave despite his triumph. "I swear it will be a great deal more than just nice. Let me show you. I swear I'll stop if you want me to," he added.

Please don't ask me to stop. Please, please don't ask me to stop.

Minerva swallowed hard and then nodded. "Yes, then."

He made a sound of satisfaction, leaning forward to kiss her mouth once, hard, before tugging her hips closer to the edge of the seat and holding her thighs open.

"I don't think you have the slightest idea how beautiful you are," he said, aware of the reverent way he spoke, "or what you do to me. I want to know you, every part of you, every freckle," he said, smiling and pressing a kiss to the place on her inner thigh were one such tiny speckle of colour patterned her perfect skin.

Minerva gasped, her breathing coming faster as his lips moved inexorably closer, soft, open-mouthed kisses and the touch of his tongue inching towards their goal. At last he was there, his mouth watering as he tasted her.

Minerva cried out, though it did not sound like a complaint, so he did it again, and again, his tongue seeking out and finding all the softest, most secret places. Her hands sank into his hair, holding him in place, and he grunted with satisfaction, wanting her to guide him, to show him how to please her best. He'd do anything to keep those delicate, wanton sounds ringing in his ears, making him burn. His only desire was to bring her everything she wanted. She was so perfect, so delicious, and he took his time, never wanting the moment to stop, savouring her and the erotic little sounds she made as she squirmed beneath him. He smiled, pleased beyond reason, holding her thighs apart, keeping her still so he could explore every decadent inch of her at his leisure. This was not something to rush and he kept his touch slow and caressing, coaxing her gently towards the height of pleasure and alight with joy at the honour she had given him. She trusted him with this, with her body, and that made something in his chest ache with need. His heart pounded harder as he noticed her breathing become erratic and realised she was close.

Yes. Yes, please.

Her hands clenched in his hair, so hard it hurt, and he willed her not to stop, to take everything she wanted as her body tightened beneath him.

"Inigo," she cried out, dazed and shocked as she bowed taut as the climax took her.

It was too much, his triumph in her pleasure was too great, and he snatched at the fall of his trousers, freeing his cock and taking himself in hand. He barely even touched himself, shattering as she did, giddy with the sound of his name on her lips as she came for him. *Oh God, oh God.* Nothing had ever felt like this, and he hadn't even been inside her. He eased her through her climax, gentling his touch so as not to overwhelm her sensitive flesh, but drawing every last shuddering wave from her body until she was boneless and pliant.

Inigo sat back on his heels, shaken by the force of everything he felt, undone by the swell of tenderness that swept over him as he regarded the results of his attentions. Minerva sprawled in the chair, shameless and exposed to him, her eyes closed and her skin flushed, a slight smile curving her lush mouth. With hands that were far from steady, he found a handkerchief and cleaned himself up, buttoning his breeches once more, not wanting to shock her too badly. He stared down at her, terrified by the enormity of his emotions, knowing he could not let her leave his life now she'd insisted on making herself a place in it.

Yet he didn't know how, didn't know... *anything.* His heart was slamming in his chest and he wanted to hold her, so he did, burying his face against her breasts, his arms going around her waist, holding her tight to him. He felt like a fool. She was the virgin, it was her first real sexual encounter; it was Minerva who ought to be seeking comfort, not him, but his world had tilted on its axis and he felt as if everything was suspended on the edge of a cliff.

Don't let me fall.

"Oh, my," she said, sighing with content, blissfully unaware of the turmoil she'd wrought.

She stroked his hair and he closed his eyes, never wanting it to stop, never wanting her to leave.

"That was…." She gave a soft huff of laughter. "You were right, it was so much more than *nice*. What an inadequate word."

It *was* inadequate for something that had broken his defences and left him the one exposed. How was it she had given so much and it was him who'd been made vulnerable. He'd been so certain it was merely lust for forbidden fruit, then he had *prayed* it had been only his desire driving him to want her… now though. When he'd told Solo about the first time Minerva had kissed him, his friend had asked if it had been a nice kiss. The only words Inigo had brought to mind had been apocalyptic, cataclysmic, and he'd been right. *Abandon all hope ye who enter here,* yet stupidly hope was the thing she'd given him back. She'd upended his beliefs about everything he wanted. He'd begun to question his motives, his morals, his entire outlook on life, which was appalling enough, but to dream of more, to believe in the fairy story he'd once *known* was a lie—to hope… It was the worst and most dreadful fate he could imagine, to be given a chance to hope once more, with no guarantee it wouldn't be ripped from his grasp again and leave him broken beyond repair.

He closed his mind to the future, to his fears, wanting only to revel in this moment in case it was all he would have. Her skin was like silk beneath his head and he nuzzled into her breasts, kissing them, wanting to stay like this forever. His mouth sought her nipple and sucked, teasing it back to a peak as Minerva sighed. He trailed kisses up over her collarbone, up her neck, wishing he had the time to take her to bed, and consigning her friends to the devil. They'd be back for her soon and he had no idea how he would look them in the eye, but he'd not think on that, not yet. Inigo found her mouth and kissed her, tender kisses that revealed too much that he needed to keep hidden, to guard something of himself, no matter how small and pitiful.

She drew back, holding his face so she could look into his eyes and he almost turned away, not wanting her to see what she'd done.

"On a scale of one to ten, how much do you love me?" she asked, a teasing note to her voice as she smiled at him.

Oh, God.

Inigo felt his heart kick in his chest, panic sending his pulse into an erratic dance. He could almost feel the colour leave his face. He shook his head, unable to answer, praying she would not insist on him putting a number on something he could not, dared not quantify in such a way.

For a moment she studied him, too intently, as if she were peeling away the armoured layers he hid behind like tissue paper. Then she smiled, so gentle and understanding his throat tightened and the blood that had left him returned in a rush, making him blush like a scolded boy.

"All right," she said, pressing a kiss to his lips. "But you will have to tell me, eventually."

Later, he prayed. Much, much later, but he distracted her with kisses and his hands on her until he'd chased such questions from her mind.

Chapter 11

I'm sorry, Tilda, darling, but I think perhaps you have misinterpreted my reasons for marrying Gordy. I know I told you it was the sensible thing to do at the time. I made it appear that after six seasons I was desperate. Well, that was partly true, but not why I did it.

I wanted him, Matilda. I've wanted nothing so much as I wanted him the first moment I laid eyes on him. I was motivated by desire, not good sense, so for heaven's sake do not take my actions as a reason to do the sensible thing, because the last thing I was when I suggested Gordon marry me instead of Bonnie, was sensible.

—Excerpt of a letter from Mrs Ruth Anderson to Miss Matilda Hunt.

Still the 21st January 1815. Beverwyck. London.

"Prue, really, stop pulling so hard. You will yank my arm from its socket," Minerva grumbled as her cousin towed her up the stairs.

She'd known it was coming. There had been no escaping it. Poor Inigo had looked so damn guilty he'd barely been able to meet Prue's eye. Rather shockingly, Minerva hadn't felt the least bit guilty. In fact her, overriding emotion was one of happiness bubbling up inside her, and a terribly smug smirk kept trying to escape by curving her lips up at the corners.

Finally, they got to Prue's bedroom, where Minerva was hustled inside, and the door closed behind them.

"What happened?" Prue demanded, arms folded.

Minerva's eyebrows went up. "None of your business," she retorted.

Prue goggled at her. "None of…? Minerva, I allowed you to visit the bloody man on the understanding that you'd not do anything foolish."

"Oh, it wasn't foolish," Minerva said, giving a blissful sigh and sitting on the edge of Prue's bed. "It was… it was marvellous."

"Oh, my lord!" Prue threw up her hands. "I will have him chopped up into little bits," she said, surprisingly savage considering Prue was usually so level-headed.

"For heaven's sake, Prue." Minerva shook her head. "He didn't ruin me. I'm still… still…."

"If you can't say it, how can you be certain you *are* it?" Prue asked, scathing now. She folded her arms tighter, her cheeks glowing a little more brightly. "Do… Do you even know what…? Has Aunt Phyllis ever explained—"

"Good heavens, no!" Minerva said, her mind rebelling against the idea of her Mama ever instigating such a conversation. "No, Harriet gave me this fascinating book…."

Prue groaned.

"And Bonnie filled in the gaps, so—"

"Oh, heaven help me."

Her poor cousin looked so outraged that Minerva could only laugh. "Are you trying to pretend that you and Robert didn't… well, *you know*, before you were married."

Prue's cheeks coloured. "I'll have you know I was a virgin on my wedding night."

She put up her chin, full of righteous indignation.

Minerva just quirked an eyebrow at her and Prue huffed.

"What I did or didn't do is neither here nor there. Robert wanted to marry me and he's a duke. What's more, I didn't need anyone's permission or good opinion. Even if this man feels strongly enough to want to marry you, what exactly are you going to do about your mother? You're not yet one and twenty, I might remind you. She can still forbid the match."

"Only until July," Minerva muttered, tracing the ivy pattern on the counterpane with a fingertip, well aware that Prue was right.

Inigo had told her from the start he had no intention of marrying her. He didn't believe in love or marriage, or even monogamy. She was risking everything for a man who'd warned her repeatedly that he'd never be what she wanted him to be. The realisation burst the happy little bubble she'd been floating in, and she fell back to earth with too much force.

Minerva blinked, her eyes burning, and then she remembered the moments after he'd made her feel… feel like she was flying. She'd never known such pleasure was possible, even though Bonnie had been quite vocal on the subject. Better than even the heights he'd taken her to, though, had been the way he'd held her afterwards. It had meant something to him too, she knew it. He'd not wanted to answer her question, either, though she knew that was likely because he'd not wanted to hurt her at such a time by telling her nothing had changed. Her heart sank. At the time she'd thought… she'd hoped… but now, now that the heat of their passion had faded and she was not with him, it seemed a lot less certain than it had that he would ever really care for her.

She looked up to discover Prue had crouched down before her and was holding her hands.

"Min, I just want your happiness. You know that, don't you?"

Minerva nodded.

"Have you really thought about it? I mean, assuming for a moment that he offers to marry you. Have you thought about what your life will be like? Once upon a time you had your heart set on marrying a duke and—"

Prue held up a hand to stop her as she opened her mouth to object.

"And whilst I know that was to please Aunt Phyllis, you must admit you have expensive tastes. You like pretty gowns and jewels and going to balls, and all the things you enjoy now. Those things cost a great deal of money, love. Don't you remember how you hated economising before I married Robert? The way you would sigh over all the things you couldn't afford. If you marry this man, that may well be the way you live for the rest of your life. He's not a gentleman. He'll not be invited to all the parties you attend now, and he won't be able to buy you the things you want. I know that it seems mercenary to point this out, but you must have your eyes wide open, Min. After the honeymoon is over, your love will need to be strong enough that those things don't signify."

Minerva blinked hard, unable to stop the tears from falling as she made a small sound somewhere between a laugh and a sob. "It is, though, Prue. I love him. I love him so much and I… I'm frightened he won't ask me. I'm frightened he doesn't feel the same."

"Oh, love."

Prue sat on the bed beside her and gathered her up, hugging her tightly as Minerva held on and prayed she hadn't put her faith in a man who wouldn't ever reciprocate her feelings.

***

22nd January 1815. Church Street, Isleworth, London.

Inigo jolted. Something was banging inside his head. He groaned and raised a shaky hand to his temple. It felt like a bloody brass band marching back and forth across his brain. The pounding came again, and this time he opened his eyes, finding them settling on a wooden rack filled with boiling tubes. *Huh?* He blinked, trying to focus, utterly disorientated.

His stomach roiled and his head throbbed as he peeled his face from his work bench. Hell and the devil. He'd drunk himself into a stupor in his lab and not even made it to bed. The pounding came again, this time accompanied by someone cursing his name.

"Inigo, damn you. Let me in, I'm getting soaked out here."

Inigo groaned as he realised it was his front door that was being assaulted, and Solo was quite capable of breaking the bloody thing down if he got mad enough.

"Coming," he muttered, staggering towards the door.

Somehow, he slid back the bolt and opened it, almost staggering back as the daylight seared his eyes and burned his brain.

"Christ," Solo said, curling a lip at the sight of him. "What happened? Did something explode?"

"Only my brain," Inigo said with a groan, trying and failing to close the door without making a sound.

Solo snorted and took off his greatcoat, which was dripping rivulets of water onto the wooden floor.

"Hell, man. It's bloody freezing in here. Can't you at least domesticate yourself enough to light a fire? I suppose it's too much to ask if there's any coffee?"

"It is," Inigo agree, following Solo out to the kitchen. "But feel free to make some if you can find it."

Inigo ignored the muttering and cursing and only winced as Solo moved about the kitchen. His friend coaxed the stove back to life and had coffee brewing in short order. For a man with money and a title he was remarkably self-sufficient, but Inigo supposed life in the army did that. It had also given him a bullet which had almost cost him his leg, and Inigo could tell the cold, wet weather was bothering him as his limp was more pronounced than usual.

The good thing about Solo was that he didn't feel the need to make small talk, and so silence reigned until he sat down at the table with a pot of coffee and the remains of a sugar cone. Inigo grimaced as Solo applied the sugar nips to break off several generous chunks, throwing a couple into each mug before pouring the coffee on top. He stirred the mugs and slid one across the table to Inigo. It was hot and very strong, and Inigo drank it down as his stomach protested. Solo poured him another cup in silence, added more sugar, and handed it back again.

"So," he said, studying Inigo curiously. "What has you drowning your sorrows so deep you're struggling to surface again?"

Inigo gave him a black glare over the rim of his mug. "Perhaps I was celebrating."

There was a snort at that idea. "You don't do celebration, to my knowledge. Far too frivolous, and I've never seen you more than mildly foxed, let alone half seas over, which you must have been to look as wretched as you do. So, let's have it. What's wrong?"

Inigo groaned and set the mug down, putting his head in his hands.

"That bad?"

"Worse," he croaked. "So much worse."

When he spoke Solo's words seem to hover somewhere between amusement and real concern. "Oh, that's the problem is it?"

Inigo looked up, unnerved by the sudden understanding in his friend's voice.

"What?" he demanded, panicked by the idea his inner turmoil was so easy to read.

"Didn't I say you were in deep trouble?" Solo replied, his lips twitching. "So, your admirer got more than a kiss this time, did she?"

Inigo fought to keep his expression neutral, but could not fight the heat that climbed the back of his neck.

"Oh, ho, you poor bastard. She's got you tied up in a pretty knot hasn't she?"

Inigo swallowed, torn between confessing all and telling the irritating sod to go to the devil.

"What's she like?"

It was tempting to just tell him to shut up, but there was something in Solo's eyes that told him he could trust the man not to amuse himself at Inigo's expense. Well, at least no more than usual. To his chagrin, Inigo discovered he wanted to talk about her, to tell someone else about Minerva Butler and the devastation she'd caused in his life.

"Beautiful," he admitted, wishing he hadn't sounded quite so wistful. "Ridiculously beautiful, not to mention foolish, innocent, too bloody young, and far above my touch."

"Ah," Solo said, understanding. "Her parents won't like the match."

Inigo scowled, folding his arms. "Who said anything about making a match?

Solo just snorted and shook his head, his gaze unwavering. Inigo huffed.

"I can't marry a girl like that. Even if I wanted to," he added, with more defiance than truth, but Solo was annoying him.

"Oh, you want to, else you'd have not drunk yourself into a stupor last night."

"She's deluded," Inigo snapped. "She's woven some ridiculous romantic fantasy about me, and comes here to… to look after me, like she's taken in a bloody stray dog. I don't want her pity, and I don't want to marry someone who will wake up to reality too late and despise me for what she refused to see from the start."

Solo stared at him before sitting back, one hand still curled about his mug. He picked it up, staring down into it as he spoke. "How long have you been in love with her?"

Inigo started, something that felt a lot like fear curling about his heart.

"I'm not… I never said…."

The pitying look Solo gave him made Inigo's stomach twist into a knot.

"You didn't need to."

"No." Inigo shook his head. "It's lust. It's just I've never wanted anyone this badly before. You know how I get if something catches my attention. I get obsessive. I need to know everything, to discover *everything*. It's the same thing, this wanting to be with her every moment, needing her with me. It's only that, a new obsession. It's not…."

Solo's gaze was unwavering, and Inigo clamped his mouth shut.

"Who is she?"

Inigo shook his head. "I may not be a bloody gentleman, but I'm not such a cad as all that."

"Oh, come now. I won't ruin the girl by tattling. Surely you can trust me?"

There was silence as Solo refilled his mug.

"What about you?" Inigo countered. "Did you find someone willing and able to fill the position you required?" he asked, a mocking tone to his voice.

Solo frowned at him. "Don't talk like that. I did, yes, and...."

"And?"

His frown deepened. "And she's very lovely. A lady. I.... Don't talk about her like she's...."

"I'm sorry," Inigo said at once, guilt tangling in his gut.

That he, of all people, should taunt either Solo or whatever woman he'd found to agree to his arrangement was a testament to exactly how badly Minerva had disturbed his thinking. If they were both consenting adults, it was no one's business but their own, and Inigo ought to be the last person to mock Solo for it.

"Forgive me."

There was a huff of laughter. "No need. You're in a bad way, my friend. I think you should concentrate on your own troubles."

"What do you think I've been doing?" Inigo said, nettled. "I can't work, I can't sleep. I lurch from day to day counting the minutes until I can see her again." The admission shocked the hell out of him, as much as it evidently did Solo. "Well, say something!" he demanded, incensed now. "Don't you have some advice for me, at least?"

Solo nodded. "Go and buy a ring, and do it quickly."

Chapter 12

Dear Miss Fernside,

I am writing to confirm that the work to the cottage is coming along nicely. I believe all will be ready by the end of January as we agreed. That being so I wondered if you would like to arrange whatever furniture, curtains etcetera you prefer? I have arranged credit for you at the places indicated below so you may choose whatever you see fit. I would like you to be comfortable in your new home. Please rest assured that the credit is in your own name and arranged by Mr Briggs. There is no question of any scandal attached to it as he has always been your man of business.

I also wanted to say I enjoyed our meeting. I look forward to furthering our acquaintance and hope you do not feel too uneasy or have too many misgivings about the future. I beg if there is anything that troubles you, that you will let me know.

—Excerpt of a letter from Solomon Weston, Baron Rothborn to Miss Jemima Fernside.

22nd January 1815. Beverwyck. London.

Matilda sidestepped a puddle heading towards the other women who were huddled before a shop window, perusing a new display of spring bonnets. At least the rain had stopped for their little shopping trip, though the streets were wet and mucky. When she looked up, she found Minerva beside her, her expression filled with remorse and anxiety. Matilda sighed as Minerva moved closer.

"I'm so sorry, Tilda, I ought never—"

"No," she said, interrupting her apology. "You ought not, but neither should I. I'm not your mother, or even your cousin. I had no right to speak to you so."

Minerva smiled and took her arm. "But you are my very dear friend, and you're frightened I will be hurt."

Matilda nodded and covered Minerva's hand with her own. "I am frightened."

It was true, though the truth ran far deeper. She was frightened for them both, and more than a little jealous. Minerva was risking everything for the chance to be with the man she wanted, desired, maybe even loved. She was throwing caution to the wind with hardly a backwards glance, and Matilda envied her courage, her determination to grasp what it was she wanted, even though she knew it wasn't the same for her.

Mr de Beauvoir would be lucky to have Minerva. She was from a good family and she had a handsome dowry. A woman like that could open doors for a man who would find them firmly closed to him now. The man who haunted Matilda's dreams would gain nothing by association with her. He'd already diminished any value she might have and, even then, that value would never have been great enough for him to consider marriage.

Men like him did not *simply* marry, certainly not to please themselves, let alone for love, or at least, rarely. It was a business venture, the joining of two great families to produce an entity wealthier and more powerful than before.

Men like him.

She sneered at herself for not even being able to refer to him by name to herself when she thought about her dreams, about all the impossible things she wanted.

The Most Honourable Lucian Barrington, Marquess of Montagu.

Lucian.

She wondered if anyone ever called him that. It seemed impossible. He *was* Montagu. He was the title, and no one could ever forget it. Except perhaps his niece. Miss Phoebe Barrington had called him Uncle Monty. She smiled at that, smiled as she remembered how those cold features had softened when he'd looked upon the little girl. He'd seemed almost human.

"Penny for them?"

Matilda laughed a little as Minerva drew her attention back to her. "I'm not certain they're worth nearly so much."

"You were thinking about him."

Matilda looked at Minerva and wished she could deny it. "Well, it's hardly a difficult thing to guess at. I think about him more than is good for me. To think about him at all is more than is good for me!" she added with some heat.

"It doesn't matter though, does it?"

Matilda shook her head. They'd fallen back behind their friends, Prue and Bonnie and the others chatting merrily some way ahead as they made their way down Bond Street.

"You've been back to him? To your Mr de Beauvoir?"

Minerva nodded. "I have."

"And you will go again. No matter what." It wasn't a question. Minerva just smiled, which was all the answer Matilda needed. "What's it like? When you are together?"

Her heart squeezed at the dreamy look that settled over Minerva's expression.

"Bliss," she said, laughing a little as she turned back to Matilda. "Worth anything at all."

"Really?" Matilda turned then, taking Minerva's hands. "You really mean that? Anything?"

Minerva's eyes grew brighter. "I think so. I love him and, no matter what comes of it, I… I can't regret that. Perhaps I'll never have everything I want, but whether I'm forced to marry another or never marry at all, I'll know what it felt like to have everything I've ever dreamt of, if only for a little while."

Matilda swallowed. "You're very brave."

"Or very stupid," Minerva allowed, the way her smile faltered telling Matilda the girl was not ignorant of how badly things might go for her if they were discovered, or if her lover did not do the decent thing by her.

Matilda smiled, praying Minerva would get everything she dreamed of. It had always been her goal, after all, to see all her friends settled, all ten of her chicks with nests of their own. She'd told herself that would be enough, that she'd find her happiness through them. She'd be an auntie to all their babies, the doting maiden aunt who always had a sweetie hidden in her pocket and smelled vaguely of peppermint. Her throat ached from the effort of not screaming.

It wasn't fair.

Why could she not have what she wanted, at least for a little while? Montagu wanted her. He wanted her badly and she wanted him. She could be his lover. Maybe she could keep it a secret, like Minerva was doing, and it wouldn't ruin her utterly. Perhaps after….

Perhaps what? She'd pretend it never happened and marry Mr Burton? Her stomach roiled at the idea. That was something she could never do. It was one thing to marry Mr Burton because she felt she had no other choice, to pretend pleasure in his company that she didn't really feel, but to come from her lover's bed to his.... No. She had to choose, and she'd made the right choice. The sensible choice.

Minerva might have a chance at happiness. A slim one, but the possibility was there. There was no such chance for Matilda, and she knew it. Montagu would never marry her. Even if by some miracle he wanted to, he couldn't, and she had no illusions on that score. The possibility of the marquess marrying damaged goods was ridiculous. There'd be an almighty scandal, his pristine bloodline tainted, and didn't all the *ton* know how seriously his family had always taken that? The world knew the Barrington family had been ruthless for generations, and the current marquess was the culmination of that relentless climb for power. An impeccable lineage, wealth, and power. They said even Prinny feared him because of the secrets he knew, the hold he had on some of the greatest families of the *ton*.

Matilda knew more than its fair share of tragedy had visited his family, leaving him the last of his line. He had to marry soon and secure that illustrious bloodline by producing an heir. When he considered his prospective brides, Matilda would not be among them. She was already too old, many of her best childbearing years behind her, not to mention being unsuitable. All she was good for was to warm his bed.

Nothing more.

She'd do well to keep that in the forefront of her mind. The trouble was it had always been there. She reminded herself of it daily, and it didn't change a blessed thing.

Forcing herself to abandon the subject, Matilda gave her attention back to her friends. Jemima was in good spirits today. Apparently, the financial difficulties she'd been experiencing were over and her aunt's legacy was generous enough for her to furnish her new home in comfort. So, they went with her from one shop to the next, ordering curtains and linen and rugs, and a variety of miscellaneous items she'd need to begin her new life in the country. There was something about the whole affair that made Matilda uneasy, though she couldn't put her finger on what. Except perhaps that Jemima seemed nervous, cagey almost, when she discussed the cottage. Matilda had suggested going to stay with her for a week or two to help her settle in, and had been a little hurt to be gently but firmly rebuffed.

As Jemima was currently staying with her, it seemed odd that she did not wish for her company, but perhaps Matilda was reading too much into it. She was so tangled up in her own mind she could only see danger lurking at every corner for the rest of the unmarried women among them. No doubt Jemima was looking forward to having a place of her own. It was only Matilda who was terrified of being left all alone, foolish creature that she was.

She paused in front of a shop window to admire a bolt of pure white cotton gauze. An embroidered sample with sequins and gilt thread was beautifully displayed beside it, and Matilda imagined how a ball gown would look, sheer and ethereal with that glittering embroidery heavy about the hem and bodice.

A shadow cast over her, blocking out what little sun had fought past the grey clouds and Matilda looked up, hardly even surprised to see Montagu reflected in the window glass. For a moment she wondered if she'd finally lost her mind and dreamed him up, but no. Like a bad penny, he seemed to turn up whenever her thoughts were on him. To be fair, she supposed he'd have had difficulty turning up when her thoughts weren't on him. How depressing that was.

He was standing behind her, not too close, but anywhere in the same vicinity was too close for her sanity and good sense with this man.

"It's exquisite. I should like to see you wear it," he said. "I'd buy it for you, if you'd let me." His voice was low, intimate, and even though she looked at his reflection, she could see the desire to do so reflected in his eyes. It must irk him no end that she wasn't something he could just buy in the same way.

"I can buy it for myself, I thank you. Money is not something I lack for, as I'm sure you know."

She said it to shock him, but he didn't look remotely disgusted by unladylike behaviour. How shocking to be speaking of money in front of him, yet he seemed rather amused.

"How vulgar we are today," he remarked, lips twitching a little which only irritated her the more.

Why? Why did she want him so badly? Why was it only when she was sparring with him like this that she felt alive?

"Well, that's no doubt what you expect of a woman only fit to be your mistress. Doesn't vulgarity come with the position?"

Frustration at her own idiocy made the words harder and uglier than she'd intended, but it was too late to regret them.

He frowned, and she turned away from the shop front to look at him, finding a troubled expression in his eyes. "It is you who sees vulgarity where there is none. I treat my mistresses with the greatest respect. It does not make you less of a lady to me."

"Less of a lady?" She gaped at him, astonished. Bearing in mind the way he'd ruined her by being alone in the same room that seemed an outrageous statement. "You're unbelievable," she said, at a loss for anything more comprehensive. Her nerves were too frayed, her emotions too compromised. "And as I understand it, all your paramours have been married ladies. Society gives such women a deal more leeway. I assure you, once you cast me aside and your name no longer protects me, it shall consider me vulgar in the extreme. Unless I find another suitable protector. I suppose that remains an option for all the years my face is kind enough to keep me safe."

His expression darkened. "I told you, you need have no fear the future. You would be wealthy beyond anything you now have. I would guarantee your comfort."

"Why are you not putting as much effort into finding yourself a wife?" she demanded, heart pounding now as she fought to keep herself calm, her voice mild, for fear of making a public spectacle of herself.

"That is my duty to the title. I have little say there." His words were cold and hard, and she could read nothing from his face, but every inch of him was rigid with tension. No doubt she had not the right to speak of his wife and he was disgusted she should even refer to her, whoever she may be.

Matilda made a sound of disgust, hoping it was fierce enough to cover up the fact she was close to tears as she turned away from him. To her horror, Montagu caught her arm. She gasped, glancing around to see if anyone had seen. He let her go at once, looking a little shocked himself at having done such a thing in public.

"I marry for the title. Not from choice, but there are some things I *can* choose for myself, and I would not be so certain of my growing bored with you, Miss Hunt. No one has ever…." His jaw clenched, the words cut off. "You are not like the others."

She laughed at that, hearing the break in the sound and clenching her fists, willing herself to stay calm. "Yes, because none of the others said *no*. The moment I capitulate, I become just the same as the rest of them."

He opened his mouth but didn't get to reply.

"Lord Montagu."

They both turned as Minerva addressed him and Matilda could only commend the young woman's courage as Montagu's displeasure at the interruption blazed from him, his silver eyes glacial with annoyance.

"How lovely to see you," Minerva continued, ignoring her frigid reception. "Have you been fencing at Angelo's?" Minerva took Matilda's arm, tugging a little, subtly gesturing to the fashionable group of women heading towards them, their avid gazes fixed on Lord Montagu, and Matilda.

Montagu followed Minerva's gaze and glowered a little, but his attitude to Minerva was far warmer when he spoke again.

"I was, Miss Butler. I visit twice a week at least."

"And Gentleman Jackson's?"

Matilda glanced at Minerva in amusement, wondering at her nerve in questioning the man so closely. With regret she realised she wanted to know the answer rather too much. Men stripped down to box, did they not?

"I find boxing inelegant and brutish," the marquess replied, and Matilda was astonished to discover a slight smile at that wicked mouth. "It is not my preferred pastime. May I have the honour of escorting you both to your next engagement?"

He offered Minerva his arm first. She nodded and placed her hand upon his sleeve.

"Miss Hunt?"

Matilda sighed, not wanting to touch him, or rather wanting to too much, but she had little choice as they were all under scrutiny.

"Thank you, my lord. You are most kind," she replied, unable to keep the sarcasm from her voice.

With trepidation, she took his arm, wishing her gloves were not so fine, and his coat not so well fitted. The muscle beneath her fingers was hard and well defined and, whether or not he boxed, the marquess did not appear to be a man who shirked physical exertion. Awareness burned through her and she kept her face turned away from his.

They walked to where the other ladies had paused before a haberdasher, and their faces were priceless as they saw Montagu escorting them down Bond Street.

"I believe this is where I take my leave," he said, after giving a polite nod to the others in response to their curtseys.

All but Prue, of course, who outranked him and stared daggers at him, her dislike apparent.

"Your grace," he said, with every show of courtesy, before turning and leaving them alone.

Prue glowered at his back before linking arms with Matilda.

"That man," she muttered, giving Matilda a sideways glance.

Despite everything, Matilda could not help but laugh.

"Yes," she said with a sigh. "That man."

Chapter 13

My Lord Duke,

I was given leave to approach you directly by your uncle, Baron Fitzwalter, who assured me of your interest in the subject of steam locomotion. I am enquiring as to your interest and support for my company and investment in passenger locomotion. After having seen Mr Trevithick's demonstration in Bloomsbury some years ago, I remain convinced of the need to invest in this astonishing invention at the earliest opportunity. Our long term intention would be to lobby parliament for authorisation to run a railway to be used both for the transportation of goods and passengers.

If you believe this may be a subject that interests you, I should be glad to discuss the matter in greater detail.

—Excerpt of a letter from Mr Gabriel Knight to His Grace, The Duke of Bedwin.

23rd January 1815. Church Street, Isleworth, London.

Inigo stared at his bedroom ceiling and sighed. Usually he'd have been up for hours by now. He slept little, his brain reluctant to leave whatever it was he was working on alone for longer than was necessary. At least he'd written up his report for the investigation, though his paper on the new element he'd discovered was barely a third of the way through. That he wasn't desperate to write up every aspect of his most significant discovery to date was not lost on him. He was in a bad way: lost, drowning in an obsession so overwhelming, so all-consuming, that he hadn't even bothered trying to work this morning. He couldn't focus. Today he'd just given in, not bothering to get out of bed and allowing himself to remember the extraordinary afternoon he'd spent with Minerva. To say he was longing to see her again was such an understatement it was ridiculous. She filled his mind and, every time he breathed in, it felt as though she had bruised his chest, the ache that had settled there was so profound.

An obsession, he told himself again. *You know how you get.* It was no different from when he'd passed out cold last year because he hadn't eaten or slept for three days. That had been during his experiments burning diamonds and charcoal, which was so expensive it had damn near ruined him, and would have if the findings hadn't been so incontrovertible. This was no different—hardly different at all, in fact—when he thought of the many faceted diamond, and beautiful Minerva. He couldn't stop remembering how glorious she'd looked in the moments after she'd reached her peak, with the taste of her on still his tongue.

Oh, God.

He groaned as his body stirred to life. The need to see her again, to be with her, touch her, it consumed his every thought until he believed he'd run mad. It had become so bad he was giving Solo's advice serious consideration.

Go and buy a ring, and do it quickly. The fellow had likely only been joking. If Solo had known the young woman Inigo was speaking of was the Duchess of Bedwin's cousin, he'd have been appalled. Solo was a good fellow, not a snob like many of his ilk, but even so… a titled gentleman approving such a match for a well-bred lady seemed not only unlikely but ludicrous. Not to mention the fact that Inigo would be taking advantage of her. She was too young, too inexperienced about life and men. Good God, she was only twenty, making him ten years her senior. Not that he felt it in her presence. It always appeared she were the one in charge, the one who took control, intent on taking care of him, protecting him. Why, he could not fathom, and for some mad reason he didn't even object. He *liked* it.

Muttering, he swung his legs to the side of the bed and forced himself to wash and shave. He at least had a woman to do his laundry now, determined that Minerva should not find him looking like a complete wreck whenever she next took it upon herself to appear. The clean shirt was ironed and smelled fresh, and he'd just tugged it over his head when there was a knock at the door. Cursing, he snatched up a pair of trousers and hurried down the stairs in bare feet, doing up the buttons as he went. If this was Solo back again….

He yanked open the door, and his heart leapt with delight and with such force that he could not control the smile that broke over his face.

"Minerva!"

She flew inside, dropping the basket she carried at his feet, and he barely had time to close the door before she was in his arms.

"Darling!" She hung off his neck, pulling him down for a kiss.

Inigo did not need a second invitation. He wrapped his arms about her and held her to him as tight as he could as he kissed her, urging her lips apart for him to savour her properly and tugging at the ribbons of her bonnet. He cast the irritating thing to the floor without a second glance.

"Why do you taste of strawberries?" he asked, his voice gruff as he buried his face against her neck.

She laughed, and the sound rioted through him, making him feel lightheaded and foolish.

"Because I had strawberry jam for breakfast. I brought some for you too, as you have such a sweet tooth."

"I'd rather just taste you," he murmured, nipping at her ear.

"That can be arranged," she said, staring up at him with such undisguised desire that the need to have her, to make her his, overwhelmed all else.

Go and buy a ring, and do it quickly.

It was ridiculous, outrageous. There were so many reasons it was a terrible idea he couldn't even begin to list them. Yet the desire keep her with him always, or at least until his obsession abated, was undeniable. He'd given her fair warning. He'd told her time and time again not to keep coming back to him, not to pursue him so relentlessly, but she had. Now it was too late. He was in the grip of an obsession so vast he could not fight it, could not resist it. He had to have her.

"Come to bed with me."

He couldn't take the words back once spoken. If she'd hesitated, or shown the least bit of reluctance, he might have been able to stop things, for now, at least, but the sigh of pleasure and the look in her eyes were explicit enough.

"Yes."

He stared down at her, down into eyes of impossible blue, into a face that lured him into wanting what he'd always believed nothing more than a mirage. When he was with her, it didn't feel like an illusion though, he could not see the lie he'd always been certain was there when people professed themselves to be *in love.* It seemed natural and perfect and just as it ought to be. It was only when she was gone that his cynical mind got to work and made him doubt, and then the rest of the world seemed to join in, to stand against him, against *them*, against everything he wanted and hoped for. *Hoped.* God, he was a bloody fool.

"Yes, Inigo," she said again, raising a hand to his cheek.

He realised he hadn't moved but was standing in the dim hallway, enraptured by her face. He let out a breath.

"You ought to leave now, before it's too late, before I—"

She lifted onto her toes, clutching at his shirt and raising her mouth to his. When she let him go, her words were a soft breath against his lips.

"I ought not have kissed you all those weeks ago. I ought not have kept writing to you when you kept telling me not to. I ought never to have come here. Yet I *did* kiss you, I did keep writing, and here I am. I am not leaving now, my love."

My love.

He'd never been anyone's love. Never had anyone *to* love him, or at least been obliged to care, for love was a myth people insisted on believing, was it not? He'd told himself that for so long, that love was a pretty lie, that it didn't exist. He'd been content enough, with his work filling every corner of his life. He *had* been content. Hadn't he?

Her words shivered over him like a caress, sliding under his skin and into his bloodstream, potent as the finest liquor, setting fire to his heart. It wasn't love, he reminded himself, needing to keep that clear in his mind if nothing else. He was far gone enough to believe such foolishness. For her it was desire, as unlikely at that seemed, for him, desire that had become obsession. He kept reminding himself of that too, but the lines were blurring, and he felt himself wanting the myth.

There were too many things he wanted to say but had no words for. It was too difficult to even understand himself, let alone explain this yearning for her, this terrifying need to have her with him when he'd never had anyone. Instead he took her hand and led her up the stairs to his room, knowing he was the worst kind of wicked bastard. He'd put it right, he promised himself. Marriage was lust with a ring on its finger, he'd been right about that, but now he understood the need to conform.

It was one thing to look at the world and sneer at its rituals and foolish ideas on morals, and the idea that other people had the right to dictate who they could take to bed with them. It was another to

To Experiment with Desire

force an innocent like Minerva to defy convention and let them tear her apart for his beliefs. So he'd take her innocence, for if he ruined her, Bedwin and her cousin and her bloody mother would have to allow the marriage to go ahead. It was a vile thing to do and they'd despise him for it, but that would always be the way of things. He could live with that. Though the admission made his chest tight with anxiety, he did not think he could live without Minerva in his life, not and keep his sanity intact.

She walked into his bedroom, looking around with interest, not that there was much to see. It was at the back of the house, with a view over the garden, which had been a wilderness since Inigo had moved in five years ago. He had no idea of what to do with a garden, though he enjoyed seeing greenery outside, especially after so many years of grotty rooms facing onto brick walls and filthy backstreets.

"You don't spend much time in here," she said, smiling at him.

It wasn't a difficult thing to surmise. Apart from the bed and a chest of drawers, the room was all but empty. No rugs or pictures on the walls, nothing that made it a comfortable part of his home. It was simply a place to sleep when he could no longer stay awake. He'd never brought a woman here. The only women in his life had been the kind you paid for. It had never occurred to him to court a woman, he'd never had either the time or the inclination. His arrangement with Harriet had been practical, not romantic. He hadn't the slightest idea about romance, which made him feel at a disadvantage. Perhaps he ought to have asked Solo, but….

He was being bloody ridiculous.

At least the sheets were clean.

"No," he admitted, putting a hand to the back of his neck, feeling awkward now. "I… don't sleep a great deal, and…. No," he said again, frowning.

She smiled at him, and the beauty of it, of *her*, pierced his heart. She was like the diamond. It had hurt his heart to destroy the beautiful little stone, tiny and perfect as it had been, but to prove his theory it had been necessary. When it had gone, he'd felt remorse, but he'd been triumphant too, having proved it was another form of carbon. Would he destroy Minerva with this obsession, this need to take everything from her?

The idea frightened him, more so when he realised that he could not stop it happening.

"Second thoughts?" she guessed, moving towards him and placing her hands on his chest.

How did she do that? How did she read him so easily, and why wasn't she the one who was nervous? She ought to tremble and blush, uncertain of what to do, yet it was him acting like a skittish virgin. Cross with his own foolishness, Inigo told himself to get a grip and cupped Minerva's face in both hands, refusing to notice that they were far from steady. He lowered his mouth to hers and, the moment their lips touched, all uncertainty—and any possibility of doing the right or honourable thing—evaporated.

Minerva sighed against his mouth and he was undone, pulling her closer, deepening the kiss even as his hands unfastened the buttons on her pelisse. He drew back with difficulty, but was too desperate to get the clothes from her not to give the job his full attention. She stood still, watching him, so intent as she allowed him to move her this way and that to pull each garment from her body. By the time she was in nothing but her shift and stockings, Inigo was breathing hard, and her cheeks were flushed a dramatic shade of pink.

He stood back, wanting to savour the moment, drawing out the anticipation even though his body was clamouring for more, to touch and taste and lose himself in her.

"Well, don't stop now," she murmured, breathless as she looked up at him with a glimmer of mischief in her eyes.

Oh, God, the blue of her eyes. Whenever they were apart, he told himself they could not possibly be the shade he remembered, and every time he saw her again, he realised they really were that ridiculous shade, even more vivid than he'd dared believe.

"So eager for me to ruin you?" he asked softly, reaching out and touching her cheek with the backs of his fingers.

"Yes," she admitted with a little laugh. "I suppose I am."

Inigo sucked in a sharp breath, as surprised and pleased by her candour as always.

"You're not nervous at all?" He stared down at her, perplexed by her surety, her certainty that what she was doing was right. Had he ever been that certain of anything, of anyone? Yes, he realised. He'd known from the start that she was dangerous to him, he'd been certain that she would change his world and it had terrified him. With good reason. He was certain now too, certain that he must keep her with him, make her his, for always, in whatever way that needed to happen.

"Why would I be nervous?" she asked, sliding her arms about his neck. "I know you won't hurt me. I trust you."

Guilt stabbed at his chest and he shook his head. "You ought not, *I* ought not—"

She pressed a finger to his lips, frowning. "That's not what I meant. I know you don't believe in love, or marriage. I accept that. I mean... I'd very much like to change your mind, but you've always been honest with me, and so I know I can trust you."

Inigo groaned. It was too late. He could not fight this obsession, could not fight his desire for her, but he would make it right. He would make everything right for her. After. Unable to wait a moment longer, he reached for the hem of her chemise and lifted it, tugging it over her head. It dropped from his fingers, not that he noticed, not now that she was revealed to him.

She was still wearing her stockings, tied with pretty blue ribbons. When she moved her hand to tug at a neat bow on the front of one thigh, Inigo stilled the movement.

"No," he said, his voice ragged. "Keep them on. I like them."

"Oh." She sounded surprised by that, but his attention was too caught to say any more.

He couldn't breathe. He wanted… so much, *everything*, though he didn't know how to tell her. He had no idea how to explain how beautiful she was, or how to express everything he felt in this moment.

He reached out a tentative hand, feeling like the grubby orphan boy he'd been, one who'd broken into an exclusive gallery, about to lay his dirty fingers on some priceless work of art. Her skin was so warm, so fine, and he could not stop the soft exclamation that left him, betraying his wonder at the liberty she was allowing him. He traced the curve of her hip with a fingertip, intrigued as she shivered beneath his touch. Retracing the same path, he moved up towards her breast, outlining the full curve before circling the pink bud of her nipple, furled tightly now as she shivered again.

"Take your hair down," he said, watching as she moved to obey him, her slender fingers seeking out each pin until her blonde hair fell about her shoulders in a tumble of shiny curls.

"So strange," he said, reaching to touch one silky curl, tugging it and watching it spring back with rapt attention.

"What is?" she asked, and he could hear the smile in her voice, wondering at it, at her simple happiness when it didn't seem the least bit simple to him.

"It hurts to look at you," he admitted, wondering too late if he ought to have told her that, if it gave too much away, but he was too perplexed not to ponder why that was.

He looked back at her to see her eyes were glittering, as though she might cry. He scowled, not wanting her to cry, but realising she wasn't the least bit unhappy as she blinked, and a smile curved her beautiful mouth.

"Where does it hurt?" she asked.

He lifted her hand and placed it against his chest, over his heart.

"Here?" she asked.

Inigo nodded, smiling in return, because it was impossible not to.

"Me too," she whispered, laughing a little as a tear slid down her cheek.

"Don't cry," he said, the ache intensifying despite her smile, despite the delight in her laughter.

"I can't help it," she said, the words filled with amusement. "I'm so happy I feel like I might burst."

Inigo took a deep breath, testing the way the ache intensified as he inhaled, as though it was a physical reaction, not just emotion. He put his hands to her face again, smoothing the tear away with his thumb and then leaning in to kiss her, once, softly, before drawing back, watching as his hands slid over her, down the elegant length of her neck, over her shoulders, smoothing over the tender curve of her breasts, her tiny waist, to her hips. He fell to his knees then, feeling it only right, one ought to worship a goddess on one's knees. Minerva, goddess of wisdom. The gentle swell of her stomach beckoned him, and he pressed a kiss against it, closing his eyes as his palms moved down her hips. Her breathing hitched, and he continued to press kisses over her skin as he explored, reaching around to cup her behind.

"So perfect," he murmured against her belly. "So beautiful."

She stroked his hair and he sighed, lost in the pleasure of being with her. It all seemed so difficult, so complicated if he stopped to think about it, but if he didn't think, if he just let it happen…. It was so easy.

He looked up at her, caught in her eyes all over again, the strangest sensation sweeping over him, like drowning in an ocean of Prussian blue, and doing it on purpose, willingly. Turning his attention back to the lush body before him, he trailed a finger through the silky dark gold curls at the apex of her thighs.

"I think you liked it when I kissed you here," he said.

She gave a little huff of laughter.

"You only *think* so?" she queried, her amusement obvious. "Goodness. Whatever do I need to do to convince you?"

"Ask me to do it again," he suggested, grinning now as she flushed, the colour staining her lovely skin from her cheeks to her breasts.

"Wicked man," she murmured, tugging at his hair. "You're just trying to make me blush."

"Not just trying." He chuckled as she pressed her hands to her cheeks.

Inigo moved closer to the sweet nest of curls, never taking his eyes from her as he pressed a kiss to her most delicate skin. He moved back again, raising one eyebrow.

"Oh," she said on a sigh.

Biting back a smile he moved in again, this time touching her with his tongue, a barely there caress that had her clutching at his hair again.

"Oh, yes, do it again," she said, breathless and demanding all at once.

A thrill of desire shot through him and he did as she asked, teasing her gently as her breathing picked up speed. With a devilish glint in his eyes, he stopped again, loving the outrage in her expression.

"What?" he asked, all innocence.

"Inigo!" There was a whiny quality to his name, and he laughed.

"What, love? What do you want me to do?"

"Do it again," she murmured, glaring at him a little.

"Do what again?"

"Oh, you're wicked!" she exclaimed, burying her face in her hands.

"Do what again, Minerva?"

"Kiss me," she demanded, still hiding behind her hands, the words muffled.

"Where?"

She peered through her fingers at him, her eyes narrowed. "You know where," she said, and then huffed as he didn't move.

She slid one hand down, between her legs and Inigo watched its progress with his lungs locked down tight, he couldn't breathe, desire a white hot shimmer under his skin.

"Here," she said, parting the curls for him.

"Oh, God," he moaned, leaning in again and tasting heaven as she sighed with relief.

He eased her legs farther apart as her hand sank into his hair and his tongue slid between her soft folds to find the sensitive bud hidden within.

"Inigo!" she exclaimed, clutching at his hair again, hard now as he gave a villainous chuckle and carried on tormenting her, delighting in the erotic sounds she made, and in the decadent taste of her.

"This," he murmured, nuzzling her inner thigh, "is the sweetest thing I have ever tasted."

"Better than cake?" she asked, a dreamy note to her voice that pleased him immensely.

"Better than cake," he agreed, unable to keep the smile from his face. "Better than strawberry jam or anything else you might have packed in that basket you keep filling for me. This is my feast, the thing I hunger for."

He returned to the sweet task of tormenting her, sliding his fingers over her slick skin and pushing one inside her.

"Inigo," she cried, swaying so that he had to put his arm about her, steadying her. "I… I can't stand… I can't… like this."

Inigo got up at once, picking her up in one swift movement and carrying her to the bed. He put her down, taking a moment to enjoy the sight of her there, in *his* bed, and allowing the primitive, possessive sensation that rose in his chest to savour the moment.

"You're wearing too many clothes," she said, plucking fretfully at his shirt. "Take them off."

"You're very autocratic," he remarked, still grinning like a fool as he tugged his shirt over his head.

He felt ridiculously happy, as though there was champagne flowing in his veins, bubbling up inside him, opium filling his head and his lungs, intoxicating him until this all seemed like some wonderful, mad dream. Too perfect to be real, to be anything it was possible to hold on to, though he was damn well going to try.

"I think you like it," she observed, making him realise she was a deal more perceptive than perhaps he'd given her credit for.

"I do," he admitted. "I like it when you tell me what you want from me, when you instruct me how to give you pleasure. I like giving it to you even more."

She gasped at that, covering her mouth with her hand. "The things you say."

"I'm telling you the truth," he said, undoing the buttons on the fall of his trousers. Her gaze fell to where his hands worked and his cock twitched in anticipation, the heat in her eyes making him want everything all at once and yet to take his time too, to savour every moment.

"How long do we have?" he asked, knowing it would not be enough time, no matter how long it was.

"All day, until six," she said, glancing up at him before returning her gaze to where his hands lingered at the buttons on his trousers.

"Thank God." He sighed and pushed the trousers down his hips, leaving them where they fell as he stepped out of them and towards the bed, towards the heated look in her eyes.

Minerva had turned onto her side and was staring at him in wonder.

"You're much bigger than I realised."

Inigo gave an inelegant snort at that and Minerva flushed scarlet.

"No, I... I didn't mean that," she said, a little indignant. "I meant... all over. Your clothes always look a little too big, as though you've lost weight, and so I never... I never realised. My... what broad shoulders you have."

"I can't help but feel that sentence ought to end with *Mr Wolf*," he said, feeling every bit as wicked as Little Red Riding Hood's hungry villain.

Minerva giggled, and the sound pleased him so much he wanted to make her do it again. He climbed onto the bed, stalking his way up the mattress to her.

"My, what big eyes you have," Minerva said, as Inigo loomed over her.

"All the better to see you with," he growled, sweeping her with a lascivious look as his body tightened with need.

She laughed again, just as he'd wanted her to, and he revelled in it, in her attention, her pleasure in him.

"My, what big hands you have," she murmured, as he palmed her breasts, squeezing and caressing them, tweaking the sensitive peaks of her nipples as she moaned and shifted beneath him.

"All the better to embrace you with," he replied, keeping to his role, though he could barely speak a coherent word when he wanted to taste her again so badly.

"My," she gasped, as his hands slid lower, parting her thighs. "What a big mouth you have."

Inigo returned a wolfish grin. "All the better to eat you with."

She let out a little cry as he returned his mouth to where she so obviously wanted it and gloried in the way she writhed beneath him.

"I could do this all day," he said, nipping at her thigh as she trembled beneath him.

"Oh… Oh, I'll die," she gasped, shaking her head from side to side, laughing and pleading with him at once. "Please, Inigo, don't stop, don't stop, don't stop."

"As if I would do such a heartless thing," he said, more than content to return to his task, holding himself in check with difficulty as she sighed and moaned with increasing fervour.

By the time she reached her climax, he was beside himself with impatience. The need to take his own pleasure inside her left him half mad, deranged with desire. Her body quivered still, pliant and soft as he moved over her, finding his place between her thighs as she reached for him. He stared down at her in wonder, at the hazy, drugged light in her eyes as she smiled up at him.

"I need you," he said, his voice rough, the ability to speak lost as he pushed a little inside her. Oh God. "I'm sorry… I can't… I have to…."

She got no more warning as he sank into her with one deep thrust, his own guttural moan of pleasure drowning out her little cry of pain. Immediately contrite, he gathered her to him.

"Sorry," he begged, kissing her throat, her jawline, and stroking her hair. "I'm sorry."

Minerva let out an unsteady breath, staring up at him.

"Don't be sorry," she said, that sweet smile that had the power to turn his world upside down making his throat tight with emotion, with the enormity of everything she was giving him, trusting him with. "Inigo?"

"Yes?" he said, praying she wouldn't ask him to stop, to tell him she'd changed her mind, forcing the word out though he was beyond conversation, beyond the need to do anything but move inside of her.

"Ten," she said, stroking his face with such tenderness he could not possibly form a reply.

Instead, he buried his face into the curve of her neck and moved. The pleasure was so intense he couldn't breathe. He gave himself over to sensation, to the rightness of being with her, knowing it would never be like this with anyone else.

"Oh, God, Minerva, Minerva, my love...."

He had no idea what he was saying, but could not stop the words from coming as the intensity of feeling overwhelmed him. He was aware of her lips on his, of her own murmured promises and declarations, and of her hands caressing his skin, holding tightly onto him.

"Don't leave me," he said, the words raw and too honest in the heat of passion as everything whited out, replaced by a climax so intense he could do nothing but ride it, crying out as he came, spilling inside her with such force he felt exposed and ragged and horribly defenceless until he dared to open his eyes and look at her.

Minerva was staring at him, breathing hard, and then she buried her face against his chest and burst into tears.

Chapter 14

Mr Knight,

I should be interested to hear more of your plans.

—Excerpt of a letter from His Grace, The Duke of Bedwin to Mr Gabriel Knight.

23rd January 1815. Church Street, Isleworth, London.

"Minerva!" Inigo held her to him, stroking her hair and kissing her forehead, her cheeks. "I'm sorry," he said, sounding wretched. "I'm so sorry. Did… Did I hurt you? Do you regret it? I'm so sorry, love, tell me what I can do…."

Minerva shook her head, trying to control herself and finding her heart overflowing as she looked into Inigo's stricken face. She made an unsteady sound, somewhere between a laugh and a sob.

"I'm n-not crying," she managed though, as there were tears streaming down her face, he could be forgiven for looking perplexed. "At least, I a-am c-crying, but only because I'm so… so…. *happy*," she wailed, and then buried her face against his chest again, laughing and hiccoughing and still crying like a madwoman, and good heavens, if this didn't put him off her for life, she didn't know what would.

With a supreme effort, she took herself in hand, drew in several deep breaths, and wiped her face on the bedsheet.

"It's all right," she said, sounding a little less hysterical, though Inigo still looked shocked and uneasy.

She took another deep breath and let it out before biting her lip and trying not to laugh. Inigo was staring at her, so bewildered it was adorable.

"You did nothing wrong," she said again, calmer now as she stroked his face.

"Are you certain?" he asked, looking unconvinced. "I didn't hurt you? I know I'm a selfish bastard, I ought never...."

She silenced him before he could finish that sentence by the simple expedient of pressing her mouth to his. Just as she'd hoped, he returned the kiss, and she sighed, delighted to discover how tender he could be.

"It was wonderful," she said, letting out a contented sigh as he shifted onto his back and drew her against him. Minerva cuddled into his side, perfectly content. He held her close and she rested her head on his shoulder. "So wonderful that it... it was a little overwhelming. I'm sorry if I startled you."

He was silent for a long moment before he spoke.

"It was wonderful," he said. "And overwhelming."

There was something in his voice that told her he meant that, and Minerva closed her eyes, happier than she could have believed possible.

"I'm so sleepy," she said, smiling, still a little dazed by everything that had happened.

"Sleep, then," he said, turning to kiss her forehead.

"But I don't want to miss being with you," she said, though the effort of keeping her eyes open was becoming harder.

"I'll be here when you wake up," he urged, his hand stroking up and down her back, a soothing movement that was perfectly blissful. "I won't let you sleep all afternoon, I promise."

"Oh, very well then," she murmured, and fell promptly asleep.

***

Minerva awoke to the pattering of rain on glass, the room bathed in shadowy grey as the weather had closed in, stealing any light from the afternoon. She looked up to find Inigo watching her, and smiled.

"Good afternoon, Mr de Beauvoir," she said, feeling silly and happy and rather wonderful.

"Mr de Beauvoir?" he repeated, one eyebrow raised. "Isn't that a little formal in the circumstances, *Miss* Butler?"

She laughed, reaching up to trace the shape of his lips. "Kiss me."

He obliged at once, a deep, languorous kiss that she felt all the way to her toes. She sighed as he lifted his head, his eyes darker than ever as he regarded her.

"Have you been watching me sleep?" she asked, finding her mouth curving at the idea.

"Yes," he admitted. "It's fascinating."

Minerva blushed, wondering if such scrutiny was a good idea. "Heavens, did I do anything embarrassing? Oh, please don't tell me I snore," she exclaimed, horrified by the idea.

He chuckled and shook his head. "Nothing of the sort. You sleep very neatly, with pretty little sighs and an enigmatic smile at your lips. I'm desperate to know what you were dreaming about."

She grinned at that, running a hand over his chest and tangling her fingers in the coarse hair there, following the trail down a little way as his stomach twitched and jumped beneath her touch.

"Ticklish?" she asked, delighted by her discovery.

Inigo snatched her hand away. "Answer my question and I'll answer yours."

"Ah, but I already have my answer," she teased him.

"Tell me," he murmured, nuzzling into her neck and nipping her skin.

"Why, I was dreaming of you, of course," she said, sighing as he kissed a path up to her mouth.

"Is that why you looked so happy?"

There was something in the question that she couldn't read, but she answered him honestly, watching his face as he looked down at her.

"Yes."

Inigo closed his eyes and let out a breath. "Will you come back tomorrow?"

"Yes."

"And the next day?"

"Yes."

"And…?"

"And for all the days you want me, Inigo."

He stared at her, some emotion in his eyes she desperately wanted to understand but didn't feel able to push for. If she asked him, asked for the answer to her question, *how much do you love me,* she feared she would scare him away, or get an honest answer she wasn't ready to hear. She believed she'd felt the emotion within him today, knew in her own heart that he loved her, at least a little, and that was enough for now. So instead she gave him her answer again.

"I love you."

He stilled, and she wondered if perhaps she ought not have said it so bluntly. She'd already told him that, on their scale of one to ten, she had reached ten. If she didn't know that the natural philosopher in him would strongly object, she would have admitted that she'd passed ten some time ago and had reached some unfathomable number she couldn't even contemplate. There was tenderness in his eyes as he reached to touch her face, though. When he cupped her cheek and bent to kiss her, it was with every expression of gentleness, of love, that she could want. The kiss was slow, lingering, sending pleasure racing over her skin in a series of exquisite little shivers as he drew the hand he held back down, to touch his arousal. Minerva curved her hand about him, intrigued as he gasped and rested his forehead against hers, apparently pleased by her touch.

"Like this?" she asked, as he nodded, eyes closed, his breath hitching as she moved her hand over the silky skin, enraptured by his expression, the fierce concentration. Minerva sighed, her own body stirring in response to his obvious pleasure. "I wish I could be here always."

"Here?" he asked, covering the hand that was caressing him with his own.

Minerva chuckled. "I wasn't thinking of anything quite so specific, but yes. I want to touch you whenever I like, which is all the time, if you hadn't realised."

He made a low sound that thrilled her as it rumbled through his chest. "If you were here all the time…."

"Yes?"

There was a desperate exclamation, not quite a laugh. "Oh, God. I'd never work again. I'd never eat nor sleep. I'd never be able to do anything but touch you, kiss you. I'd become the world's leading expert on Minerva Butler." He kissed her shoulder, touching a fingertip to her skin and then traced it across her collarbone. "I want to map every freckle, to know what makes you different to everyone else, to know why it is I find you so intriguing… everything about you."

"Everything?"

"Everything."

"I'm not sure I know everything myself," she said, watching his face with interest, wondering how much of what he said was true, how much of it just said to amuse her. "I'm still discovering things about myself."

"Then we'll figure them out together," he said, before sucking in a sharp breath as she tightened her grip on him. "Not just a pretty face," he murmured.

She smiled at that, loving the power she held over him in this moment as he closed his eyes and gave a soft moan. Giving him a little push, she got him to turn onto his back and tugged the bedcovers from him.

"Christ, it's cold in here," he complained, but she only smirked at him.

"Hush, I want to look at you."

He grumbled but said nothing more, though she could see his skin prickle with cold.

"Perhaps I ought to warm you up?" she said under her breath, considering to herself how wonderful he'd made her feel earlier as she shifted down the bed and pressed a kiss to his erection.

He jolted, swearing in shock, which she surmised was a good reaction, so she did it again, and again, and teased the plump head of his shaft with her tongue, which had him gripping the sheets and breathing hard. Fascinating. She did it again, running her tongue up and down the length of him before taking him in her mouth and sucking gently. That wrung such a cry of pleasure from him it startled them both.

"Did I warm you up yet?" she asked sweetly, staring up at him.

"Holy God, you will kill me," he growled, before pulling her up the bed and turning her onto his back. "I want to be inside you. Can you...? You're not too sore?"

Minerva shook her head, too eager to care for any minor discomfort.

"Please," she said, raising her hips in invitation. "Please."

"Oh, God," he moaned, as he sank inside her again. "Oh, yes."

***

"Your bed will be full of crumbs."

"Don't care," Inigo mumbled around a large bite of savoury pie.

Minerva hadn't wanted to leave the bed, but Inigo's stomach had been growling so ferociously it had been impossible to ignore, though he'd been quite willing to do so. She'd had to resort to tickling him to get him to let go of her long enough to scurry down the stairs and grab the basket. Now, they sat up in his bed, in a tangle of sheets, working their way through the well-stocked basket. Lovemaking gave one a tremendous appetite.

Inigo continued to surprise her. Since the last time she'd been here, it was as though he'd stopped fighting her and whatever was happening between them. A love affair, she supposed, or at least, that's what she would call it. She loved him. Prue would be furious with her when she realised Minerva had come here again, but it didn't matter. Her poor mother would never get over the shock if she ever found out. Idly, Minerva daydreamed about what her life might be like if Inigo *wanted* to marry her. She pushed the thought away. There was no point in dreaming of things she would likely never have, no matter how much she wanted them.

Inigo had told her from the beginning he'd not marry her, and she didn't want him unless it was what he wanted too. She could think of nothing worse than having a man forced unwillingly into marriage. Any affection or regard, or the tentative hopes she had that perhaps he loved her a little bit, would die under such circumstances. He would resent her for the loss of his freedom, and she could not bear that, could not bear for him to look at her with anything less than the warmth she saw in his eyes now. It would break her heart.

"Where were you born?"

The question took her by surprise, and he smiled as she paused with a piece of cake halfway to her mouth.

"I want to know about you, about your family. Where do you come from? Do you have brothers and sisters? What do you like to do?" His lips quirked. "Other than hunting down poor, defenceless natural philosophers and driving them out of their minds?"

"Is that what I did?" she asked, her eyebrows going up.

Inigo snorted. "You deny it?"

Minerva grinned. "My friend Ruth accused me of hunting you, too," she admitted. "But yes, I denied it. I said it wasn't a hunt, but a siege. I told you I wanted your heart, didn't I? So I took it hostage and I won't give it back until you admit it belongs to me."

He frowned, avoiding her gaze and staring down at his hands. "But if it belongs to you, you'll keep it anyway. What do I have to gain?"

Minerva reached over and popped a piece of cake into his mouth. "My undying love and devotion, which you have anyway, so nothing at all, I suppose." She kissed his cheek, rifling in the basket for the sweetmeats she'd packed for him. "But I have no brothers and sisters, I was born in Kent, and it was just my mother and I until Prue came to live with us. My father died when I was a month old, so I have no memory of him."

"I'm sorry."

Minerva shrugged. "I'm told he was a hero in a Flanders campaign, but he was injured out there and died of his wounds."

"You're from a titled family, though, is that right?"

Minerva nearly choked on her cake. "If you were to hear my mother talk, perhaps. She is a distant relation to Viscount Trent, though she has used that vague connection with more tenacity than you might think possible. She's single-minded, I'll give her that."

Minerva watched Inigo's dark eyebrows draw together. "She wants the best for you."

"She wants the best for her," Minerva retorted, and then regretted it. "No, I ought not say that. She's a rather silly creature and she puts far too much importance on things like titles and wealth, and for a long time I did too, because she always told me how vital it was, but it isn't. I know that now. What's the use of being a duchess, or wealthy beyond your dreams, if you're unhappy, if you can't share it with someone you love?"

"Your cousin seems happy enough as a duchess."

Minerva gave a little cry of triumph as she found the box of sweetmeats. "That's because she's head over heels in love with her duke," she said, laughing as she handed him a candied treat, studded with fruit and nuts. "She'd have married him if he'd been penniless, never mind without a title. In fact, it was the title that frightened her most, I think, but anyway. She was the one who taught me the important things in life are the ones we can't pay for."

Inigo was staring at her, a troubled look in his eyes, and so she reached for him, taking his hand and pressing it to her breast, over her heart.

"It's what's in here that's important, Inigo. I don't care about money and titles. I'm in love with you because… because I'm in awe of your intelligence, because you fascinate me and make me laugh and challenge me, and I've met no one like you before in all my life. Your views about men and women being equal, the way you believe the world ought to be, and your belief in me—that I could understand the same things you could if I only I had the education—these things made me fall in love with you. I need nothing else."

To Experiment with Desire

He was quiet for a long time as she held his hand against her. She'd put on his shirt for her foray down the stairs, and there was a possessive gleam in his eyes that suggested he enjoyed seeing her wear it. Now, she wondered if she'd said too much.

"I like having you here, with me," he said. "I've never brought anyone here before… a woman. I've never…"

He chewed on his lip, clearly uncertain of how to say what he wanted, perhaps afraid of offending her.

"Talk to me, Inigo. I don't mind what you tell me, only that it's the truth."

He let out a breath and nodded. "I've never had a lover, someone I cared about, or… or who cared for me. No one has ever…." He cleared his throat and took his hand away from where she'd pressed it to her but kept hold of her hand. "I'm not good at friends, at being close to people. In the foundling hospital it was… difficult. The other boys didn't much like me and I didn't like them. I had a friend once, for a while, but he left and after…."

He shrugged, and there was such eloquence in that hopeless gesture that Minerva's eyes filled as she realised how alone he'd always been.

"This," he said, gesturing to the room about them, "this house cost every penny I'd saved from the moment I started earning money. I never went out, did nothing but work, though I loved my work more than anything, so I never minded, but this place…."

Minerva waited, aware he was trying to tell her something important.

"It made me feel real." He laughed, shaking his head. "Does that sound stupid?"

She shook her head, unable to speak as her throat was too tight, and she didn't want to embarrass him by crying.

"It does to me, but it's true all the same. It was like I finally existed when I bought this house, like I'd achieved something that made me into a real person." He huffed out a frustrated breath. "I can't explain it better than that, but the point is this. It took me years to accomplish. This little house, barely furnished, it's the height of my achievement."

He dropped her hand and scowled, looking away from her and Minerva shifted around the bed, embracing him from behind and resting her head on his shoulder.

"Inigo, you started with nothing and no one, and this house is only a tiny part of it. Your name is famous, you're one of the most respected men of science in the world. You weren't born with a title and a fortune at your fingertips, and so everything you've achieved only makes you that much more remarkable. Your financial worth is the least important part of everything you've done."

"I know that," he said in disgust. "But my science won't stop people from cutting you in the street or put this house in a better part of town, or enough money in the bank to buy you the things you are used to. How much did that dress cost?" he demanded, gesturing to the expensive pelisse and gown he'd taken off, an angry note to his voice. "Do you even know?"

Minerva blanched as she realised she had no idea.

"Inigo," she began, but he got off the bed and surged to his feet.

He crossed the room, tugged on his trousers, and snatched a clean shirt from the chest of drawers.

"Go home, Minerva. Go and marry a rich man and leave me be."

"Inigo, please…."

He was out of the door before she could say anything else and her heart broke, knowing it was his pride that was smarting and not knowing how to fix it. She let out an unsteady breath, more than anything she wanted to go after him but suspected it would be best to leave him alone to calm down. She'd pushed enough for one day, and it had been a perfect day until the last few minutes. With regret, she realised it was growing late and her carriage would return for her all too soon. She made the bed, and checked for crumbs, repacking the basket before she got dressed and fixed her hair as best she could. Once she was respectable again, on the outside at least, she made her way downstairs to the kitchen, unsurprised to discover it empty. He'd be in his laboratory now.

It was hard to fight back the temptation to go to him, but she did, and lit the fire so it would be warm for him later, putting the rest of the food in the pantry. She hoped he'd remember to eat some of it. Once everything was done, Minerva put on her pelisse and reached for her hat, which she'd found abandoned at the bottom of the stairs. There were a few minutes to wait yet, but she supposed she'd best be ready at the front door.

She was halfway down the hallway when he called out to her.

"Minerva?"

She turned, immediately swept up in a fierce embrace as he held her to him. Minerva said nothing, just stroked his hair, aware of the tension singing through his body.

"I don't want you to go."

"I don't want to go either," she admitted, feeling her heart soar with his angry, almost grudging admission.

"You'll come back?" he demanded.

She drew back a little to look at him, to see the intensity of his expression, and put her hand to his cheek. He covered it with his own hand, pressing a kiss to her palm.

"Of course I'll come back. I'll always come back if you want me to, Inigo."

"You're mad," he muttered, and then let out a harsh breath. "Tomorrow?"

"Tomorrow," she agreed. "But the afternoon. I'll likely be in trouble with Prue for today's little adventure, and it will be difficult to get away, but I will try my best to come, and as early as I can manage."

He stared down at her, his expression dark and troubled. "Madness," he murmured, shaking his head. "Both of us, out of our damn minds."

Minerva laughed. "Speak for yourself," she said, giving him a kiss. "I'm perfectly sane, and very much in love."

She felt a jolt of anxiety at the unhappy sound he made.

"You're wrong." He looked tormented and furious now, and she could not help but worry for him. "It's… it's lust and obsession and… and—bloody hell! —I feel like I'll go mad if I must wait until tomorrow to see you again. That can't be right. It cannot be normal!" he exclaimed, running a hand through his hair, making it stick up in all directions.

Minerva refrained from telling him it was normal if you were in love with someone. He seemed to struggle with the changes she'd wrought on his life, and it was enough that she had something to hope for. She would not force the idea upon him. The sound of a carriage drawing to a halt meant their time was up and she turned to kiss him, comforted by his anguished groan as he let her go.

"I try my hardest to come to you tomorrow, Inigo. Don't forget to eat some supper. I put it all in the pantry for you and lit the fire in the kitchen. I love you."

He folded his arms and scowled, and she could only smile, delighted that he was so unhappy at her leaving.

"Thank you," he said, still grudging as she reached for the door. "I won't forget."

Chapter 15

Miss Hunt,

Believe me when I tell you there is no need to chastise me for this letter. I know quite well that I ought not write it. I know you will delight in telling me how furious you were to receive it, but I still hope that there is a small part of you that welcomes it.

I am still bewitched. You will not accept my gifts nor my advances and yet I know my touch did not disgust you in those moments we found ourselves trapped behind a curtain. Of all the ridiculous situations to find ourselves in that one is worthy of being replayed on the stage, and would have been if we'd been discovered, God forbid. I still cannot think of that night without a mixture of amusement, outrage and such desire I fear I will run mad.

I must see you.

I will be at the British Institution tomorrow afternoon. Perhaps you will be so kind as to indulge me. I have no expectations of you changing your mind. I only wish to be in your company for a short while.

M.

—Excerpt of a letter from The Most Honourable Lucian Barrington, Marquess of Montagu to Miss Matilda Hunt.

24th January 1815. South Audley Street, London.

"A letter? Anything exciting?"

Matilda jolted, crumpling the letter behind her back and wishing she could stem the blush that rose to her cheeks. She turned to face the fire instead, as Jemima came into the parlour with Helena in tow.

"No, not really," she said, sliding it into the pocket in her skirts. "To what do we owe the pleasure, Helena?"

Helena grimaced and shook her head. "I'm hiding from Robert and Prue."

"Oh, dear. What have you done?"

There was an indignant huff as Helena sat down. "Why do you imagine I've done anything?"

"Because we've made your acquaintance," Jemima said with a placid smile.

Helena glared at her and then shrugged. "I can't argue that, I suppose, and it *is* partly my fault. But, I ask you, how would you fare against Minerva Butler's determination to ruin herself for that wretched man?"

"What's happened?" Matilda and Jemima asked in unison as they sat down on either side of her.

"Prue found out that Min spent the whole day with Mr de Beauvoir yesterday, and she's furious. Not only because the foolish chit went there alone in broad daylight again, but because I helped her go with no one noticing. Robert doesn't know why Prue's furious, only that she is and that it's mine and Minerva's fault, and so he's angry with us for upsetting her in her *delicate condition.* Honestly, though, I've seen military men less delicate than Prue in a temper. She's scary."

"What is Prue going to do? Will she tell your brother?" Matilda asked, worrying for Minerva and what might happen if the duke found out.

"I don't think so, not yet anyway, but Prue doesn't know the madwoman is intent on going back to him again this afternoon. I told her I can't continue to help her ruin herself, assuming the damage isn't already done," Helena muttered, sounding angry, though the worry in her eyes gave away her real emotion. "But I wanted to be out of the house so I couldn't be coerced into helping her again, and then blamed for doing it."

Jemima nodded and covered Helena's hand with her own, but Helena looked to Matilda.

"Am I a bad person? A bad friend?"

"No," Matilda said, smiling at her. "You want to help her, and protect her too, but you can't do both. Minerva is a grown woman, though, and we all make our own choices. She knows the risks."

"You approve?" Helena said in outrage.

Matilda felt her blush returning and wondered if that *was* what she meant. No, she didn't approve; she was terrified for Minerva and what might become of her if she was discovered having an affair with de Beauvoir. Yet she admired her. She had the courage of her convictions. She'd decided on what she wanted, and would do everything in her power to take it for herself and damn the consequences... and the consequences would undoubtedly damn her.

"Not approve, exactly," Matilda said, choosing her words with care. "But I understand, and... and, if I'm honest, I rather envy her."

Helena stared at her in shock.

"She loves him, Helena," Matilda said gently. "More than she's afraid of what will happen to her. I… I would like to know how that feels."

Helena frowned, but it was the sharp glint in Jemima's eyes that made Matilda look away.

"Well, then," Jemima said after a rather tense silence. "What shall we do to occupy ourselves this afternoon?"

Matilda bit her lip, knowing it was madness just as well as Minerva knew it, and for once allowing herself to act without thinking it through. "Well, I… I was considering a trip to the British Institution."

***

Inigo stared at the tray of glittering, shockingly expensive rings before him and scowled. He had no idea what to choose. He wanted to buy something with diamonds and sapphires, something that would sparkle like Minerva's eyes, but if he was to have any chance of supporting a wife, he could not spend nearly everything he had on a ring.

"I just want a wedding ring," he said, glaring at the man behind the counter, who was clearly not interested in his business now as another customer had entered the shop.

The new fellow was a dandy, dressed to the nines, and obviously a great deal wealthier than Inigo.

"A wedding ring," the impatient jeweller said, nodding as he watched the newcomer take a jewelled fob watch out and flick it open with a pointed sigh.

A new tray of rings appeared, plain gold or silver bands this time.

"That one," Inigo said in a rush, panic crawling up the back of his neck.

"An excellent choice, sir," the jeweller said with an insincere smile that made Inigo want to upend the tray and throw it at him.

Why was he doing this? What had happened to his life? He didn't want to get married. He didn't want a wife and a family and… and suddenly he was thinking about Minerva carrying his child and his hands were shaking. Sweat prickled down his spine as too many conflicting emotions surged in his chest. Longing, terror, and guilt. No matter what he wanted, he had to protect Minerva. Thanks to his complete lack of sense yesterday, she might already be pregnant. They must marry, no matter what he wanted. That he couldn't bear the thought of getting through a whole day without seeing her was irrelevant. His obsession wasn't a reason for marriage; keeping her safe was the only reason that mattered.

The jeweller came back with the ring in a small blue velvet box and Inigo handed over the money. He snatched up the ring and shoved it into his pocket before hurrying out of the door. Once outside, he drew in a deep breath, willing the cold air to steady his nerves.

"Inigo?"

He turned, cursing whoever it was before seeing Solo hail him from across the street. Knowing he'd not escape now, Inigo crossed the road, fastidiously avoiding the squelchy filth that yesterday's rain had washed into mucky puddles, and nodded a greeting to Solo.

"I don't believe it," Solo said, a crooked smile at his lips as he regarded the jeweller's shop on the other side of the road. "You took my advice."

Inigo huffed out a breath. "I didn't have a lot of choice."

Solo frowned at that, nodding towards a chop house a few doors down. "I'm famished," he said. "Come and eat and you can tell me all about it."

He hesitated, considering how long it would take him to get home. It was only half past ten, but he needed to be back in plenty of time in case Minerva came around earlier than she'd suggested.

"Have you eaten breakfast?" Solo demanded with a sigh.

Inigo rolled his eyes. "What is this overwhelming need everyone has to make me eat? You're not my bloody mother."

"That's why, you fool," Solo retorted. "You've had no one to look after you but you're not capable of doing it yourself."

"I'm thirty years of age!" Inigo protested. "I've managed so far."

Solo gave him a long, considering look that Inigo didn't doubt took in a hastily tied cravat and crumpled coat. To his mortification, his stomach decided that would be a good moment to join in and gave an audible grumble. Solo raised one eyebrow.

"Fine," Inigo muttered, cross for no reason other than he'd felt cross when he woke up and the feeling hadn't dissipated.

He'd been cross that Minerva wasn't beside him, cross that he missed her so badly, cross that she couldn't come that morning, cross with her family for keeping her from him and ever crosser that they'd allowed her to come after him in the first place. Everyone was causing him aggravation, and he longed for the time when he'd been all alone with only his experiments for company. Life had been so very simple. Empty and lonely, perhaps, but simple.

They found a table in a relatively quiet corner of the busy chop house and ordered lamb chops, potatoes, peas pudding and two glasses of porter. It was delivered with remarkable speed and they ate in companionable silence for a while, for which Inigo was grateful. He knew it wouldn't last.

"So, you bought a ring?"

Inigo stabbed a potato with his fork and scowled at it. "Yes."

"When are you going to ask her?"

He shrugged. "Today, tomorrow, what does it matter?"

Solo rolled his eyes. "Do you even have any idea what you're going to say?"

Inigo chewed the potato, glowering at Solo and wishing he'd mind his own business. "What's it to you?"

Solo sighed and returned his attention to his dinner. "Because I'm afraid you'll mess it up, and then I'll be stuck with watching you tumble into a big dark hole when you realise what an ass you've been."

Inigo stabbed another potato, frowning. "I've ruined her. She's got no choice."

Solo stared at him in disbelief and then rubbed a weary hand over his eyes. "You really do not understand women, do you?"

"What?" Inigo demanded. "She might be with child, and no matter what else she's an intelligent woman. The answer is obvious."

Inigo felt uneasy as Solo just shook his head and returned a pitying expression.

"Have you told her you love her?"

Inigo opened his mouth to object, but Solo forestalled him.

"Don't even bother denying it. I've heard all about the *lust with a ring on its finger* argument and whilst I'm not pretending there's no truth in that, there *is* truth in how you're acting, too. You love her, and if you don't tell her so when you ask her to marry you, you really are an ass."

Inigo shook his head, too stubborn to consider it. "I don't know what love is, what it looks like, but I understand lust and desire. That I recognise."

"And that's all it is?" Solo remarked, setting down his knife and fork on his empty plate. "You feel nothing else for her?"

The jumble of feelings he'd been fighting when Solo had hailed him rose back up, threatening to choke him, and Inigo pushed his plate away, suddenly queasy.

"Look, you don't have to admit a damn thing to me, Inigo," Solo said. "God knows I'm no advert for happy ever afters, but I'm not such a blasted fool as not to recognise that this woman is important to you. You're one of the few people I give a damn about in this world, as depressing as that is to admit. I'd like to think you could succeed where I failed."

Inigo thought about that for a while before returning his gaze to Solo. "You didn't fail."

There was a bitter laugh, as Inigo had known there would be.

"Oh, I failed so many people in so many ways it's hard to credit, but that's neither here nor there. I won't fail you by keeping my mouth shut, even though you'd prefer it if I did."

He got to his feet, tossing some coins onto the table for the meal and laying a heavy hand on Inigo's shoulder.

"Good luck," Solo said, before heading for the door.

Inigo watched him go, his gait uneven as it often was in such cold, damp weather. He reached into his pocket and drew out the little velvet box. He opened it and stared at the simple gold band, nestled against its bed of blue silk. A ripple of fear shivered through him as he considered asking Minerva to marry him. Other than the fact that he'd ruined her, Inigo could think of no earthly reason she should do such a thing.

She loves you, said a little voice in his head.

"There's no such thing as love," he muttered, snapping the box shut and putting it away.

To Experiment with Desire

Minerva was caught up in this destructive obsession, just as he was. That was all. Eventually, those feelings would burn out and disappear, like that blasted diamond he'd destroyed. When that happened, she'd find herself married to a man way beneath her, one who could not give her all the things she wanted and deserved, and—when she realised it—it would crucify him. The idea of Minerva looking at him with anything less than the adoration he saw in her eyes now made his chest tight with misery.

He told himself it would be better to lose her now than to face the agonising slow death he knew was inevitable as he watched her accept that her feelings had been an illusion. How would he bear it when he saw the scales fall from her eyes and her affection for him diminish by increments? The trouble was, he couldn't let her go. Though every argument told him it would be best for him, he could not do it.

Letting her go was so terrifying he couldn't even consider it, though keeping her with him frightened him just as much. Yet, there was one empirical fact that swayed the scales firmly towards marriage. He'd ruined her, she might carry his child already, and he was damned if he'd be responsible for another fatherless bastard in the world.

***

Matilda looked around the grand building that was the Pall Mall Picture Gallery, or British Institution, and tried to keep her attention on the paintings. Jemima and Helena wandered ahead of her, talking in low but animated tones as they perused the pictures. Matilda stared up at the jostle of images, sky hung, side by side and on top of each other until her gaze landed on one by Thomas Lawrence, whom she greatly admired. She'd considered commissioning a portrait of her brother and Alice with their first child when he or she had arrived, as she thought it would be a lovely present for them. This portrait was of a rather dashing hussar, his sword slung over his right shoulder in a nonchalant pose, all the gold braid on his uniform gleaming, and the fur on his cape so real she felt she could reach out and find it soft to the touch.

Matilda jolted as something equally soft brushed her hand and looked down in surprise to find it had been grasped by a little girl, who was beaming up at her.

"Why, Miss Barrington, how nice to see you," Matilda exclaimed, as delighted to see the lovely child as she was chagrined by the way her heart leaped about in her chest like a mad rabbit.

For, if Miss Barrington was here, so was her Uncle Monty.

The child beamed at her, her blonde ringlets framing the angelic face and blue eyes that reminded Matilda so forcefully of her closest relative. She wondered just how beautiful Montagu had been as a child.

"Good afternoon, Miss Hunt."

Matilda forced herself to remain calm as she turned to regard Lord Montagu and curtseyed to him. As ever, he was impeccably dressed in a dark blue coat with a snowy white cravat, the usual large, single diamond pin glinting among the pristine folds. He held a silver-topped walking stick in one gloved hand. There was no hint in his eyes of the desperate need to see her of which he'd written, or of the desire that made her fear he'd run mad. He was as cool and precise as he always was. No doubt it was all a game to him, and he felt nothing at all. It was certainly easy to believe.

"Do you like the pictures, Miss Hunt?" Phoebe asked, staring up at her. "I like the one of the horse best, do come and see."

She tugged at Matilda's hand, and Matilda was powerless to refuse her.

"It's a Stubbs," Montagu told her, giving her a sideways glance. "Whistlejacket. She's rather taken with it."

Matilda smiled and nodded, wondering what on earth she was doing. "Are children usually allowed in the galleries?" she asked quietly.

"Some children," Montagu replied with a quirk of his lips.

Matilda laughed. Of course.

"Thank you for coming."

She looked around at him, surprised by his soft tone, the sincerity in his voice.

"I hardly need tell you it was against my better judgement."

"Hardly," he agreed.

"Look, isn't he beautiful?" Phoebe said, pointing at the huge painting of the chestnut stallion.

"Very handsome indeed," Matilda agreed as the child stared at it a moment longer before moving along the gallery to stare up at another painting, this time of a monkey.

"Phoebe looks well. Happy." She studied Montagu's face before he answered, transfixed by the change in his austere expression as he looked upon the little girl.

He could love, then… at least, he could love this little girl.

"You think so?"

It seemed to be a genuine question, one with something that sounded like concern behind it, and Matilda continued to survey him.

"Yes, I do. Why?"

He was silent for a moment, his blond brows drawn together. "It is often lonely for such a child and I…" he gave a surprisingly self-deprecating laugh. "I am hardly ideal parent material."

Matilda tried to imagine Montagu playing with a doll's house or reading bedtime stories, and failed utterly, though the idea made something inside of her ache with a sudden sense of emptiness.

"She has playmates?"

Montagu hesitated before nodding and she was struck by how different he seemed today. He was usually so forcefully in control of himself and the conversation.

"Yes, but...."

He stopped, and Matilda sensed he'd say no more on the subject, but she couldn't resist pushing a little.

"But?"

He glanced back at her, frowning. "I'm too overprotective. Children can be cruel and, the last time we had young guests, there was a falling out. She was upset. I've been rather concerned about repeating the incident."

"That's only natural, I suppose," Matilda said carefully, aware of the exclusivity of this moment of candour and not wanting to do or say anything to end it. She knew Phoebe was his only living kin, his family having been touched by too many tragedies. "But children fall out all the time, and are best friends a moment later."

He nodded, looking unconvinced.

"I worry for her," he said, a dark look that Matilda did not understand clouding his eyes.

"She's your only family. Of course you worry for her. You're a devoted uncle and want to do what's best for her, that does you credit."

He glanced at her and shook his head, a smile that had no humour in it curling his lip. "How you can say such a thing?"

"What?" Matilda asked, perplexed by the bitterness of his tone.

"I have not always been kind to you, Miss Hunt, and I know that whatever is between us is there against your will, your judgement, your hopes for the future. Yet *you* are always kind.

Fair. You have a generous heart. I do not deserve your understanding, and yet I want it, very much."

Matilda stared at him, astonished, and knew she was in very grave danger. Panic rose in a sweep of colour as she recognised the feeling in her heart for what it was. She had to get away.

"I'm going to marry Mr Burton." The words escaped her before she'd even really registered them, forced from her in a jumble as the intensity of her emotions threatened to have her do or say something very, very foolish indeed.

Montagu stilled. Was it only her imagination that made her believe he blanched? The colour left his face so quickly she couldn't be certain it was not a trick of the light. The day was dark and grim, the daylight in the gallery not so bright as one would hope for viewing pictures, but surely Montagu looked pale, did he not? Did it truly matter to him? He turned away from her and her scrutiny.

"You don't give a damn for Mr Burton," he said and, though the words were quietly spoken, she could hear his anger.

"He's a decent man," she retorted, finding she could hardly breathe.

Montagu made a harsh sound. "He'll suffocate you and snuff out all that makes you vibrant and alive. You must be the model wife for a man like that, perfect in every way, and heaven help you if say or do anything he doesn't agree with."

Matilda fought down a prickle of unease, remembering Mr Burton's obvious disapproval when she'd helped Harriet and Bonnie. They had proved that Lady Frances had tried to trap Kitty's fiancé into marrying her instead, and Mr Burton had not been pleased. She thought of all the times he'd made his displeasure clear when she'd danced with any man but him. It was only natural, she told herself; he was protecting her. Yet there had been glimpses of something proprietary that *had* made her uneasy.

"You would say that," she retorted all the same, nettled that he could undermine her decision with such ease. "And I suppose you'd be different, oh, but I forgot, I would never be your wife, so it's hardly the same."

"With me you'd be free!" Montagu swung around, grey eyes glittering with such fury that Matilda drew in a sharp breath, but Phoebe came running up to them and he clamped his mouth shut, forcing a smile to his face for his niece.

"Have you decided if the monkey is eating oranges or peaches yet?" he asked, sounding quite calm and in control of himself.

"Yes, definitely peaches," she said, grinning up at him and showing a perfect set of dimples.

Ridiculously, Matilda wondered if she'd inherited them from her uncle. If she had, Montagu had never smiled with such unrestrained pleasure as to make them visible.

"I'm glad we cleared up that mystery, Bee."

Matilda felt her throat tighten at the tenderness in his voice as Montagu touched a hand to the girl's cheek. He turned abruptly away, walking to the other side of the gallery and leaving them alone together.

Phoebe watched him go, a tiny frown between her pale eyebrows, the expression such an echo of Montagu's that Matilda's breath caught.

"What's wrong?" Phoebe asked, looking up at her.

Matilda heart clenched, struck that the girl should pick up on her uncle's mood with such ease.

"There's nothing wrong, love," Matilda said, crouching down to the little girl, who was still watching her uncle.

He was staring at a painting, though she doubted he saw it. Every inch the ice-cold, untouchable nobleman, she reminded herself. He was far from her reach. Phoebe glanced uncertainly at Matilda and then back to Montagu.

"Are you sure?" she asked, taking Matilda's hand and glancing back at her uncle. "He…." The little girl lowered her voice, and looked around to check no one was close before speaking again. "He gets sad sometimes, though I'm not supposed to tell anyone. But you won't say anything, will you? You're his friend." She hesitated, giving Matilda an oddly penetrating look. "He has got no other friends, you see. He's not at ease with most people, but I think he likes you. You *are* his friend, aren't you, Miss Hunt?"

Matilda swallowed, hard. "I… well…. Yes. Yes, I suppose we are friends, and of course I won't tell a soul, not ever, but… but what do you mean? Everyone is sad sometimes, Phoebe."

Phoebe shook her head. "Not like him. I don't like it when he's sad. He tries very hard to pretend he isn't, but I can always tell because he tries *too* hard. His eyes don't look the same. It's like he's not really there, like he's gone somewhere else."

Matilda stared after Montagu, willing away the urge to go to him, trying to squash the feelings she'd told Helena she wanted to experience and now wished she'd never hoped for.

"*Are you lonely?*"

"*I do not lack for company.*"

She'd sensed it in him before, something untouchable and desolate, but he'd not answered the question and, when she'd pressed, he'd evaded it altogether.

There are some things I can choose for myself.

He'd chosen her.

You are not like the others.

Matilda looked up as Montagu returned to them. His face was a mask of indifference, closed off.

"Phoebe, go and look at the monkey again. I think perhaps they were oranges after all."

"But, Uncle…."

Montagu raised one eyebrow just a fraction and Phoebe sighed.

"Yes, Uncle." She walked away, dutifully returning to the painting.

Matilda waited as Montagu watched her go.

"Have you accepted his offer?" There was no emotion to the question, he may as well have been enquiring if she thought it would rain again.

Matilda stared at him, trying to find a crack in the mask, some clue to what it was Phoebe had meant about him being sad.

"No," she said, when his expression remained aloof. "He hasn't asked me yet, but he's going to."

Montagu nodded.

"Thank you for coming today," he said, scrupulously well-mannered. "I hope you enjoy the rest of the exhibition."

Matilda watched, a little astonished as he gave her a polite nod and walked away, collecting Phoebe before leaving the gallery. She let out an unsteady breath, her thoughts all in a jumble, her throat tight with anxiety and regret. Well, that was that, then. She was safe from Montagu, just as she'd hoped. He'd leave her be now, surely?

She walked to stand by the window, discovering it overlooked the front of the gallery. Looking down, she saw Montagu emerge a few minutes later, holding Phoebe's hand as their carriage moved forward. They stood, waiting as a footman opened the door and put down the step. Phoebe looked up at her uncle, staring at him in silence, and then covered the hand that held hers. Both tiny white-gloved hands held Montagu's larger one in such a tender gesture of comfort that Matilda's eyes burned.

Chapter 16

Mr Glover,

I read your report with great interest. I want comparisons to other mills in the country to discover if safety standards are as poor as they would appear to be in the two you have investigated. I also want the names of all those injured. I would ask you to continue your investigations at the mills located in Derbyshire with all haste and return your findings to me without delay. I suspect you will discover more of the same. I have made funds available should you need to employ more men and to cover any further expenses. Speed is essential, no matter the costs involved. The personal information I requested also remains a priority.

I expect to hear from you in no less than a week.

—*Excerpt of a letter from The Most Honourable Lucian Barrington, Marquess of Montagu to Mr Richard Glover.*

24th January 1815. Church Street, Isleworth, London.

Inigo sat, drumming his fingers on the kitchen table. He'd lit the fires in both his bedroom and the kitchen, laid the table ready for lunch, and tried to work on his paper for a full hour before conceding defeat. He took out his watch, glared at it when it still insisted it was gone three o'clock, and muttered a curse under his breath. Where the devil was she?

A knock at the door had his chair screeching across the kitchen tiles as he stood up and ran for the door. Wrenching it open, Inigo scowled to see a messenger boy in the Duke of Bedwin's livery.

"For you, Mr de Beauvoir," the boy said, handing over a letter bearing the duke's seal.

Inigo's stomach somersaulted. Had Bedwin discovered his affair with his wife's cousin? Perhaps this was to inform him he was being called out. Before he could tear it open, the boy leaned forward and withdrew another letter from inside his jacket.

"And this one is from Miss Butler," the lad whispered with an accompanying wink that only made Inigo scowl harder.

Good God, the reckless little fool! Now she was bribing Bedwin's staff to send messages? He flushed hot and cold in quick succession.

"Wait," he said tersely, closing the door and ripping open Minerva's letter first.

My darling Inigo,

I'm so sorry. Prue is standing guard and I simply cannot get out of the house today. Tomorrow will be easier as she is going with Bedwin to visits friends. Bedwin is holding an impromptu and informal dinner tonight though, and he has sent you an invitation. Please accept it, my love. There are to be some important men here tonight and you may have another opportunity to talk to him about your work. It will be torture to see you and not touch you, but better than not seeing you at all. Do come.

With all my love,

Minerva.

Inigo let out an unsteady breath before opening the letter from Bedwin and discovering an invitation for this evening. He scrawled a reply and opened the door again, pressing a coin and his acceptance into the boy's hand before grasping his other wrist.

"And if you breathe a word about that other letter to another living soul, there won't be a place in the whole country safe enough for you to hide in."

The boy grinned at him, shaking his head. "Don't you worry, none, mister. Miss Butler's a good 'un, I won't ever tattle. She did me a kind turn once and I ain't forgot."

Inigo nodded and let the boy go, seeing sincerity in his eyes. "Thank you."

The boy nodded and then hesitated, narrowing his eyes. "You gonna do right by 'er?"

"Yes! Not that it's any of your business, cub," Inigo retorted, fighting back a surge of guilt under the boy's judgemental gaze.

"Well, that's all right and tight, then." The cheeky blighter doffed his hat and stuck his hands in his pocket, whistling as he walked off.

***

The evening of the 24th January 1815. Beverwyck, London.

Inigo tugged at his coat and fought the urge to yank at his cravat, which was bloody strangling him, as a footman announced his name.

There were more guests than he expected, perhaps a dozen, though there was only one that he was interested in seeing. He glimpsed a sunshine yellow gown and his breath caught, but before he could move forward a hand gripped his arm.

"Inigo?"

He turned, and met piercing dark blue eyes and a chiselled, handsome face with a familiar cynical expression.

"Gabe?"

"Didn't blow yourself up yet then, professor?"

Inigo gaped, looking the impeccably dressed man up and down in astonishment. "I heard the rumours about the notorious Mr Knight," he said, shaking his head in wonder. "And I knew it was you, I just knew it."

"I told you I'd make a success of myself. No matter what."

"Christ, you even sound like a bloody toff," Inigo said, laughing a little.

Gabriel snorted. "Not quite, but as near as I can get without feeling like a complete prick." He looked Inigo up and down, grinning now. "Not too shabby yourself, Professor. You're famous."

"Not as famous as you," Inigo remarked, accepting a drink from a passing servant.

Gabriel gave a wry smile. "My bank balance is famous. I'm glad you're here, though. I've been wanting to speak with you. I think we can help each other. I need an alchemist."

Inigo rolled his eyes. "We had this conversation when we were boys. I can't turn lead into gold, you numbskull, so don't ask me, and I'm a natural philosopher, not a bloody alchemist."

"I see you are as charming and pedantic as ever," Gabriel said, grinning. "I can't imagine why so many of the boys wanted to beat you up. For the record, I wasn't going to ask, you jawed me to death the last time explaining why I was so addled to believe such a thing possible. I do, however, need a *natural philosopher*."

"What the devil for?" Inigo said, his eyebrows going up.

He rolled his eyes as Gabe touched his nose with one finger. Gabriel Knight had ever been thus. In the foundling hospital, it was Gabe who could get stuff… for a price. He traded information in return for goods and, even as a lad of twelve, he had been big enough and damn near insane enough to take down a guard by himself. Mostly he was too clever to use his fists unless it was inescapable or worked to his advantage. Knowledge was power and Gabe had learned to use bribery, his wits, and an innate instinct for making money. Inigo knew Gabe was one of the main reasons he'd survived the orphanage with all his limbs intact. They'd not been friends exactly, but Gabe had looked out for him, protecting him from too many beatings, and Inigo would not forget that. Admittedly, that was because Gabe found Inigo was useful to him, being cleverer than the adults who ran the place by the time he was ten, but still.

"We'll talk another time," Gabe said, patting Inigo's shoulder. "But I'll make it worth your while."

He winked at Inigo and sauntered off.

"A friend of yours?"

The familiar voice had Inigo's heart beating double time as he turned towards it. His breath caught as he saw Minerva, and all the reasons why she would be out of her mind to settle for him crashed down upon him with force. She was stunning. The yellow dress brought out the gold in her hair and, set against those eyes, she was the embodiment of a summer's day. He couldn't speak, couldn't think, could do nothing but stare at her and despair at how damn hopeless it was to feel this way. It was like longing to embrace the sun, though you knew you'd be burnt to cinders before you even got close.

Minerva looked back at him and then blushed, glancing around to see if they were observed.

"Inigo," she whispered, her voice pleading. "Stop looking at me like that."

With a herculean effort, he tore his gaze away from her.

"Sorry," he managed, his voice sounding odd and scratchy.

"I don't mind," she said, a soft note of amusement in her voice. "Only everyone will know what happened between us if you don't stop."

Inigo cursed himself, knowing she was right and trying desperately to take himself in hand.

"Forgive me, Miss Butler," he said, once he could say something halfway intelligent. "May I say how… how exquisite you look tonight."

"You may."

The look of pleasure in her eyes at his compliment almost undid him all over again, but he downed the drink he held and gestured a servant over to give him another.

"Am I to take it you know Mr Knight?" Minerva asked him.

Inigo narrowed his eyes. "Yes. Do you?"

Minerva looked far too pleased by the note in his voice which was not jealousy, but she mistakenly seemed to believe was.

"We were just introduced this evening," she said, taking a sip of her drink and looking around the room. "I have a friend who finds him rather fascinating, though," she added, giving him a speculative glance.

"Tell her to run far, far away," Inigo said softly.

"Why?"

"Because women love him and there's never been one yet who's held his interest for above an hour, as far as I know. He's dangerous to any well-bred lady. He despises aristocrats, but he'll use them in any way he can to get what he wants."

"And what does he want?"

"Money. Power."

Minerva looked troubled by that and he hoped her friend wasn't as reckless as she was. He might be a bastard, but Gabriel was ruthless.

"You know him well?"

Inigo shrugged. "We grew up together."

"The foundling hospital?" Minerva said in surprise.

"Yes," Inigo agreed, doing his best not to look at her as he spoke, for his hands were itching to touch her, to slide over the butter-soft satin that encased her breasts, to pull her to him. He let go of a breath, trying to concentrate on the conversation. "We lost touch over the years, but I very much doubt he's changed."

Minerva's gaze moved over the room to where Lady Helena was standing, speaking with Lord St Clair. Inigo cursed, realising Harriet must be here too. Not that he bore her any ill will, nothing of the sort, but Harriet knew him better than most and he didn't doubt their circle of Peculiar Ladies shared all the latest gossip. Did that mean she knew about him and Minerva? As he watched, Harriet appeared, moving to take St Clair's arm. The earl turned, covering her hand with his and sending her such a look that Inigo felt an odd sensation in his chest. St Clair loved his wife. It was an odd realisation, to see the difference between something that was pure lust, and the strange mixture of adoration, desire and… and something else. Familiarity?

He wondered how it would be to attend an evening like this with Minerva as his wife, and felt as if he'd had the air knocked from his lungs, his longing for it was so fierce. Was that what love was?

While St Clair's attention wandered, so had Lady Helena's, and Inigo saw her stare across the room, her gaze fixed intently on Gabe. Oh, holy God. That was a disaster looking for a place to happen. Relieved to have someone else's fate to dwell upon for a moment, he focused on that.

"It's Lady Helena."

Minerva looked up at him, a question in her eyes.

"The friend who is fascinated with Gabe—Mr Knight, I mean. It's Lady Helena."

Minerva bit her lip and then nodded.

"Tell her to stay away," Inigo warned her. "He has no scruples. He's too damn rich to fear anyone, and ruining a duke's sister is not something he'd have any scruples about."

Minerva blanched but gave a taut nod. "Thank you for the warning. I'll tell her, but—"

"But she's just as pig-headed and self-destructive as you are," Inigo finished with a weary sigh.

Minerva flashed him a mischievous smile. "You've not destroyed me quite yet, Mr de Beauvoir," she said, a wicked glint in her eyes as she moved away from him to mingle with the other guests.

***

Inigo wondered whether it had been Minerva's intervention that had him sitting next to the duke as he was far from the most illustrious guest, but he was grateful. Bedwin had already implied he had an interest in Inigo's discoveries and would be open to sponsoring him to further his work. The duke had also said he would be in touch to discuss it further in the coming weeks. This happy turn of events did not entirely make up for the way Harriet had been studying him during the meal. He felt like one the samples he examined under a microscope, hardly daring to look in Minerva's direction for fear of confirming everything Harriet was pondering behind those delicate spectacles.

"I wish I had attended your lecture last year, Mr de Beauvoir," Harriet said, snapping his attention to her now the duke was concentrating on his dinner. "I had read Lavoisier's experiments with diamonds and his conclusions, but to discover graphite also burns to form carbon dioxide was quite a coup. So you discovered another form of carbon. Fascinating."

Inigo opened his mouth to reply to what he knew, with Harriet, would become a fascinating conversation, when he saw her stiffen, her lips settling into a thin, white line. He followed her gaze to see one the guests, a Dr Murphy, looking at her with distaste.

The doctor turned to speak to a Mr Hammond, his strident voice attempting an undertone yet still loud enough to carry down the table. "I have oft remarked the perils of educating females beyond what is natural. It damages the ovaries and leads to infertility and sometimes hysteria. A dangerous affliction, especially for one yet to produce a family."

"I'm sure Her Grace would be interested in that argument, Dr Murphy," Inigo said, making sure Duchess Bedwin could hear him at the far end of the table. "I believe, as a successful writer, she can be taken as a model for the educated woman."

As Her Grace was also very clearly pregnant, it was a forceful enough argument in any circumstances. As she was now staring daggers at Dr Murphy, Inigo took a malicious satisfaction in his discomfort.

"Ah, yes," Dr Murphy said. "Well, there are sometimes remarkable exceptions that prove the rule." He gave Duchess Bedwin a condescending smile and Inigo saw her knuckles whiten around her water glass. "I believe you are a proponent of education for women, Mr de Beauvoir?" the doctor said, his expression conveying everything he thought of that opinion.

"I am," he agreed, settling in for the inevitable argument.

"Yet, you must observe that females are a far more tender species than the male. They are easily upset, their minds disordered when overly stimulated and, as the bearers of the next generation, that frailty must be protected."

"If women are silly and prone to fits of the vapours, it is because of a lack of education or proper focus," Inigo said, his indignation at the man's attitude making his temper flare despite knowing better. "Nearly every foolishness exhibited by *some* women can be attributed to the fact that everyone around them insists on treating them as children, that combined with the tedium of having no useful purpose beyond bearing children themselves is bound to cause hysteria. Any sentient being would become hysterical in the face of such boredom. I might add that, if women are as frail and delicate as you suggest, it's a wonder humanity has lasted this long."

There was a spectacular silence.

"This is what becomes of allowing a lowborn fellow like that among his betters," Dr Murphy said in a low voice, glaring at Inigo.

"Bedwin," Her Grace called from the far end of the table. "I like Mr de Beauvoir very much. He talks a great deal of sense. Do sponsor his work. Harriet admires him tremendously, and you know how often you've remarked on how clever the countess is." She flashed Dr Murphy a brilliant smile. "Tell me more about why women are hysterical, Doctor. I must share it with my friends when we meet next week. I can hardly wait for the fascinating conversation that will follow."

Dr Murphy turned a vivid colour that reminded Inigo of strontium salts burnt on a naked flame. He wasn't sure that particular shade of red was healthy, but could not deny his satisfaction in seeing it.

"Darling." Everyone looked to see St Clair addressing his wife. "Ought I to join Bedwin in sponsoring Mr de Beauvoir? I know how much you admire his work, and you know I live to please you. Perhaps he'd be willing to help you with the book you were speaking of in return?"

Harriet beamed at her husband. "What a wonderful idea," she said, obviously delighted. "I was so impressed by that book you lent me, Mr de Beauvoir. I believe Miss Butler read it too.

Conversations on Chemistry, by *Mrs* Jane Marcet. It was so effective in explaining scientific principles in straightforward language that I was toying with the idea of writing something similar but tackling different subjects. Perhaps we could explain some of your work in terms which the general public, and *especially* women," she added, sending a fierce glare towards Dr Murphy, "would be comfortable reading and understanding."

"I should be delighted to participate in such a project, Lady St Clair," Inigo replied as Harriet grinned at him.

He glanced next at Minerva, which was a mistake. The expression of pride in her eyes made his heart feel most peculiar, as though it were expanding in his chest. He looked away and returned his attention to his dinner, resolving to try to keep his mouth shut for the rest of the evening.

Inigo knew he was about to ruin his own prospects. The offers from Bedwin and St Clair would be swiftly withdrawn when he proposed to Minerva and they discovered their affair. They'd likely try to take Minerva from him and away from any possible scandal, at least until they were certain she didn't carry his child. She'd be married off, quickly and discreetly to someone more worthy of her. He wasn't about to sit by and let that happen, but he knew such powerful men could ruin him with ease, and then what could he offer her? Despite everything he stood to lose, he couldn't regret it.

Once, he would have sold his soul for the kind of financial support the duke and the earl's backing would give him, but now, as badly as he wanted it still, it paled in comparison to Minerva. Without her, the rest held little value for him, and if that wasn't the most terrifying thought he'd ever had he didn't know what was.

***

"Good Lord, I'm worn to a thread," Helena complained as they made their way up the stairs. "The conversation at these dinners of Robert's is so deadly dull."

Minerva stifled a yawn. It had been a long night, with most of the men dominating the conversation with business matters. She'd been unable to share more than a few words with Inigo, either, which was likely for the best.

"You're just irritated because you were the other end of the table from Mr Knight."

"Well, you're just smug because you're bursting with pride over Mr de Beauvoir," Helena countered, sticking her tongue out.

Minerva laughed, unable to deny it. "Oh, but you must admit he *was* marvellous."

Helena chuckled and let out a sigh. "I must," she admitted. "I've always hated that Dr Murphy, but he's very influential, sadly, and my brother likes to keep up to date with all that's happening in the world. That's the only reason Mr Knight was here too, of course, for you know my brother doesn't like him. Happily, I think Robert saw tonight what I've been telling him for ages about the loathsome Dr Murphy. If he didn't, I suspect Prue will explain it to him in excruciating detail," she added, making Minerva smile.

"Well, I can't see him being invited back any time soon."

"Thank heavens! You must be thrilled at Mr de Beauvoir's success this evening. With both St Clair and Bedwin sponsoring him he'll be a force to be reckoned with."

Minerva nodded, though she was troubled, too. She knew it was likely Bedwin would withdraw his support once he discovered that she was Inigo's lover. St Clair had never been a fan of his in the first place and his support had been given to please his wife more than anything, so there was every chance he would follow suit. Before, it had only been Minerva risking her future to be with him, but now… now she might jeopardise his whole career if they were discovered.

"Well, I'm off to bed. Goodnight, Min."

Minerva looked up, her unsettling thoughts pushed to one side for the moment as she regarded Helena.

"You will remember what I said about Mr Knight, won't you, Helena?"

Helena rolled her eyes. "Pot. Kettle. Black," she said succinctly.

"It's not the same," Minerva said, moving closer and lowering her voice. "Inigo tried to keep me at a distance, to protect me. From what he said of Mr Knight, he'd be only too pleased to ruin you. He hates the aristocracy, and you're as aristocratic as he'll ever get close to. Inigo has known him since they were boys, Helena, and he says the man is dangerous. For heaven's sake, I know I'm being reckless, but that's just madness."

Helena looked back at her and raised one, perfectly arched eyebrow. "No, darling. That's a challenge."

Chapter 17

Dear Miss Hunt,

It is with the greatest regret that I must inform you I will not be in London next week as I had hoped. I have some unexpected business in Derbyshire which needs my immediate attention. This means I must cancel my appointment to call upon you.

I hope I need not explain further how very disappointed I am.

I pray that you will excuse me, but rest assured of my regard and admiration. I will hasten to London at my earliest opportunity.

—Excerpt of a letter from Mr David Burton to Miss Matilda Hunt.

25th January 1815. South Audley Street, London.

Matilda stared down at this morning's letter with chagrin. She was not relieved, she told herself sternly. She took a moment to remember Mr Burton's face and all the things that had made her like him. When they'd met, she'd thought him charming and attentive, polite, and she'd thought he had kind eyes. He'd shaken that first impression a time or two, but there was really nothing she could put her finger on. Many men were a deal more overbearing than he was. She was just being foolish, looking for excuses, and that had to stop. It really did. It was only that Jemima had left that morning and she was feeling blue devilled. Nothing more.

Jemima had her new cottage and a new life awaiting her, and it was quite all right that she wanted to settle in by herself. Jemima's future as a spinster seemed to hold no fears for her, and Matilda admired her for that, for not panicking and feeling the desperation to marry as soon as she could. Admittedly, she was younger than Matilda and did not have her reputation to contend with, but if Jemima could face the future with such equanimity, surely Matilda should be ashamed for feeling such overwhelming terror at the prospect of being alone.

Besides that, there was no reason in the world that she should be hurt by Jemima not wanting her company. She'd be invited to visit soon enough.

Setting the letter aside, she finished her breakfast and readied herself to go out. She was just fastening her bonnet as the butler opened the door to Minerva. Her friend looked lovely in a bright blue gown and spencer and a charming little bonnet with blue and yellow silk flowers in a cluster on one side.

"Good morning, Min. What excellent timing," Matilda said, gesturing for her to go back outside to Matilda's waiting carriage.

"Thank you so much for doing this," Minerva said, taking her arm as they walked down the front steps. "You're really too good."

Matilda snorted and shook her head. "I'm fast coming to the conclusion I'm nothing of the sort," she said with a sigh.

"Whatever do you mean?"

Minerva took the waiting footman's hand as she climbed into the carriage and Matilda followed suit, waiting until the doors were shut behind them before she spoke again. She didn't really know what to say, but she owed Minerva honesty.

"I'm horribly jealous," she said to Minerva with a wan smile. "And in awe of your courage."

Minerva laughed at that. "Courage? I'm not sure there are many who would see my actions as courageous, and the truth is,

Matilda, I can't do otherwise. I love him and… and being without him is unbearable. There just comes a point where there no longer seems to be a choice to make."

Matilda nodded but didn't want to pursue the subject any further. The idea of feeling so fiercely for Mr Burton was so far from possible she felt a surge of guilt. The poor man deserved more than a half-hearted wife, did he not? In the hope of changing the subject, she reached into her reticule for one of the little cards Jemima had given her with her new address on.

"Jemima left for the country this morning. She asked me to give this to you and to beg you to write to her. I know she'll settle in and make friends quickly but, in the meantime, she asked that everyone keep in touch.

"Oh, of course I will," Minerva said, smiling and tucking the card away. "I'm dying to see her new cottage. It sounds idyllic."

"It does," Matilda said, turning away to look out of the window until they got to Church Street.

"I'll pick you up later as arranged," she said, smiling at Minerva and praying that everything would work out for her and her Mr de Beauvoir.

"I'll not forget this, Tilda," Minerva said, squeezing her hand before she stepped out of the carriage.

Matilda watched as she hurried to the front door and disappeared inside. The carriage moved on again and she sighed, trying to keep her mind on the shopping she was going to do, and not to remember Miss Barrington's concern for her uncle, and little white-gloved hands holding his.

***

Minerva turned onto her side, her fingers trailing back and forth through the hair on Inigo's chest. She regretted that she'd not been able to bring him lunch, but getting here at all had been hard enough. Prue had been feeling unwell and so cancelled their trip to call on friends, going back to bed for the afternoon. When Bedwin had seen Minerva going out, she'd had to lie and say she was going to Matilda's. It was partly true, for Matilda had agreed to take her to Inigo, but lying to his face had been awful and would also get Matilda into trouble with Prue if she discovered it, which was worse.

She regarded Inigo, who was dozing, one arm crooked behind his head. He seemed preoccupied today, a little tense, and she couldn't understand why. Twice she'd been certain he'd wanted to ask her something, but every time he seemed to be about to do so, he changed his mind. She feared he was thinking about his prospects. Last night's offers from Bedwin and St Clair could change his life forever. He'd never again find his work hindered by lack of funds. It would be possible for him to set up a new laboratory if he wished, with all the newest equipment and using assistants to work with him, which she knew he couldn't afford to do now. His work was his life, and if she took that from him, she'd never forgive herself. Had he come to the same conclusion? Was he trying to end things between them?

"What is it?"

Minerva looked up to find Inigo studying her.

"Oh, nothing," she said, a little too brightly. "It's just been such a lovely day."

He snorted at that, turning her onto her back and staring down at her. "You have very low expectations, Miss Butler. Bread and butter for lunch and an afternoon in my bed. There are some women who would not say that it had been a lovely day unless there had been an outing somewhere expensive, and flowers at the very least. Jewels, perhaps. They would want serious courting before giving away even a kiss."

"Ah, but those women do not know the pleasure to be found in your bed is greater than expensive jewels."

Inigo laughed, and the sound made her feel alive, and so happy she could hardly contain it. She wanted to make him laugh often and, in the light of her thoughts, that made her melancholy.

"Are you stroking my ego?"

Minerva's lips quirked into a smile as her hand slid down his chest, down his belly and lower. "I wasn't," she murmured. "But I can if you want me to."

He sucked in a sharp breath as her fingers curled about him and caressed his growing arousal. She watched his eyes darken as her own desire burned hot in an instant.

"What would you have of me?" he whispered, staring down at her. "I'm yours to command. I fear what I might do for you if you asked, or perhaps it's wondering if there is anything I *wouldn't* do that is the most terrifying."

Minerva's heart clenched, wishing it was that simple. "I want what I've always wanted from you, Inigo."

But she knew, as he leaned down to kiss her, that for him, that was the most terrifying thing she could ask him for.

***

The day went by far too fast and the sense that Inigo was ill at ease only grew as she readied herself to leave. She'd almost asked him, seeing the unhappy glint in his eyes as she fastened her spencer, but she was a coward. How Matilda could think her courageous, she couldn't fathom. She was far too frightened to ask Inigo what was wrong for fear he would tell her this affair had to end. It was selfish and craven when she knew what his work meant to him. She'd known from the start she would always come second to his experiments and she'd accepted that, but she'd thought perhaps she could keep a part of him for herself.

Instead, her own insistence that Bedwin support his work had become the means of destroying her own hopes. She could tell he was anxious and knew he didn't want to hurt her. The certainty that he was trying to let her down gently grew by the moment, but it was too soon. She wasn't ready to say goodbye. Not yet.

So she didn't ask, and every time he seemed to gather himself she chattered about inconsequential nonsense, not allowing him to say the words that would break her heart and grind her dreams to rubble and dust.

"Minerva," he said, taking her arm just as the sound of a carriage drawing up outside the house could be heard beyond the door.

Thank heavens, Matilda was early.

"I must run, darling. It was too bad of me to make Matilda bring me here. I can't compound that by making her wait for me." She kissed him, a quick press of lips that silenced his protest, opened the door, and froze.

There was a woman on the doorstep whom she recognised. They'd only met once, in Tunbridge Wells, the second time she'd met Inigo. He'd asked Minerva to remind him of an appointment to escape the woman's company. Minerva now knew that Mrs Tate was notorious and had once been the Earl of St Clair's mistress. What on earth she was doing here was one thing, but that Mrs Tate had seen her here with Inigo alone would be Minerva's downfall.

"Mrs Tate," Inigo's voice pierced the drumming sound in her ears which she realised must be her heart pounding too hard, too fast. "To what do we owe the pleasure? Have you met my fiancée? Miss Butler, this is Mrs Tate."

Minerva glanced back at Inigo in shock, but he appeared to be perfectly calm. Mrs Tate looked between them both, delighted curiosity in her eyes.

"We have met," Mrs Tate agreed, her lips quirking with amusement. "And I was here to issue an invitation. It seems you are to be the toast of London, if the rumours are correct, Inigo, and I am here on behalf of Lord Havisham. He is determined that you should give a lecture for him and his friends, as they could not attend the last one you gave."

Minerva bristled at the informal manner she spoke to Inigo, though she knew well enough that Mrs Tate had addressed him that way before, and that Inigo did not like the woman. The last time Inigo had refused point blank to give a talk for Lord Havisham, whom he'd clearly held in contempt, and so Minerva waited for him to refuse.

"I would happily agree," he said, and Minerva turned once more to stare at him, seeing a fierce glint in his eye as he regarded Mrs Tate. "If I can be assured that no one will hear of Miss Butler's visit here, at least until after we are married."

Mrs Tate pursed her lips, considering and then laughed.

"Oh, very well. Who am I to stand in the way of a love affair? My lips are sealed." She handed Inigo the invitation and turned to wink at Minerva. "Good afternoon, Miss Butler," she said with a knowing smile, before climbing back into her carriage just as Matilda's drew up behind it.

"Inigo," she said, so astonished she hardly knew what to say. "Inigo, I'm not asking for this."

That any choice in the matter had been taken from him made guilt bear down on her. She'd done this, she'd pursued him until this had been the inevitable conclusion, and now he was trapped.

"You don't have to marry me."

"Of course I do," he said, sounding rather impatient. "Don't speak a word of this to anyone. I'll call on Bedwin this evening. Now hurry up and get in the carriage before anyone else sees you."

"But Inigo...." she protested, as he practically bundled her into the carriage.

"Don't worry," he said. "I'll make it all right."

Then he closed the door and told the driver to go.

Minerva stared at him out the window, only vaguely aware of Matilda shifting to sit beside her and take her hand.

"Min, what's wrong? You're white as a sheet. What did he mean, he'll make it right?"

Minerva turned to stare at Matilda, hardly knowing what to say, and burst into tears.

***

25th January 1815. Beverwyck, London.

Inigo's stomach roiled and he thanked providence that Minerva hadn't brought a packed basket with lunch today. If she had, he felt certain he'd have cast up his accounts on the gleaming marble floor of Beverwyck's imposing entrance hall by now. His palms were sweating and clammy, his damn cravat felt like a noose, and there seemed to be ice water dripping down his back. Trust him to find himself captivated by a woman whose nearest relations included a bloody duke.

Captivated.

That was a safe enough word.

It didn't seem to encompass what he felt, but he'd decided he'd rather not dwell on that. He was feeling overwhelmed enough without studying why it was he felt like he was standing on a cliff's edge. What would he do if Bedwin refused his permission?

He didn't have any longer to consider the prospect as the butler reappeared and told him Bedwin would see him now. It was probably just as well, the way his stomach twisted at the prospect of the man's refusal indicated how devastating that news would be. He assumed, going on the fact Bedwin hadn't met him at the door, pistols in hand, that Minerva had said nothing, as he'd requested. At least he'd not been kept waiting long and it appeared that Minerva had not heard him arrive, for he'd not seen her. Hardly unexpected in a place the size of Beverwyck. A meteorite could land at the front of the house and Inigo wouldn't have been the least bit surprised if they'd not notice at the back.

He followed the butler through the house, past every trapping of wealth and privilege and the history of Bedwin's illustrious family. He ignored the paintings of snotty aristocrats who stared down their superior noses at him. It was a reminder of his position that he needed no illustration of. The butler lead him into an impressive library where Bedwin was waiting for him.

"De Beauvoir," the duke said, welcoming him with more warmth than Inigo could have expected.

The room was floor to ceiling with books, all dark wood and comfortable chairs. In normal circumstances Inigo would have found it warm and inviting.

"This is unexpected. Drink?" Bedwin asked, proffering a decanter of what looked like brandy.

Inigo nodded. He needed something to fortify his nerves that was for certain.

Bedwin turned away to pour the drinks. "If you're here to check I meant what I said about sponsoring you, you needn't worry. I'm a man of my word."

"No, it's… it's nothing of that kind. I never doubted your word," Inigo said, accepting the drink from Bedwin's hand and taking a large swallow. "Though, when I've said my piece, I fear you may wish to retract your offer. I should not hold it against you."

Bedwin frowned at him. "I hope this has nothing to do with the disagreement you had with Dr Murphy. I assure you the duchess was beside herself with joy at seeing the old goat put in his place. She's long held him in dislike, but I must confess I'd not seen quite how odious he was until last night."

Inigo grimaced. "No, Murphy is a dim-witted old fraud who has no business practising medicine, in my opinion, but that's neither here nor there."

The duke's eyebrows raised just a little, but he said nothing about this rather forthright observation. He gestured for them both to sit, but Inigo shook his head.

"No, thank you," he said, feeling that he might need to move fast if Bedwin decided to murder him.

Not that Inigo couldn't hold his own. The times when he would allow others to bully him had long since gone. He'd learnt to fight dirty and hard before he'd left the foundling hospital, but that didn't mean he liked to, and he certainly didn't feel he could defend himself if Bedwin wanted his blood. He deserved everything coming to him for taking advantage of Minerva, and he damn well knew it.

"I'll come to the point," he said, seeing the curiosity in the duke's eyes deepen to concern. "I am here to ask your permission to marry Miss Butler."

Bedwin stared at him.

"Minerva?" he said after a moment. "You wish to marry Minerva?"

Inigo nodded. "I do."

Bedwin continued to stare at him. "I was unaware that you were on such intimate terms."

There was an unmistakable edge to his words now which was hardly surprising.

Inigo cleared his throat. "We met last summer. Miss Butler expressed an interest in my work and… and we have been corresponding ever since."

"I see."

From the increasing tension in the room, Inigo suspected that he did see, all too clearly.

"So, this desire to marry Miss Butler stems purely from a formal correspondence. How romantic."

"I... We...." Inigo hesitated but knew there was little point in beating around the bush. "We have been meeting also, when... when possible. I must tell you that I hold Miss Butler in the highest esteem and will do everything in my power to make her happy."

A muscle was ticking in Bedwin's jaw, which Inigo did not take as a positive sign.

"How strange," he mused. "You see, St Clair is a good friend of mine, and from what he said about your previous engagement to his wife, I was given reason to believe that your ideas on love and marriage were not at all what one would choose when considering a match for a romantic young woman like Miss Butler. *Lust with a ring on its finger* was the most positive statement you had to give, was it not?"

Damn. Damn. Damn.

Inigo swallowed. "My opinions on marriage have been brought into question since meeting Miss Butler."

Panic rose in his chest. He knew that this man had the power to destroy his future in every way, if he so chose. The faster the tension between them climbed, the more the anxiety inside him built, destroying any chance he had to make a coherent argument. Putting what he felt for Minerva into words was something he would never achieve. It had been hard enough to admit it to himself, but here, now, with Bedwin staring daggers at him... impossible. He put his empty glass down and took a deep breath.

"She *must* marry me," he said, desperation forcing him to rely on the one argument he hoped might prevail, even if it earned him a beating. He could hardly protest in the circumstances.

"You bloody bastard!"

The duke lunged forward, grasping Inigo by the cravat and propelling him against the wall with such force that the air was knocked from his lungs.

Inigo stood, staring back at him, praying that the man would let him make things right, no matter how he punished him for his actions.

"I will ask you two questions, before I demand that you name your seconds," Bedwin growled, tightening his hold on the cravat until Inigo could hardly breathe. "Is she in love with you?"

Inigo let out a breath of laughter, that at least he could answer honestly. "God knows why, for I don't have the slightest idea, but yes… yes, she loves me."

Bedwin tightened his grip on the fabric about Inigo's neck, and he gasped.

"And you?" the duke demanded. "Do you love her?"

The question made Inigo's heart crash about in his chest with far more force than any concerns that he might face a beating or a duel, and Inigo tried not to panic. He thought about his life before Minerva had exploded into it, bringing all the chaos and colour and happiness that came in her wake. It had been like living in muted tones before she'd arrived, as though he'd viewed the world through a dirty window. Minerva had stripped all the grime from the skewed picture he'd had of what life could be, and having that vibrancy taken from him was a greater terror than saying the words which made his chest tight with anxiety.

"Yes," he said, holding Bedwin's gaze. "And it's intolerable," he added, with perhaps more candour than he ought. "I knew how it would be from the start, and I did everything I could to put her off, I swear it. I knew I'd be lost if I let her in, and I am. I can't be without her. I just… I *can't*. I know I'm not worthy of her." He took a breath, feeling the grip on his neckcloth loosen a fraction. "I know she ought to marry someone better than me. I know she could have won a duke or some grand title for herself, as her mother wants her to, but that's not what *she* wants. She's contrary and foolish, and quite possibly a little bit mad, but she loves me, and I'll spend the rest of my days trying to make certain she never regrets choosing me."

Bedwin let out an unsteady breath and released his grip on Inigo.

"Right answer," he growled. "And if it weren't for the fact I know just how you feel, I'd still make you pay for what you've done."

Inigo stared back at the duke, hardly daring to hope he'd understood correctly. "Then... then you'll let us marry?"

"Let you?" Bedwin repeated and then gave a harsh bark of laughter. "I've little choice if there's a chance you've impregnated her, you stupid bastard. However, if Minerva echoes everything you've told me, no. No, I won't contest the match, though I may find other ways of making you pay," he added darkly.

Inigo nodded, knowing this was inevitable. It was not a surprise, and he'd prepared himself for that. He'd just have to work a deal harder and take jobs that held little interest for him but that paid well.

"I assumed you'd no longer want to sponsor my work."

Bedwin snorted and rolled his eyes, looking dreadfully un-ducal. "And how do you propose to keep a lady like Minerva in the style to which she's become accustomed if I don't?"

Inigo felt the colour rise at the back of his neck, and stood a little taller as indignation burned in him. He knew he'd never be able to afford everything Minerva deserved, but he *had* warned her, and she'd said....

"Oh, don't look so stricken," the duke said, a little gentler now. "You're a brilliant man, Mr de Beauvoir and I should be happy to sponsor you. I find it a fascinating prospect, if you must know, and you must put up with me demanding you explain and show your findings at regular intervals. That, along with attending whatever charitable events I see fit to send you to, and an openness to work in certain projects I have an interest in, will be your penance. I know a man of your talents will find there are many ways of increasing his income. Minerva's dowry is not inconsiderable, either," he added.

Inigo scowled and waved that away. "That's Minerva's, to do with as she sees fit."

Bedwin nodded and smiled at him, which was so beyond anything he'd hoped for that he finally allowed himself to breathe easy. It appeared the worst was over.

"Well, then. I suppose we had better send for Minerva and allow her a say in the matter, before we tie this up to our own satisfaction."

Inigo watched as he rang the bell, the panic rising in his chest once more. He'd not considered that. He'd assumed that once he had arranged things with the duke, that would be that, but no.

"You would allow her to refuse me?" Inigo said, his voice a little unsteady sending a longing glance at the empty glass he'd set down.

Bedwin returned a pitying look and took his empty glass away for a refill. "I would not recommend it, but I would allow it, if she did not feel you could make her happy."

Inigo considered that in mute horror until the duke handed him his drink. Inigo took a large swallow.

Apparently, the worst was far from over.

The butler who'd shown him in appeared again.

"Jenkins, please ask Miss Butler to join us," Bedwin told the man, who bowed and left them.

Inigo's hand searched out and found the little blue box in his pocket and he clutched it in his palm like a talisman. She'd say yes, wouldn't she? She said she loved him. She wanted to be with him, surely that was enough. He cursed himself as he realised it was far from enough. What if she'd seen sense and come to realise what it would mean to marry him? What if she'd realised it was just a lot of romantic nonsense, just as he'd realised it was nothing of the sort? *Oh, God.* He felt sick and hot and uncomfortable and he wanted to see her, longed to see her, astonishingly even more than he wanted to turn and flee in the other direction.

The butler reappeared alone and Bedwin gave him a quizzical glance.

"Well?" he asked.

"It appears Miss Butler is not in her room, your grace, and has not been seen since earlier this afternoon."

Inigo's heart lurched.

"What do you mean?" he demanded, suddenly anxious. "Where is she?"

Jenkins, or whatever his name is didn't so much as blink. "We are doing our best to ascertain that information," he replied, with perfect calm.

It appeared he would say more when there was a knock at the door.

"Come," Bedwin called.

A young woman hurried in and dipped a curtsey. "Begging your pardon, your grace, but we just found this in Miss Butler's room. It's addressed to you."

The girl handed it to the duke, who dismissed her, but Inigo didn't miss the grim expression on his face as he broke the seal and tore it open.

Inigo waited, beside himself with trepidation, for as long as he could bear it.

"Well?" he demanded, wondering how long a heart could go on beating at the current rate his own was managing before it gave out.

Bedwin cursed, running a hand through his hair before thrusting the letter towards Inigo.

"You'd best read it."

The duke's sour tone did not make him feel any better. Inigo was vaguely aware of the duke speaking to the butler and asking the staff to discover when and where Minerva might have gone, but as soon as he saw the familiar curly handwriting his gut clenched with fear and regret, and he could hear nothing but Minerva's voice as he read.

Dear Robert,

Please forgive me for all the trouble I have caused you. I must point out, however, that it is I alone who have caused the trouble. Prue knew nothing of my plans outside of the fact I was infatuated with Mr de Beauvoir, and poor Inigo—Mr de Beauvoir—did his very best to make me behave myself, but it was no good.

I think perhaps I fell in love with him the very first time we met last summer, at least a little bit, and it's been growing worse with every week that passes. I love him quite dreadfully, you see, but I'm afraid I behaved very badly and pursued him despite his best efforts to dissuade me. That being the case, I cannot allow you to hold him responsible for what has happened.

A woman called Mrs Tate saw me leaving his house this afternoon and to protect my reputation Inigo introduced me as his fiancée. I know he plans to call on you intending to offer for me, but I shan't accept. He doesn't love me, or at least if he does it is unwilling. His work is the most important thing to him, which I quite understand, as he is a brilliant man and it would be cruel and unjust to punish him for something which was not his doing. I won't trap him into a marriage we would both come to regret, and I won't see him suffer for my mistakes.

Dearest Robert. I shall come home at once if by some miracle you still wish me to, but only if you swear to me you will not withdraw your offer to sponsor him. I will not risk losing a discovery that might change the world, because of my stupid selfishness. Punish me by all means, but don't punish him and everything that he might achieve with your support. I will forward you my address in a few days, once you have had time to consider the matter.

I am so sorry to be such a trial to you after everything you have done for me and hope you can find it in your heart to forgive me. Please tell Prue not to get upset, and that I am so sorry I've been such a little fool.

Minerva.

"Oh, God," Inigo said, remorse sweeping over him with the icy force of the north sea. "Solo warned me I'd mess this up, and he was right."

"Rothborn?" Bedwin queried. "What has he to do with this?"

Inigo swallowed down the emotion tangled in his throat. "I was going to ask her to marry me before Mrs Tate discovered her at my home," he said. He held out the little blue box he'd been clinging to as proof. "I had the ring, but… but I was too bloody afraid. Solo warned me I had to tell her why I wanted to marry her, but I…. When Mrs Tate left, I just told her I'd make it right, I never said… I never told her I wanted….” His voice shook a little and he clamped his mouth shut.

It was a surprise to feel a reassuring hand settle upon his shoulder.

"She can't have gone far," Bedwin said. "We'll find her, and she's promised to be in touch in a few days so I think we can assume she's safe."

Inigo nodded, not the least bit reassured. "I pray you're right, for if anything happens to her, I'll never forgive myself."

"I do understand just how you feel, you know," Bedwin said with a wry smile. "Prue led me a merry dance before I got her to marry me. A fraught carriage ride through the dark in search of a missing lady is not a new experience."

"Then I can only hope your good fortune rubs off on me," Inigo said, wishing he'd just listened to Solo when he'd had the bloody chance instead of being so damned pigheaded.

"I'll do all in my power to see it does."

Inigo nodded his thanks, too overwhelmed to speak for a moment.

"Would the duchess know where she'd go, do you think?"

The duke shook his head. "My wife has been feeling unwell this afternoon and must be unaware of her cousin's flight, and I intend to keep it that way until she's found. I won't have her fretting herself to death, it's bad for the baby. We can, however, speak to her friends."

"Miss Hunt," Inigo said, remembering. "Miss Hunt picked her up in her carriage this afternoon. She might have gone there."

Bedwin nodded. "Then that's where we'll start. Come along, there's no time to lose."

Chapter 18

My dearest Aashini,

Do you plan to return to London soon? I miss you dreadfully. It seems all my chicks have flown the nest, except for Helena, and we have never been especially close. I believe a duke's daughter has little need for my particular brand of chaperonage, such as it is. Jemima seems to have embraced the life of a spinster with no regrets and no need for company and I can only admire her and wish I was strong enough to follow suit.

If you haven't heard already, I believe that there will be an announcement between Minerva and her Mr de Beauvoir. She caught him at last it seems or will do once he has tracked her down. The poor man was here with Bedwin last night in a fever of anxiety. I don't believe Minerva to be in any trouble so do not worry for her. Whether or not she meant to, she has played her hand superbly and Mr de Beauvoir is so obviously besotted it was painful to see his worry. I will give you the full story if you will come and visit me. See how cruel and wretched I have become in your absence that I must blackmail you into coming to me.

Darling Nate has invited me to stay and I will go when the baby is due if I can be a comfort or help to Alice, but I dare not go too soon. They are so blissfully happy, and I would hate myself if they ever suspected how dreadfully envious I am. How simple it seems for them to have it all.

A home. Love. A family.

Now Jemima has gone I am all alone and the truth is I'm frightened. I'm frightened I might do the sensible thing, and terrified I might not, but more than either of those fears I do so hate being all by myself.

—Excerpt of a letter from Miss Matilda Hunt to Lady Aashini Cavendish.

26th January 1815. Mitcham Priory, Sussex.

Inigo rapped at the front door of the ancient priory. It was an impressive stone building in the shape of a T and surrounded by a moat. The weight of history seemed to cling to the walls, giving a sense of solidity, of having always been. Inigo had always liked the place, which was strange. He preferred things to be new and modern, but there was a comfortable shabbiness to the priory that seemed to welcome visitors, which was odd as its owner was as prickly as the towering, twisted yew tree that dominated the front of the building.

Inigo waited and rapped again, knowing how few staff Solo kept at the vast place, although it needed a veritable army to keep it in order. The man preferred solitude to order and knowing how much he prized order in all things that was saying something.

At length, the housekeeper found her way to the front door and took him inside, showing him into Solo's study with a promise to track down her eccentric master as quickly as she could.

Inigo poured himself a drink, though it was barely midday, and settled himself in to wait with no expectation of seeing the man himself anytime soon. If Solo had taken himself off with a book, he'd have found somewhere he'd not be disturbed, which—

in a labyrinth like Mitcham Priory—could mean he'd not be discovered until he got hungry and deigned to show himself again. Not that it mattered. Inigo could wait to hear *I told you so*.

Once again, he cursed himself for a fool. If only he'd told Minerva his feelings, they could have saved all this nonsense and heartache, and his heart did ache. It was the strangest thing, and for the first time in his life he understood the idea of heartbreak. He'd always believed it a hysterical reaction to something inevitable, because the end of a love affair, whether by choice or circumstance, had to be inevitable, or so he'd believed. That a large, fleshy organ like the heart could break or shatter like glass had been incomprehensible.

It was so strange to discover he had been so wrong. He was used to being the man with the superior mind, to being able to understand with ease concepts that the average person couldn't fathom. Yet, all along, they'd been looking at him with a mixture of amusement and pity for not understanding that which they had known to be true. Even Harriet, whose intellect he admired, could not convince him that love existed. Yet how could he have known when he'd never seen it? It wasn't something that was quantifiable, he couldn't measure it or weigh it or test it over a naked flame and, when people spoke of it, he recognised nothing of what they told him. It just sounded like desire, the kind created by nature to ensure the continuation of the species.

There had been no love in evidence in the foundling hospital, a certain amount of care perhaps from *some* of the adults, and friendships between the boys, but love? He'd never seen that. He'd not found it as an apprentice, nor in the hard slog to educate himself, working all hours to earn money for books, for equipment, for something that was his own. There had been only himself and his own determination to succeed. It had never occurred to him how lonely he'd been until Minerva had crashed into his life, chipping away at the wall he'd built to hide behind.

Well, now that wall had been torn down leaving his heart exposed and vulnerable, and all too ready to shatter at the slightest impact. The duke had been as good as his word, and they'd visited all of Minerva's circle of Peculiar Ladies, all that were in town at least, but no one knew where she was. There were suggestions she might have gone to visit Mrs Kitty Baxter in Ireland, or perhaps to Scotland to Ruth Anderson, but Inigo knew if he went haring off in one direction he'd inevitably discover she'd gone in the other, and so he could do nothing but wait and pray she would give Bedwin her address as promised.

As soon as he discovered her address, he would take himself to her and throw himself upon her mercy. She had said she was dreadfully in love with him in that letter, and he could only pray that it was enough for her to overlook his stupidity. That she had been willing to sacrifice herself, her reputation, and her future for him had made all the emotions he'd refused to experience in the past rise inside him in a tangle so vast he felt he was drowning in them. No one had ever cared a jot for him before, and now this. It was humbling and extraordinary and he didn't feel equal to it, but he was damn well going to try. He'd come from nothing and nowhere with no one to help him. Now he'd put the same effort into making sure that Minerva was happy and loved, and had everything he could give her.

***

It was growing dark when Solo finally turned up. Inigo had been standing by the window when he saw him emerge from a narrow path that appeared to disappear behind a hedge. To his surprise, Solo seemed to be in a good mood, a slight smile at his lips so out of character that Inigo could not help but wonder what had put it there. The light was fading from the skies and dark clouds were rolling in, promising a heavy downpour and perhaps an accompanying storm.

He turned away and walked to the fire, staring down into the flames as he waited for his friend to appear.

"Thought I might find you here, you stupid arse," Solo said, sounding unreasonably cheerful when he finally strode into the room.

Inigo frowned. "Why on earth would you expect me?"

"Because you messed things up, like I knew you would."

Inigo glowered and huffed but he could hardly deny it. "If that's the extent of your help—"

Solo waved an irritable hand to silence him. "Oh, it's not, believe me. We will sort this out properly, and you'll owe me a very large favour."

"Anything," Inigo said at once and then stopped. "Wait, how do you know I messed things up? It only happened yesterday and…" He stared at Solo and then let out a breath. "You've seen her."

Solo nodded. "I have."

Inigo crossed the room wanting to shake the bloody man into telling him everything. "Where is she? Is she all right? Is she angry with me? Will she see me?"

There was an exasperated tut and Solo rolled his eyes. "Calm down, man. She's perfectly well, and yes, I have no doubt she'll see you, and yes, I will send you to her presently."

"Now!" Inigo demanded, heading for the door. "Let's go. I have to see her at once."

"Not so fast."

Inigo turned, incensed by the delay. "Solo, please, for the love of God, I'm dying here. Take me to her."

Solo's expression softened a little. "I thought you didn't believe in love?"

"Don't," Inigo said, shaking his head.

They both knew he'd been a fool and he'd endure all the mockery Solo wanted to give out, but not now, not tonight when everything seemed to hang in the balance. He was too raw, too brittle to take it without shattering.

"Very well. I can see you have reconsidered." Solo's wry smile was gently teasing rather than mocking but Inigo still looked away. "Before I tell you where to find her, I must have your word as a gentleman that you will tell no one I led you to her."

"I'm not a gentleman," Inigo replied, perplexed, before realising he'd taken it rather too literally, as always, when Solo let out an impatient breath. "But you have my word as your friend that anything you tell me will remain in confidence if you wish it."

"I do," Solo replied, giving Inigo a hard look. "The lady I spoke to you about, the one with whom I have a… a private arrangement."

"Yes?"

"It appears she is one of the… *Strange* Ladies?" he said, frowning.

"Peculiar," Inigo corrected. "They're the Peculiar Ladies."

Solo snorted and shook his head. "Yes, those. Anyway, in short your Miss Butler is a friend of the young lady I have an understanding with. Miss Butler appeared on her doorstep yesterday evening. Your beloved is now conscious of my involvement, but has been sworn to secrecy, and I expect you to do the same. None of the other ladies are aware of our arrangement and my… *friend*… wishes for it to remain that way. You will respect her wishes or I'll not give you her address."

"Confound you, of course I'll respect her wishes!" Inigo exclaimed, having been pushed beyond the limits of his patience. "I'll never speak her name again and deny all knowledge of her under pain of death if you wish, but for the love of God tell me where Minerva is!"

Solo gave a little huff of laughter, but his eyes were warm when he next spoke. "It will be easier if I draw you a map. You must take a lantern and, for heaven's sake, don't go pounding the door down. They won't be expecting you, as I couldn't be certain you'd come here and didn't prepare them for the possibility."

Inigo nodded, too eager to see Minerva to dispute anything. As Solo sat down at his desk and drew a simple map, a rumble of thunder murmured overhead.

"I'm afraid the weather is closing in," Solo said, looking at the dark shapes of trees thrashing back and forth in the dimming light outside the window. "Perhaps it might be best to wait until morning rather than—"

"Give me the bloody map!" Inigo exploded, wondering how much more he had to tolerate before he could see Minerva.

Solo sighed and went back to work.

***

Inigo cursed, as many filthy, foul words as he could unearth, which was a considerable number as it turned out. Being born in the gutter had an effect on one's vocabulary. They were satisfying now as he squinted down at the increasingly soggy scrap of paper on which Solo had drawn his map. His lady friend was a Miss Jemima Fernside, and he had bought and renovated a dilapidated cottage for her. There were other properties on the priory estate, but this one had certain advantages. Although it was not within the priory's borders, but on the outskirts of the nearest village, it could be easily reached with discretion via a path through the priory's gardens and a hidden entrance in the back garden. Miss Fernside could therefore, with care and some luck, keep her reputation intact, and no one would be any the wiser about her gentleman caller. That was fine in daylight. In the dark with the devil of a storm raging and rain lashing down so hard Inigo had been drowned in seconds, it was a little more challenging.

Lifting the lantern, Inigo saw at last the large oak tree he'd been looking for and knew he was close. Hefting the sack he carried back onto his shoulder, he wondered if he'd entirely lost his mind. Solo certainly appeared to think so when Inigo had explained what he wanted. Not that he cared. All that he cared about was making Minerva agree to marry him and, if he had to make an arse of himself to do that, he was more than willing. So, he put his head down and pressed on through the howling wind and the rain, until the little glow of lamplight ahead of him confirmed he had reached the entrance to the cottage garden.

Trying his best not to shiver, though he was bloody freezing, he made it to the front of the house. Mindful of what Solo had warned him, he knocked gently, though he wanted to break the bloody door down. Acting like a caveman would likely not help his cause, though, so he stood up straight and tried his best to look civilised and non-threatening. Going on the gasp of alarm given by the young woman who opened the door, he'd failed miserably.

"Is Miss Butler here?" he asked, aware that he'd come out without his hat and the downpour had plastered his hair to his head. The rain dripped onto his shoulders in rivulets. "Please," he added as the woman's eyes grew wide and round. "I am Inigo de Beauvoir. I must see her."

"Inigo?"

There was a muffled exclamation from behind Miss Fernside, and suddenly there she was. Something tight and uncomfortable that had been growing steadily since that appalling interview with Bedwin unknotted just a little at the sight of her.

"Inigo!" the word was a squeak of surprise. "Where did you come from? How did you know…? My word, you're soaked to the bone! Come in before you catch pneumonia."

Inigo shook his head and swung the sack down the floor in front of him.

"Good heavens," Minerva said, staring at the black sack, and at the fact he was no doubt covered in soot.

To his relief, Miss Fernside melted away to give them some privacy.

"I'm sorry," Inigo said. "I'm so sorry for the mess I made of this entire situation, but I've never believed in romance and so the need to be romantic has never been something I've had the opportunity to practise."

"Romantic?" Minerva said doubtfully, blinking and clutching her shawl a little tighter about her shoulders.

"Yes," he said with an emphatic nod. "Romantic. You deserve that after… Oh, God, Minerva I wish I'd just told you the truth but every time I tried…."

He paused as she reached out and put a hand on his shoulder. Despite standing under the awning of the front door, he was still dripping from head to toe, as though her very own rain cloud had come down to visit. Gloomily, he reflected it was an apt description.

"Inigo," she said, her tone gentle. "I've explained everything to Bedwin. There's no need to marry me… truly."

"Yes, there is!" he shouted, making her jump, but he couldn't hold back now. "There's a desperate need. It's life or death, do you hear me?"

He grasped hold of her arms, praying she could see the anguish in his eyes.

"W-Whatever do you mean?" she asked, paling in the flickering lamp light.

"I mean that I'll die if you don't marry me," he said, knowing this was the moment to bare his soul. It was awful and terrifying, but losing her was far, far worse. "I'm in love with you, Minerva. I didn't realise at first because… because I didn't recognise it. I thought it was obsession, the kind of obsession that grips me when I work, and I can't stop until I have an answer."

"But you love your work, Inigo," she said, her voice soft and her smile so full of tenderness that his heart clenched.

"Yes," he admitted. "But I love you more, so much more. It's terrifying how much more. I love you than anything else in my life. My God, Minerva, there isn't anything else but you. I'll never be able to work again if you don't put me out of my misery and agree to marry me."

He stared at her, watching her throat work as she swallowed. Her eyes seemed very bright, her cheeks flushed, and Inigo thought he'd seen nothing so lovely in all his life.

"What's in the sack?" she asked.

Inigo frowned. "It's… It's a romantic gesture."

Minerva stared down at it and bit her lip. "It's a sack of coal, isn't it?"

He nodded. "I can't afford diamonds yet," he said, rubbing the back of his neck and feeling more idiotic than he could credit, but he ploughed on all the same. "But I'll do my best for you, Minerva. I'll give you everything I have, everything I can, and perhaps there will be times when it will be no more than a coal fire to keep you warm when it's cold, but the moment I can buy you diamonds, I swear I will."

"Oh, Inigo."

He staggered as she launched herself into his arms and kissed him. Her lips were so warm against his chilled skin, her body soft and supple against his frozen frame, and he clung to her, kissing her with everything he had, holding nothing back.

"I love you," he said again, once he could bear to lift his lips from hers. "In case I didn't make that clear. I love you so much, with all my heart."

"I know," she said, with a little hiccoughing laugh as she wiped a stray tear from her cheek. "Do you know, Helena warned me you might give me a sack of coal? She was right, but it's better than diamonds, Inigo, truly, because it's your first romantic gesture, and it was for me. I love it. I love you."

"I'll practise," he promised her solemnly. "But you might have to teach me what *is* romantic, because I think it might be a while before I get the hang of it."

"I think you have a fine idea already, my love," Minerva said, her voice quavering.

Inigo wasn't certain if she was laughing or crying, but she looked happy, so he let it go.

"Then you *will* marry me? Because you haven't answered the question yet," he said, unable to stop worrying until he had an unequivocal response.

"Of course I will!" she said, shaking her head at him. "But, for heaven's sake, come inside before you freeze to death!"

Inigo ducked under the lintel and into the cottage. Minerva led him to a small parlour, where a fire was blazing in the grate. It was cosy and cheerful, and the young woman who had opened the door to him was sitting beside the fire. She looked up and smiled, her expression warm.

"Mr de Beauvoir, I'm so pleased you came."

"I'm afraid you might be less pleased when I've dripped a puddle onto your carpet," Inigo said ruefully.

"It's of no matter," Miss Fernside replied, shaking her head. "Is everything well, Minerva?"

"Everything is perfectly wonderful," Minerva replied. "Oh, Jem, we're getting married!"

The young woman leapt from her chair with a little cry of delight and embraced Minerva.

"Oh! Oh, how wonderful," she said, snatching a handkerchief from her sleeve and dabbing her eyes with it. "I'm so... so happy for you both."

Inigo smiled, rather touched by the sincerity of the woman's pleasure in the news. He'd not expected to be greeted with such enthusiasm, bearing in mind that Minerva would lower herself in society by marrying him.

"I only hope my mother doesn't make a fuss," Minerva said, taking his hand. "I'm not one and twenty until July, and we'll need her permission."

"Bedwin has promised to speak to her," Inigo said, praying the duke had as much influence as he seemed to believe.

"Bedwin?" Minerva echoed. "So... he approves?"

Inigo could not blame her for the doubt in her eyes.

"Approves might be stretching it a little," he admitted. "But he will support us."

"Oh, but Inigo—"

"And," he interrupted, holding up a hand to stop her, "he won't change his mind about sponsoring me, though he seems to have some diabolical form of punishment in mind for having...."

He felt his cheeks scald as he remembered they were not alone.

"For having compromised me?" Minerva finished for him, grinning at his obvious discomfort.

"Hmph," Inigo replied with a nod, relieved that Miss Fernside had busied herself with tending the fire, endeavouring to give them privacy.

"Well, that's wonderful news. I'm so relieved, but I still don't understand how you knew I was here," Minerva said, staring at him in wonder.

"I didn't," he admitted and let out a breath. "It's a long story but, in short, I had always planned to ask you to marry me, Minerva, even before Mrs Tate arrived."

He brought out the little box with the wedding ring inside and showed it to her.

"Oh!" Minerva said, pressing her hands against her heart. "Oh," she said again, and then sniffed and wiped her eyes, which Inigo took to be a good sign.

It appeared she cried when she was happy, which was something he would have to get used to.

"Solo—Lord Rothborn—is a friend. He knew how I felt for you, and he warned me to make my feelings clear before I asked, but… but then that woman turned up and…." Inigo sighed. "I made a mess of things and, when I couldn't find you, I came down here to seek his advice while I waited for you to send your address to Bedwin. You cannot imagine my joy when he told me you were here."

"Oh," Minerva said, looking a little shy. "I think I can. I think perhaps it was how I felt seeing you on the doorstep."

Inigo stared at her, wishing they were alone so he could take her in his arms.

"Well." Miss Fernside said briskly, as she got back to her feet and replaced the bronze poker in its stand. "This is all wonderful news, but you must leave now, Mr de Beauvoir. My reputation hangs by a tenuous enough thread, without having strange men visiting my house at all hours of the night."

Minerva sighed with regret but nodded her agreement.

"She's right, though I wish it were otherwise. You really must go, but I hate to send you out in the rain again." She clutched at his damp sleeve, looking up at him with beseeching eyes. "Promise me you'll have a hot bath and make yourself warm again. Perhaps the housekeeper could make you a hot toddy or something to keep out the chill? I should be wretched if you fell ill on my account."

Inigo felt a surge of pleasure as it occurred to him there was someone in the world who cared about him, who would worry for him and want to look after him if he was sick. Minerva would be there for him, no matter what, and that was a strange and wonderful realisation after a lifetime of being alone.

"Promise me, Inigo," she said sternly.

Inigo hadn't answered her but was just standing staring at her like a fool.

"I promise," he said, feeling the smile curve over his mouth as happiness spread through him.

Chapter 19

My Lord Marquess,

Our fears are confirmed. In one mill alone, six dead in the past four years and over sixty mutilated in that same period. The overseers are brutal, and accidents stem from uncovered belts, shafts and flywheels. The atmosphere is acrid, a mixture of machine oil and thick dust that is forever irritating the throat, nose and eyes. Adults endure a sorry enough plight, but the children in this place are the most pitiful I have ever seen. Pale, nervous and slow, their misery is written upon their faces. The worst of all are the mule scavengers. These wretched little creatures are sent to recoup the cotton wastage gathered on the floor underneath the working spinning mule. The youngest child I have seen was four years of age, indeed none was older than eight as they would be too large to fit in the confined space. They are working for up to 16 hours a day and are beaten if they fall asleep.

My lord, if there is hell on earth then I believe we have found it. Something must be done.

—Excerpt of a letter from Mr Richard Glover to The Most Honourable Lucian Barrington, Marquess of Montagu.

29th January 1815. Beverwyck, London.

They were married three days later, by special licence, at Beverwyck.

Minerva experienced the entire service in a daze and suspected Inigo felt the same. He looked overwhelmed, any misgivings she might have had about him regretting their marriage overturned whenever he looked at her. There was such love in his eyes, such warmth, that she felt the glow of it burning inside her.

There had been no time to get a dress made for the occasion, and so she had chosen the yellow gown that Inigo had liked so much. It was her own favourite, too, and matched the joyous sense of hope that carried her through the day as though in a dream.

Robert had given her away and both she and Inigo had been astonished at how warmly he had welcomed Inigo and stood by them. Standing before the curate now, Minerva bit back a smile as Inigo stuttered through his part. The curate had spoken sharply to him twice already, as Inigo seemed to drift off whenever he looked at her, losing track of what was happening, and the frustrated clergyman was forced to repeat himself. They made it to the end of the ceremony at last, the curate looking almost as relieved as Inigo, and Minerva could not hold back her laughter. It was not at all proper to laugh at such a serious moment, she supposed, but when Inigo beamed at her she didn't give a fig what anyone else thought. He knew she was laughing with wonder and happiness, and he knew because he felt the same way.

Her laughter died as he leaned in and kissed her, a chaste kiss with so many looking on, but the promise in his eyes made colour leap to her cheeks and her blush was as maidenly as anyone could hope for, despite the fact she was far from innocent.

Except those who were too far away to make the service at such short notice, many of the Peculiar Ladies came to celebrate the event.

"I'm so delighted everything worked out for you, Minerva," Matilda said, giving her a hug, her eyes wet with tears.

Minerva had seen her weeping during the ceremony and felt a pang of anguish for her friend. She'd seen her talking in hushed tones with Aashini, and was glad she and the viscount had returned to London. The two women had always been close.

"It will for you too, Matilda. It must," Minerva said. "There's no one that deserves a happy ever after like you do. I cannot believe there isn't one waiting for you."

Matilda laughed. "Well, it's very well hidden is all I can say, but never mind that. This is your day and I couldn't be happier. I'd say I hope your husband knows how lucky he is, but I think everyone here can see that he does."

Minerva could only agree as she greeted all her friends, brimming with joy. Whenever she turned and caught Inigo's eyes, the tender expression he cast her way made her long for the day to be over. Lord Rothborn had stood as Inigo's best man, and Minerva watched as he and Jemima carefully avoided each other. She'd been shocked to discover Jemima's arrangement with him, but he was wealthy and handsome and seemed a decent enough sort, if brusque, and she knew she was in no position to judge. Though she worried for her friend's reputation and happiness, she had no right to voice her concerns after everything she'd done to be with Inigo. Besides, Jemima wasn't a fool, she knew the risks she was taking and—bearing in mind her options—there was little choice for her. Minerva could only hope that Lord Rothborn would see her as more than his mistress once he got to know her better.

"Well, you got him, you wicked creature," Bonnie said, drawing her attention away from Jemima.

Minerva laughed, and turned to her friend to find her eyes sparkling with mischief.

"And there I was thinking you were such a ladylike little creature."

Minerva snorted. "Being a lady is overrated."

"Well, you'll get no argument here," Bonnie said with a wink. "But then I never was one to begin with. How is your mama taking the news?"

Minerva pulled a face. Her mother was the only fly in the ointment, though after the initial hysteria had passed and the doctor had sedated her, she'd taken it quite well.

"She'll live. So long as Bedwin softens the blow by allowing everyone to believe they are thick as thieves, her pride will recover, I'm sure."

Bedwin had been an absolute lamb, in fact, and Minerva knew she could never repay him for all he'd done to smooth their path. Mr and Mrs de Beauvoir would never be welcome among the highest sticklers of society, but she found that was no loss. Bedwin's public support of both their marriage and her husband's career would have a huge influence on how others treated them, and for that they owed him a debt.

The wedding breakfast was lavish enough to satisfy even Minerva's woeful mama but, as Minerva stole a glance at her husband, she could tell he was keen for all the fuss to be over.

"We'll be able to leave soon," she whispered to him, smiling at he turned to her with a frown.

"I don't want to spoil your day," he said, shaking his head. "We can stay as long as you want to."

Minerva let out a happy sigh.

"What a lovely man you are," she said, pleased with the tinge of colour that pinked his cheeks. "But I'd like to go home, with you."

"Home," he said, such wonder in his eyes that her throat grew tight. "Yes." He nodded, reaching for her hand and holding it tight. "Yes, I want to go home."

It was another hour and a half before they made their escape. Everyone wanted a moment with the happy couple, and there were so many toasts and well wishes it would have been churlish to cut them short. Bedwin's carriage carried them back to Isleworth and the handsome red brick house on Church Street.

Inigo put his hat to one side on the plush velvet seat and ran a hand through his hair as tiny bits of rice cascaded to the floor.

"Why did they throw rice at us?" he asked, perplexed.

Minerva laughed and picked some stray pieces from his shoulders. "It's supposed to represent rain, which is a sign of prosperity, fertility, and good fortune."

"But it *was* raining," he said, still struggling with the concept.

"It's tradition, love."

"Oh," he said, nodding, which was apparently explanation enough. He stared at her and reached out his hand, stroking his fingers down her cheek with such adoration that Minerva thought her heart might burst from happiness.

"Mrs de Beauvoir," he murmured.

"It's a lovely name."

"French," he said, a touch of sadness in his voice. "My parents were French. It's the only thing I know about them."

"I'm sure they loved you very much, Inigo. They couldn't fail to. I know I do."

"I've never felt this way before," he said with a little huff of laughter. "I…. It's a little overwhelming."

Minerva leaned in and kissed him, drawing back to study his face. "How do you feel?"

"Happy," he said simply. "Ridiculously happy."

"Me too," she said, and snuggled against him until the carriage drew up outside his house.

"Welcome home, Mrs de Beauvoir," Inigo said, sounding so pleased with himself she could only laugh with delight as he handed her down and then swung her up into his arms and carried her inside.

He kissed her, setting her down with care but holding her to him for a long moment. When he finally broke the kiss, Minerva was breathless and dazed, and it took her a moment to realise his home seemed different.

"It's so warm," she said in surprise.

He nodded. "I wanted the place to be nice for you. I know you'll want to decorate and furnish it yourself but, in the meantime, your cousin Prue and your friends… well, they helped me arrange a housekeeper and staff. They've cleaned the place through and lit the fires, and bought new linen for the bed…."

"Oh," Minerva said, a little anxious. "The housekeeper—"

"Is not here now," Inigo said firmly. "She'll be back in two days, but the pantry is stocked for an army and we won't be leaving the bedroom before then, fear not."

"How perfect," she said with a sigh as Inigo chuckled.

"If I remember correctly, it's you that is perfect, but I feel the need to check, just to be certain."

He took her hand, tugging her up the staircase.

"And if I'm not perfect?" Minerva asked, hurrying behind him.

"Impossible," he said, drawing her across the landing and into his room.

"How lovely!" Minerva stared around to discover her friends had put beautiful new covers on the bed in a glorious sunny yellow. A fire was blazing merrily in the hearth, and candles were lit, chasing away the gloom of a January afternoon. "It's my favourite colour," she said, moving to the bed to touch the soft counterpane.

To Experiment with Desire

"Mine too," Inigo admitted. "Ever since I saw you in that yellow gown the night I came to dinner. I'd seen nothing so beautiful in my life."

Minerva laughed and ran to him, flinging her arms about his neck. "Nor I, when you put the odious Dr Murphy in his place. I was ready to burst with pride."

Inigo drew her closer against him, his arms holding on tight.

"Are you real?" he asked softly. "Are you certain I didn't dream you up?"

Minerva tugged at the ribbons on her bonnet and cast it aside onto the chest of drawers before moving out of his embrace. She stepped back, very aware of Inigo's eyes on her as her hands fell to the buttons on her pelisse. This followed much the same fate as the hat, as did her gloves.

"I think you ought to check, just to make certain," she said, turning to present the fastenings up the back of her gown to him and giving him a coquettish smile from over her shoulder.

"What a sensible idea. I think perhaps a series of experiments, to determine whether you really exist, and if I am therefore the luckiest fellow alive, or simply delusional." Inigo slid his arms around her waist and pulled her against him. "I really am, you know, the luckiest fellow alive, I mean."

"I'm so glad you think so," she said, "because I'm afraid you're stuck with me."

There was a low chuckle before he turned his attention to the fiddly buttons. It took some time, and a little cursing, but soon the yellow dress fell with a swish of satin and Minerva stepped out of it. Turning, she faced Inigo and held his gaze as she slid her petticoats down and undid the laces of her corset. Finally, she pulled the chemise over her head.

"Shall I leave the stockings on, Inigo? I remember you liked them."

Inigo swallowed, his gaze falling to the matching yellow ribbons holding the stockings in place.

"Yes," he said, his voice husky. "I do like them."

Minerva moved towards him, pressing herself against him and shivering as his cold watch chain and buttons met her warm skin.

"I was right," Inigo said in a whisper. "You are perfect."

"Ah, but am I real?" Minerva replied, smiling at him and glorying at the wonder in his eyes.

The way he looked at her made her feel beautiful and powerful, and as if she was the only woman in the world. For the life of her, she could not understand how anyone could choose a fortune or a fancy title over a man who looked at you in such a way. How lucky she was that Prue had helped her see sense, and how very much she might have missed.

She gasped as Inigo arms went around her, crushing her to him while he kissed her, his mouth at once tender and demanding. He let her go a moment later, breathing a deal faster than he had been.

"You appear to be real, but I think it requires further investigation," he said, with every appearance of gravity.

"Oh?" Minerva said, excitement coiling in her belly. "What kind of investigation?"

"Hmmm," Inigo said, moving around her, his heated gaze a brand against her skin as he circled her, prowling like something wild that might pounce at any moment.

She couldn't wait.

His fingers slid over her moved, around her waist, over her back and shoulder, down over her breast, detouring to circle one peaked nipple and then down, down her belly to the soft curls between her thighs.

"I think I must taste you next," he murmured, the words sending mad shivers racing over her and a liquid heat blooming inside.

Before she could even consider mustering a coherent answer, he had lifted her up and moved her to the bed, sitting her down on the edge.

Inigo knelt before her, spreading her thighs and leaning in to press a soft kiss to her stomach. "This is my favourite place to be," he said, a wicked look glinting at her from those striking grey-green eyes that had captured her attention all those months ago.

"Mine too," she said, feeling a wanton and terribly bold to admit to such a thing, but his expression betrayed his pleasure at her words. She watched as he ducked his head to trail his tongue over her inner thigh and sighed, lying back on the mattress and abandoning herself to the moment, knowing that he loved her, and that her pleasure was also his.

The first sweep of his tongue had her gasping and arching off the bed, so much that he slid his hands up her thighs, pushing them further apart before holding her hips down so she could not wriggle. From then on it was a hazy blur of intense pleasure, the soft, supple length of his tongue, the slight graze of his shaven chin against her most private flesh, and then the intimate caress of his fingers as he slid them deep inside her. It was a slow, intimate siege against her sanity, dismantling it by increments as the tension inside her built and built, until she was shaking and helpless and crying out, begging him for release.

Her breathing was ragged as she chased the gathering sensation that promised her peak was close, but Inigo's touch remained just elusive enough to deny her. She squirmed and bucked, trying to force his mouth closer, to give her the delicious push that would send her over the edge, but he only laughed softly, his fluttering breath a torment against her overheated skin.

"Please," she begged him, reaching down to grasp at his hair, beside herself as the sensations become too much. "Please, Inigo, please, please…."

At last he took pity, settling upon the tender bud of her sex and licking gently but with increasing speed until she shuddered beneath his touch, her vision whiting out while she rode on an exultant wave of pleasure that seemed to rush on and on until she was a pliant tangle of limbs, utterly spent, dazed and content.

As the world drifted back into focus, she became distantly aware of herself, and then of a rustle of fabric. Minerva lifted her drowsy eyelids just enough to see Inigo tossing his clothes in an abandoned heap on the floor. A low chuckle escaped her, which sounded wanton and knowing, and not at all as she expected as he climbed onto the bed, an unmistakable look in his eyes.

"Too late," she murmured sleepily, feeling like a lazy cat. "You've ruined me. I'm good for nothing now."

He snorted, shaking his head. "I married you, so you can't be ruined, and we'll see about that."

She squealed as he grabbed her and rolled her on top of him. His arousal was hot and hard between her legs, pressing against the tender flesh and she gasped with surprise as a jolt of pure sensation fired through her.

"Oh," she said, moving her hips to do it again.

Inigo closed his eyes and groaned, and suddenly she wasn't quite so sleepy as she'd thought. Her skin was wet and slick and moved easily against his silky length and Minerva sat up, bracing herself against his chest, watching him watch her, revelling in the hunger she could see in his heavy-lidded eyes. His breath caught, his hands going to her hips, guiding her movements as he rocked up towards her, intensifying the sensation. To her surprise, pleasure coiled inside her once more, quicker this time as she watched Inigo come apart beneath her.

"Minerva," he rasped, as though he was fighting for words, fighting to speak past the force of desire. "Inside you… please… need it…."

It wasn't exactly a coherent sentence, but it wasn't difficult to comprehend, either, especially when he turned her onto her back, settling between her thighs.

"Yes," she said, almost breathless as he looked to her for approval.

That little remaining breath was stolen as he thrust inside her, deep and powerful and sending her nerve endings into glittering little eddies of delight, making her shiver and sigh and cling to him as he moved inside her. Minerva closed her eyes and gloried in it, in his broad shoulders, the heat of his skin burning against, hers and the sense of completeness, of rightness, at being where she belonged, with whom she belonged.

She sighed, a long, indulgent breath of wonder while the shimmering edge of her peak came closer, chasing the rest of the world far away until there was nothing outside of the two of them and the joy they brought one another. Inigo made a harsh sound, crying out as he held her close, before burying his face against her hair. His body shook, jerking helplessly with the power of his release. The sight of his face, taut with concentration, his large frame helpless as the pleasure took control of him was enough to send Minerva over the edge in his wake, holding on tight to the only man she had ever wanted, or would ever want.

Chapter 20

Dear Minerva,

I am so very happy for you. The wedding was lovely, and I cried buckets. Your husband looked utterly dazed at his own good fortune, as well he might. I have every expectation of seeing you both settle into a wonderfully happy marriage. Do write to me soon and tell me of your plans. What is your new home like, and how is it to live with such a clever fellow?

I must thank you also for your discretion. I confess it was like being sat upon thorns to be in the same room as Lord Rothborn. I felt certain everyone should see me blush and know everything whenever I felt his gaze turn my way. He is a strange man, capable of being so very kind and yet so distant too, but I am determined to know him better. Though he does his best to thwart my efforts, I am not to be dissuaded, as he will learn to his cost.

—Excerpt of a letter from Miss Jemima Fernside to Mrs Minerva de Beauvoir.

4th February 1815. Beverwyck, London.

Matilda set her book aside and sighed. It was a dull day, the rain coming down in sheets with no end in sight. It was unlikely she would receive any callers today to alleviate the tedium and keep her mind busy. Determined not to allow herself to fall into a fit of the dismals, she took herself off to her writing desk. She'd received a letter from Aashini that morning, confirming that she would come and stay with Matilda for the weekend, and that was certainly something to look forward to. It had been so lovely to catch up with her friend at the wedding, more so to see how very happy she was. In the meantime she would content herself with writing her a reply before perusing the January edition of La Belle Assembly. Perhaps a new outfit would cheer her up, and there were always lovely illustrations of the latest styles to sigh over. That would surely keep her busy.

She'd just settled herself before a clean sheet of paper when there was a knock at the door and her butler, Baines, appeared.

"The Marquess of Montagu for you, Miss Hunt."

Matilda jolted, surging to her feet so quickly she nearly overturned the chair.

"M-Montagu?" she stammered, her voice faint, one hand going to her throat, where her heart seemed to have lodged and begun beating at a ridiculous pace. She'd never dreamed he'd call upon her at her home and to see him here, in her own parlour, was so extraordinary she was immediately sent into a flurry of nerves.

There was no mistake, though, as he strode into the room, immaculate and coldly beautiful as always. She curtseyed as he entered, at least having enough presence of mind to attend to the formalities. He glanced around to see she was alone and frowned.

"Do you not have a maid who can sit with you, for propriety's sake?"

Matilda gave a startled laugh. "It's her day off, and that you should ask me that...."

He turned back, hailing the butler who had just left the room. "Stand outside the door. I will only be here a moment."

Matilda heard Baines' murmur of agreement and Montagu walked in, leaving the door ajar.

"I will not keep you, Miss Hunt, only there is something… I have news which I must share with you that I fear you will find distressing, and so I wished to tell you in person before you read of it tomorrow morning."

"News? What news?" Matilda said, perplexed and alarmed by his presence.

She put a hand out to find the chair back, as her legs felt somewhat unsteady, but really, what news could Montagu have to share with her that she would find distressing?

"Miss Hunt, I…."

He hesitated, and for the first time Matilda felt he was uncertain of himself. This was so altogether out of character that she could not help but stare.

"Miss Hunt," he began again, and then took a deep breath. "I know what you think of me. You have never been shy in giving your opinion, and I cannot pretend that anything you have said was unfair. I have not hidden my desires from you, and nothing has changed in that regard. However, I pray that you will hear me now. No matter if you believe me false, I swear to you I did *not* do this to further my own ends. I once told you that I do not lie, and I will not do so now. I would not blame you for believing ill of me but, in acting as I have, I had only your best interests at heart."

Matilda gazed at him, unblinking and utterly lost. "Forgive me, my lord, but… but I believe I have misunderstood, or perhaps I am just being hen witted today, but I have not the slightest idea of what you are talking about."

Montagu nodded and lifted his hand, which she now saw carried a folded news sheet.

"An early edition of tomorrow's story," he said, giving it to her.

She took it, staring blindly at the headline *Hell on Earth*. She glanced at the text, gathering it spoke of the terrible conditions in a textile mill in Derbyshire. Something stirred in her mind, but the marquess' presence befuddled her too greatly to think clearly. She looked up at him, none the wiser, relieved when he spoke again.

"I admit that it was because of you I sought to investigate your Mr Burton. I had heard rumours disturbing enough to make me worry about the kind of man he was. I know it was in my best interests to discover a good reason why you ought not marry him, but I swear I did not… I did not realise…." He paused and his jaw grew tight. "I could not allow you to marry the man without knowing the truth of who he is. I am far from a saint and I know it, but this… this is wickedness," he said, gesturing to the paper she held in a trembling hand. "I pray you can forgive me for my part in exposing this, and believe that I did it to protect you and those who have suffered in such vile conditions."

Matilda stared at him and then back at the headline, scanning the text, which spoke of horrific working conditions, of deaths and injuries, and the maltreatment of children.

"Oh, my God," she said, sitting down heavily in the chair, staring at the page as the text blurred before her eyes.

It slipped from her nerveless fingers to the floor without so much as a rustle of paper.

"Matilda."

She looked up, stunned to find the marquess crouched down before her, his hands reaching for hers and holding them tight. It was remarkable to see those cold silver grey eyes fill with concern, with compassion. She'd not thought such a thing possible.

"Is there anything I can do? A glass of water? Let me send for one of your friends to come to you."

Matilda stared at him, too horrified and shaken to take it in, hardly even registering he'd used her given name, that he was still holding her hands.

"No," she said, her voice faint. She felt unsteady, sick and ill, and she wanted him to go for she was sorely tempted to throw her arms about his neck and sob at the awfulness of it. She withdrew her hands from his with difficulty, folding her arms across her stomach lest the desire to abandon herself to his care overcame her. "No. I'm perfectly fine. Thank… thank you for…."

Montagu picked up the abandoned news sheet, setting it on the writing desk beside the blank sheet of paper she'd put out.

"Thank you for exposing… for those poor, poor…."

Her voice cracked and she shook her head, pressing a hand to her mouth and taking a deep breath. The effort to steady herself was enormous, but she had to take herself in hand. It was not her who had been harmed. Her pity ought to be reserved for the wretched souls who'd died or been maimed by a rich man's greed and carelessness. It was they who had suffered, who suffered still. When she spoke again, she was calmer.

"I should like you to leave now."

Montagu stared at her for a long moment and then nodded. He got to his feet and then seemed uncertain what to do next, loath to leave her alone after bringing her such tidings. "If there is anything… anything at all I can do…?"

"I think you've done enough," she said.

She hadn't meant it as a rebuke, far from it, thinking only of the families, the children forced to endure in such abject misery, but he flinched all the same and his bow was stiff as he saw himself out. A part of her wanted to call him back, to explain she was grateful, that her words hadn't been the reproach they had appeared to be, but she was too shocked, shaken to her core, and once she heard the front door close, all she could do was cry.

***

"What are you thinking about?" Minerva asked.

To Experiment with Desire

Inigo smiled at her reflection. He was sitting on the edge of the bed, watching her pin her hair up, and seemed mesmerised by the process. Her maid would arrive today so, for now, she'd chosen a simple style. She regretted that they were no longer to be left all alone. The housekeeper had arrived early that morning, but Minerva had not seen her yet. The breakfast that had been sent up on a tray had been marvellous, though, so she was expecting great things.

"Nothing," he said, as Minerva turned on the seat to look at him.

"Don't tell fibs. Honesty, remember," she scolded gently. "I can see you are worrying, so tell me what is on your mind."

Inigo huffed out a soft laugh and leaned towards her. He reached for her hand and pulled her from the dressing table stool onto his lap. Minerva went without protest and sat down in a flurry of skirts, sliding her arms about his neck. That was too perfect a place to be not to tug at his head and demand a kiss. A fair amount of time later she sighed happily, gazing up at him with a dreamy smile.

"Now you've messed my hair up."

"So I have," he murmured, stealing another kiss.

"No, stop," she said, shaking her head and pressing a finger to his lips. "Stop distracting me."

"You started it," he protested as one hand slid up to cup her breast, squeezing and caressing in a most diverting manner, before his other questing hand tried to disappear up her skirt.

"Stop! Inigo, you're doing it on purpose," she protested, grabbing hold of his roving hand and trying to keep it still. "Now, tell me what is worrying you, or I shall tickle you again."

He glowered a little at her. "You don't play fair."

"Of course I do, you're just upset because I made you squeal like a little girl."

"I did not!"

He looked so indignant that Minerva gave a very unladylike snort of laughter.

"Did too!"

To prove her point, she wriggled her fingers into a sensitive spot on his side. Inigo gave a high-pitched yelp and squirmed away, falling back onto the bed as Minerva gazed triumphantly down at him.

"You were saying?" she said, pleased with herself.

Inigo sighed, defeated. "Fine. I squeal like a girl."

"I agree. Now, what are you fretting about?"

He stared up at her and for a moment she was lost in the astonishing depth of his eyes, the green that was almost emerald, flecked with lighter shades against the dark grey of a stormy sky.

"I'm worried I won't be able to work anymore," he confessed, his dark brows knitted with concern. "I must work, Minerva. I have a beautiful wife to support," he added, smiling at her, though she could tell he wasn't joking.

"Why on earth wouldn't you be able to?" she asked, perplexed. "You love your work. It's what you live for."

He shook his head. "It *was* what I loved, what I lived for, but now… now it's you." He reached up and slid a hand into her hair, making more of a mess of the simple hairstyle she'd managed. "I can't… how can I work when you are here, when… when I want…?" He didn't finish the sentence but pulled her down to him, kissing her hard and rolling her onto her back. His hand slid up her thigh, tugging her skirts up until he found the soft curls and the little pearl of flesh hidden within.

It was some considerable time later before Minerva could remember what it was they'd been talking about.

"Come along," she said, once she'd rearranged her clothes and done her hair again. She took Inigo's hand and led him down to his laboratory.

"Can you show me that experiment you did, please, the one where you discovered something new?"

"You want to see it?" Inigo said, looking a little doubtful.

"Of course I want to see it!" Minerva exclaimed, rolling her eyes at him. "You've discovered something no one else in the world knows about. I want to see it."

"All right, then," he said, looking pleased at her interest.

Minerva watched as Inigo set about making his preparations, and then held the sample of the chemical over heat.

"This is zinc carbonate," he said. "Zinc carbonate is a powdery solid, almost white, as you can see. When it is heated to a high temperature, it turns yellow and starts to decompose and carbon dioxide gas is evolved, which forms a white precipitate in limewater. The yellow solid left behind is hot zinc oxide. As the hot zinc oxide cools, it turns white again."

"Fascinating," Minerva said, nodding at him.

"Now, look," he said, and Minerva watched as the sample turned a bright yellow, almost orange. "This time the colour is intense and will remain even when it cools. That ought to suggest the presence of iron or lead, but there is none. There is, however, a peculiar metallic oxide, and that is something new."

Minerva smiled and watched as Inigo sat down and started making notes. He reached for a tattered book and thumbed through it, paging past a mystifying series of calculations and odd symbols and then began writing again. Smiling, Minerva tiptoed out of the room and fetched a book, then settled herself down in a corner of the laboratory to read.

She got up an hour later to fetch a cup of tea, and put one down beside Inigo with a plate of biscuits. Two hours after that she went back to talk to the new housekeeper, who was a marvellous woman in her late forties. Minerva was certain her waistline would suffer, as the woman had already plied her with more shortbread biscuits than one young lady ought to consume in a single sitting.

She returned to Inigo with another cup of tea and a slice of pie, removing the empty plate the biscuits had been on. He was still working, oblivious to the fact his lunch had arrived, though she suspected he'd find it when he looked up. This done, she had a look about the house with the housekeeper, discussing the changes she wanted to make, and which room ought to be tackled first, which passed an enjoyable couple of hours.

Now however, dinner was ready.

She had instructed the housekeeper to set it out in the dining room, a room she doubted Inigo had ever set foot in once he'd stuck a table and two mismatched chairs in there. Still, she'd made it look as nice as possible with the china Bedwin and Prue had given them as part of their wedding present. With pretty napkins and the cheery fire in the grate, and two elegant candelabras casting a lovely golden light, it looked warm and inviting. When everything was done, she returned to Inigo, sliding her arms about his waist and hugging him from behind. He looked up, appearing rather like someone waking from a dream. His smile was immediate and warm, and he turned on the high stool, opening his legs for her to come closer.

She moved into the space he made, laying her head upon his shoulder.

"I missed you," he murmured into her hair.

"Liar," she said, laughing. "You had no idea I was there."

His expression grew serious at once. "I did. I promise you I did. Every time I looked up you were there, or there was a cup of tea, a plate of biscuits, something that showed you'd thought of me. It…." He stared at her, shaking his head and letting out a breath of laughter. "It's so wonderful to have you here, I can't tell you. It's marvellous. You're marvellous."

Minerva beamed at him, hugging him tightly.

"Perhaps you'd like to help me sometimes, with the experiments?"

She looked up at him, eyes wide. "Could I?" she exclaimed, astonished he should offer such a thing to her.

"Well, only if you want to, but you seemed to be interested and you wanted me to explain that paper by Humphry Davy, but really, it would be much easier to show you."

"Oh!" Minerva exclaimed, pulling his head down for a kiss. "Oh, you are the most marvellous man."

He chuckled, obviously pleased by her enthusiasm. "We could ask Harriet to come too sometimes, if you wanted. Perhaps you could help her with the book she wants to write? I'm sure there are lots of things you would find interesting once you've learned some of the basic skills."

Minerva stared at him, blinking hard, rather overcome.

"What?" he demanded. "Surely you didn't think I'd marry such a marvellous woman and relegate her to keeping house and having babies? I mean, not that it's a problem, if that's what you'd like to do, but—"

He didn't get to say anything further because Minerva kissed him again, and then again, and then some more. She was quite certain she would enjoy decorating the house, and the idea of babies made something warm and wonderful bloom inside her, but there was plenty of time for everything. For the moment, she wanted to enjoy her husband, and their new life and all the things they would teach each other, and that was more than she had ever dreamed of.

Dinner was dreadfully late.

Girls who dare– *Inside every wallflower is the beating heart of a lioness, a passionate individual willing to risk all for their dream, if only they can find the courage to begin. When these overlooked girls make a pact to change their lives, anything can happen.*

Eleven girls – Eleven dares in a hat. Twelve passionate stories. Who will dare to risk it all?

Next in the series

To Bed the Baron
Girls Who Dare, Book 9

One desperate young woman...

Jemima Fernside is the epitome of a well-behaved lady, bred to marry a gentleman and play the part of the perfect wife. Until she finds herself alone in the world without a penny to her name. With few options available to her, Jemima has little choice but to accept a scandalous proposal to become the paid companion to a man she's never even met.

One desperately lonely man...

Solomon 'Solo' Weston, the Baron Rothborn, is sick of society, and people in general who leave him irritable and impatient. As Lieutenant Colonel of the 15th King's Dragoons, he was invalided out of the army after a bullet left him lame. Haunted by guilt, by dead comrades and a lost love, he is becoming ever more reclusive, finding escape through his beloved books.

And a passion neither of them expected to find...

When driven to seek comfort from his bleak existence, Solo believes he has little to offer but financial security in return for a lady's virtue.

But Jemima is not the kind of woman who will leave sleeping ghosts lie, and soon the past and the future don't look at all like Solo expected them to.

Keep reading for a sneak peek!

Chapter 1

Dearest Bonnie,

I am in such a lather I cannot tell you. Minerva came home today in such a flurry and I am worried out of my wits. She was seen at Mr de Beauvoir's house by Mrs Tate. Of all women! She swears that de Beauvoir has silenced her for now, and praise be he has told her he will see my brother tonight to ask for her hand in marriage. The problem is she does not seem pleased about it. She won't talk to me and there is nothing I can do. I cannot beg Robert to accept the proposal until after it happens, for she has sworn me to secrecy, and I must go to a stupid musicale this evening and you know how I detest keeping still for any length of time. I shall spend the entire evening sat upon thorns in a misery of anxiety. I only pray there will be a happy resolution by the time I get home.

—Excerpt of a letter from Lady Helena Adolphus to Mrs Bonnie Cadogan.

25th January 1815. Briar Cottage, Mitcham Village, Sussex.

The cottage was everything Jemima had dreamed of and far more spacious than she had been expecting. When first she'd seen it the roof had been in shocking disrepair, the whitewashed walls flaking and the woodwork in a sorry state. Early this morning she had left Matilda's comfortable town house full of apprehension, but now her heart swelled at the sight of her pretty new home. It had been years since she'd lived in anything but sparsely furnished rented rooms. Of late, those rooms had been damp and dingy and so cold in the winter, it was a wonder her poor aunt hadn't succumbed sooner than she had. In comparison, this was a dream come true. The thick new thatch settled heavily like a cosy hat upon half-timbered walls of brick and freshly painted lime mortar. The tangle of weeds and briar that had been the garden had been brought back into meticulous order and the neatly pruned limbs of rose bushes were clearly visible, stark and vulnerable on such a freezing afternoon. Box hedges bordered the front, meeting at the garden gate and cut with military precision, the handkerchief of lawn on each side of the path perfectly trimmed.

"He's made a fine job of it," Mrs Attwood remarked with approval.

Jemima turned to regard her companion. She still didn't know quite what to make of Mrs Attwood. Originally from Yorkshire, she was a woman in her early fifties with a good figure. She was elegantly dressed in a dark pink velvet carriage dress with ebony buttons and matching bonnet with stylish black and pink ribbons. It was a remarkably frivolous outfit for a woman Jemima thought rather intimidating. Her hair, which must have once been a rich mahogany was shot through with white, but was still thick and lustrous. A handsome woman rather than beautiful, her dark eyes missed nothing and a she had a brisk no nonsense manner which was dauting to one who'd been brought up by her timid maiden aunt. Though Jemima could not complain that Mrs Attwood had been anything but respectful to her, she was plain spoken and had put Jemima to the blush several times already. This was the first time she'd ever directly referred to the fact that Lord Rothborn was paying Jemima for her company, however, that he was responsible for her new home, all the work that had been done to it and the entirety of the contents; not to mention every stitch Jemima was wearing. Though all work had been overseen by Jemima's man of business—Mr Briggs, apparently using the legacy she'd been left by her aunt—Mrs Attwood knew the truth. Jemima's aunt had died without a penny to her name, and Jemima had been desperate enough to accept the baron's scandalous proposal.

Mrs Attwood had been employed by Baron Rothborn as Jemima's companion, there to lend her respectability, when both he and this lady knew she was anything but respectable. Not anymore.

"Yes," Jemima agreed, a little of the pleasure she felt dimming as she remembered how she would pay for the privilege of living in this lovely home. "A very fine job."

"Well, let us get inside and out of this wind, I'm fair nithered and in dire need of a cup of tea. Bessie, leave that," she said, waving a hand at their maid of all works who was struggling to hoist an overstuffed carpet bag. "The men will bring the bags in. Go and get the kettle unpacked and make us a brew."

The girl, originally employed by the baron at the Priory, cast wide, anxious eyes at Mrs Attwood and scurried away to the back of the house to where the men were carrying the luggage. Jemima gave herself a shake, reminding herself she was the lady of the house, and that she ought to stir herself into getting things done.

"Come along then," she said, striving to sound calm and in control as she took Mrs Attwood's arm and walked up the neat paved path to the front door. Happily the cottage had no near neighbours, being a good five minute walk from the village proper. However she didn't doubt that curtains had been twitching as her carriage had come through and it was only a matter of time before the first of the villagers descended upon her. She needed to be ready for them.

Not only for them.

That made her heart skip about which was most unsettling, and Jemima concentrated on retrieving the heavy door key from her reticule. They stepped through the shiny black painted front door into a narrow tiled hallway which led directly to the garden at the back of the house. On either side of the hallway was a good sized room. A formal receiving room on the right and a comfortable parlour on the left. Beyond them was to be found the dining room and staircase, and then the kitchen and scullery. There were four bedrooms and two small garret rooms. Jemima went first to the sitting room, finding it impossible to hide her eagerness.

"Oh!" Despite the circumstances she could not hold back her delight when she saw the transformation inside. Though she had chosen all the furniture herself and had dreamed of how it all might look, to see it before her gave her a little thrill of pleasure.

A fire blazed merrily in the large fireplace and the room was blessedly warm after the chill wind outside. The walls were freshly painted white, the oak floorboards scrubbed and the dreadfully extravagant rug she'd bought was thick and luxurious beneath her kid half-boots. One thing she had to say for the baron, he was no nipcheese. He had encouraged her to furnish her new home with every comfort, insisting that she buy quality and never balking at the bills. As she looked around, she noticed items that she had not bought however, small items of décor that she had thought too frivolous to spend the man's money on. These included a pair of elegant china candleholders on the mantelpiece and two porcelain figurines. A lump rose to her throat as she also noticed several lovely framed watercolours and that the recessed arches on either side of the fireplace had been fitted with shelves and filled with books. Jemima moved closer, finding the titles blur as she discovered a wonderful selection of novels and romantic poetry. Good heavens. How thoughtful he was. A rush of warmth surged through her and she scolded herself for it. That way lay danger.

Jemima knew her own weaknesses, knew she had a heart only too susceptible to romance, too easily led into tender feelings. As a girl she had often lost herself in romantic poetry or tales of heroes who rescued their lady loves from wicked villains. Too long she had dreamed of her own knight in shining armour, of *the one,* who would fall instantly in love with her and carry her away from all her troubles. Reality had crushed her dreams and brought her back to earth with such a painful jolt that she could not allow herself to indulge in such fancies again. The baron had made his position very clear. He could not offer her that. He wanted an intelligent companion to alleviate his solitude, and a woman to… to … A blush swept over her and Jemima stood closer to the fire, hoping Mrs Attwood would attribute her heightened colour to her proximity to the flames.

"Well, this is splendid," the woman said, with obvious approval. Jemima turned to find her companion stripping off her gloves and untying the ribbons on her bonnet. She put the gloves in the bonnet and set them down on an elegant chair upholstered in cream damask silk. "You have excellent taste Miss Fernside, though I could tell that the first time I looked upon you. I think we shall be very comfortable here. Such a perfect location too. Private enough not to be overlooked by the gossips and yet so convenient for the village."

Jemima's scalding cheeks burned hotter and the lady tsked, shaking her head. She moved forward, taking Jemima's hands in her own. It was such an intimate, friendly gesture from a woman she barely knew that Jemima was too startled to react.

"Why don't we call a spade a spade, my dear. You'll be more comfortable with me if you do. You are to be the baron's mistress. There's no getting away from it."

Jemima gasped and moved to tug her hands free, shocked by this forthright manner of speech. Mrs Attwood held on tight.

"No," she said, her dark eyes intent. "You'll hear me. There's no shame in surviving, Miss Fernside. We all do what we must and those who would condemn us can go to the devil if you ask me. Better a good man's mistress than to serve an army on your back. You chose right and you'll find no condemnation from me, nor that little maid neither. She talks of yon baron like he's God almighty and he's told her to keep mum. You're safe here, with us, and I'll not have you come home by way of the weeping cross once you've done what you must and there's no turning back. You've made your bed, so you may as well enjoy the comforts of the mattress. At least he's a handsome devil so it ought be no hardship."

Jemima stared at her, robbed of speech for a long moment. Then she drew in an unsteady breath and let it out again in something resembling a breath of laughter. She gave a slight nod, the most she could manage, and the hands that held hers tightened for a moment and Mrs Attwood gave her a warm, approving smile.

"That's the way lass. Now, let's have a look at the rest of the place, shall we?"

***

Solo Weston, the sixth Baron Rothborn, took out his pocket watch and checked it against the mantel clock in his study. Ten minutes before five o'clock. Miss Fernside ought to have arrived some time midmorning. He limped to the window, cursing the cold, wet weather that made his blasted leg so damned painful. Outside a dismal day greeted him. Nothing but drizzle, a low misty cloud that clung to the treetops and offered a sodden outlook upon the ancient and beautiful gardens that surrounded the Priory. The view from every window of the building was picturesque in the worst of weather, and though Solo was biased, even now on such a miserable day, it was still the loveliest place in all of England. It was also inconvenient, draughty, horribly expensive and more demanding than any mistress. He went to the chair behind his desk and sat heavily, kneading the knotted muscles in his thigh with one hand, and wondering if it would be beyond the pale for him to call upon Miss Fernside today. Surely, he ought to give her a day or two to settle in?

Yes. Two days, would be prudent.

Except perhaps two days was too long. He did not wish to insult the lady, or for her to believe him indifferent to her arrival. So… tomorrow then.

He reached for the book he'd been reading, taking out the bookmark and finding his place. It was less than five minutes before he gave up, realising he'd read the same paragraph three times without comprehending a word. The devil take it. He'd call on her today, now, before it got dark. Just briefly. Just to see she had everything she needed. He'd not stop. Not take up her time. He'd simply reassure himself all was as it ought to be and arrange a time to call again when she was settled. Decided upon this plan of action he headed for the front door.

The staff who remained at the priory had worked there all their lives, as had their parents before them. Not that there were many. When the previous baron, Solo's father, had died the house had been shut up whilst the son was away at war. On his return, half mad with grief and pain, it had been more than he could bear to have people around him. Only those he knew like his own kin had been asked to return, those who could be trusted not to gossip about the wreck of a man who had come home to lick his wounds in private. The most important of those was Mrs Norrell, the cook and housekeeper. Previously the Priory would have had an army of staff, the kitchens alone bristling with people, but Solo could not stand the scrutiny of strangers and with only him in residence it seemed pointless. So Mrs Norrell ruled the roost. She was tiny woman who barely reached higher than Solo's elbow, she was as wide as she was tall and ruled the priory in a manner the Iron Duke would have approved of.

She tsked and shook her head as she came across Solo in the great hall, shrugging into his heavy greatcoat and picking up his hat.

"Twill do that leg of yours no good to be out in this cold, my lord. You'd do best to sit by the fire. The lady will still be there tomorrow when the rain has gone."

Solo turned an icy expression upon the woman which didn't have the least effect, as he'd known it wouldn't. Having once been his nurse, she well remembered changing his clouts and smacking his arse for cheeking her. It was hard to act the high and might lord of the manner before a woman who had tanned his hide and sung him to sleep as a snot nosed boy.

"Mrs Norrell. I know you find this hard to remember, but I am a grown man and in complete charge of my own mind and person."

"Aye, and with less sense than you was born with," she said, with an impatient huff. "Ah, well. Do as you will, you always did. I'll have water heated and ready for when you get back and commence blustering about your poor leg."

Solo opened his mouth to object, he *never* blustered, let alone about his leg, confound the woman, but Mrs Norrell had stalked off back to her sacred domain in the kitchen."

"Interfering old termagant," Solo muttered as he put his hat and headed for the door.

"I heard that," Mrs Norrell yelled, before the door that led to the kitchens banged shut.

Hell and the devil, the blasted woman had the hearing of a bat! There was something supernatural about her, he was certain of it. Solo was not the least bit fanciful, he did not believe in ghosts, despite some of the odd things that happened about the priory. There was always a reasonable explanation for such things—even if he couldn't think of one himself. Yet Mrs Norrell had an uncanny knack for knowing things, for knowing *him*. He'd never outmanoeuvred her as a boy, and it was a beyond humiliating to discover nothing had changed. As Lieutenant Colonel of the 15th King's Dragoons, he was known for his brilliant military strategy and yet his blasted housekeeper ran rings around him.

Still muttering, Solo pulled on his gloves, retrieved his cane from where he'd set it down, and headed out into the cold.

Chapter 2

Dear Robert,

Please forgive me for all the trouble I have caused you. I must point out, however, that it is <u>I alone</u> who have caused the trouble. Prue knew nothing of my plans outside of the fact I was infatuated with Mr de Beauvoir, and poor Inigo – Mr de Beauvoir, did his very best to make me behave myself, but it was no good.

I think perhaps I fell in love with him the very first time we met last summer, at least a little bit, and it's been growing worse with every week that passes. I love him quite dreadfully you see, but I'm afraid I behaved very badly and pursued him despite his best efforts to dissuade me. That being the case, I cannot allow you to hold him responsible for what has happened.

—Excerpt of a letter from Miss Minerva Butler to His Grace, Robert Adolphus, Duke of Bedwin.

25th January 1815. Briar Cottage, Mitcham Village, Sussex.

By half past four the bulk of the unpacking had been done and the men who had accompanied the cart loaded with Mrs Attwood's and Jemima's belongings were thanked with tea and cakes and some extra coin, and sent on their way. Jemima was helping Bessie unpack the last of her own belongings when Mrs Attwood knocked and came in.

"What a lovely room," she said, looking around the pretty bedroom. "It will have a lovely sunny aspect, if ever the sun deigns to show itself again."

"Thank you," Jemima replied, getting up from the floor and shaking out the wrinkles in her skirts. "I hope your own room is to your satisfaction?"

"Satisfaction?" Mrs Attwood said with a tinkling laugh. "Good heavens, child. I never had such a beautiful room in my life. Grander perhaps," she said with a naughty wink. "But never so beautiful. You have impeccable taste."

Jemima blushed with pleasure. She'd always loved choosing fabric and colours but never had she been able to indulge her love for pretty things, not when it had been a choice between paying the rent and putting food on the table for so long. Not that it had always been so, but the last years weighed heavy and seemed to diminish any lighter memories that had come before.

"I'm so happy you are pleased." She might have said more, except a knock at the door sounded and Jemima looked up in surprise. Surely the neighbours wouldn't come calling on the very day she'd arrived. She glanced at Mrs Attwood who returned a knowing look.

"That was the back door," the woman said, smiling now. "So we know who it will be. I didn't think he'd be able to wait until tomorrow to see you. Such a gent too, to wait to be seen in when the weather is so poor. Many a man in his position would barge in, as he does in fact own the place. I'll see him settled in the parlour while you change your dress into something pretty. Hurry now."

Jemima stared at her, suddenly panic struck as Mrs Attwood hurried to the door.

"B-but..." she stammered. All at once she wanted to be back in the miserable little flat she'd been struggling to keep hold of these past months as anxiety coiled in her stomach and twisted her guts into a knot.

"Good heavens!" Mrs Attwood said, laughing as she came back and gave Jemima a swift hug. "He's not going to ravish you in your front room, dear. I expect he's just anxious to see you are well settled and eager to see you again. Stop looking like a virgin sacrifice or you'll make the poor man feel like a monster."

With that, she bustled out and Jemima took herself in hand. Of course, Mrs Attwood was quite correct. She was being a complete ninny. It wasn't like she didn't understand the agreement she'd entered into. She must stop being so dreadfully silly. "Bessie, get me that blue and white striped gown, the last one we put away. Do hurry, we mustn't keep the baron waiting."

Bessie paled and lunged for the wardrobe. "Oh, indeed not, Miss. A stickler for punctuality he is, what with being a military fellow. Can't abide waiting for people, nor for his dinner neither."

"Oh. Is he bad tempered then?" Jemima asked fretfully as Bessie wrestled her out of the frock she was wearing with ruthless efficiency.

"Oh, bellows like a lion he does, what and things don't go how he likes 'em. Still, tis often his leg what pains him and puts him out o' temper, so we don't pay it no mind, what with him being such a war hero. My, the stories they tell of his heroics, tis a wonder he came home as whole as he did, not that it weren't wretched bad when he first came back, but he's a good master, kind an' all, so we don't mind a bit o' bluster. Tis like a north wind, miss and soon blows itself out and then he's meek as a kitten."

Bessie, who had hardly spoken two words to Jemima before this lengthy exposition suddenly realised her nerves had led her into chattering and blushed crimson.

"Beg pardon, miss," she said, casting Jemima nervous glances as she lifted the new gown. "I didn't mean to rattle on so. Tongue like a fiddlestick Mrs Norrell says, not that I gossip, miss, for I don't. Not never. Only as you're to be... as you are... what with... well, I thought you'd like to know a bit about him," she said desperately, before tugging the dress over Jemima's head.

Once Jemima was clear of the voluminous fabric, she let out a breath. Bessie hadn't exactly soothed her nerves, but she wasn't entirely surprised by her description of Lord Rothborn. Much of what she'd said had been apparent from their first meeting, and her estimation of his better nature had grown from the thought with which he had added touches to make the house welcoming to her. The baron was a good man at heart, tempers aside, and those Jemima would learn to manage.

Bessie was just putting the finishing touches to her hair when Mrs Attwood came back.

"He's settled in the parlour, waiting for you," she said, giving Jemima a critical once over. "Lovely," she said, nodding her approval. "He'll not know what hit him when he sees you in that frock. In fine twig I must say. Now, have a little nip of brandy, for your nerves."

She proffered a small silver hip flask and Jemima took it with a frown. "I've never..." she began, but Mrs Attwood waved away her protests.

"Tis good for what ails you. Just a few sips and you'll not blush and stammer quite so much, though I suspect he'll not mind that. A gentleman likes to feel protective of a little innocent, but we don't want him feeling like a brute for stealing your virtue or some such nonsense if you overdo it."

Jemima didn't even blush this time, beginning to appreciate her companion's rather forthright way of speaking. Far better that than some farcical pretence that everything was perfectly as it ought to be. She upended the flask, taking three good swallows and then choked as the liquor burned its way down her throat.

"Good heavens!" she gasped, wide eyed.

"Well, it's not lemonade! I said sip it, not gulp it back." Mrs Attwood laughed and tugged her to her feet. "Down you go then, and remember to smile."

Jemima almost tripped down the stairs in her haste, slowing at the last step as the brandy bloomed into a puddle of warmth in her belly and eased into her veins. Oh, yes, she could see what Mrs Attwood meant now. Taking a deep breath, she gave herself a moment to gather her nerve, and headed for the parlour.

***

Solo stood by the fire. The room was exceptionally elegant, and he felt a flush of pride in Miss Fernside for having arranged it so beautifully. Not for the first time he wondered if his memory was playing tricks on him as he wondered at his good fortune. Surely, she could not have been so very beautiful as he remembered. It was perhaps a trick of the light that had given her skin that luminosity, the cold that made the blush of colour at her cheeks so sweet, and perhaps she'd used rouge to make her lips that inviting soft pink. He experienced a qualm as he considered she might have lulled him into a false sense of security. If she was beautiful, she was likely expensive and the restraint she'd shown in furnishing this house was the calm before the storm. Perhaps she'd demand diamonds and trips to the opera and the theatre. The diamonds he could manage perhaps, if he must, but the idea of the opera or the theatre made him hot and uncomfortable. The noise and the throngs of people would be more than his nerves could stand. Not to mention how awkward it would be, to be in the company of all those he used to spend time with when he was so changed... no. No, that would never do.

He took out his pocket watch and scowled at it. What was taking so long? Was she having second thoughts? Perhaps she'd escaped out the back door whilst he was waiting.

Anticipation made his heart hammer in his chest and he told himself to stop being such a damned fool. He shifted his position, taking the weight from his damaged leg as it protested at him standing for so long. Damn thing had a mind of its own, and a deranged mind at that, contrary article. It didn't like it if he sat still, but complained if he walked about too much. It was bad tempered in wet weather, yet if he sat by the fire it wanted him to get up and move. Honestly, it was like being attached to a fractious child.

He huffed, irritated, and glowered at the watch, willing the hands to move and tempted to give it a little shake. The door opened and he glanced up, and almost dropped the watch as his gaze fell upon Miss Fernside.

Good God.

His memory had been at fault. She was far more beautiful than he'd been prepared for. He clutched the watch in his hand so tight it was a wonder he didn't crush it and watched as she closed the door gently behind her and curtseyed. As she rose, as elegant as a dancer, she noted the watch in his hand and his heart kicked in his chest at the fierce blush that bloomed over her skin. By heavens, he'd never seen anything so lovely in all his days. His mouth went dry and any sensible thought vanished, likely never to be seen again. He was hot and unsettled and out of sorts. He'd wanted a comfortable companion, a woman to converse with and to bed and he'd… he'd… How would he ever hold on to her? If any man of higher rank or fortune discovered this exquisite creature was his, they'd give her a far better offer and he'd lose her. The idea made him feel ill.

"I do b-beg your pardon, my lord," she said in her soft, musical voice. "I wanted to look my best for you but I ought not have kept you waiting for so long."

Waiting? Had he been waiting? Time had suspended and he was trapped in some world in between one heartbeat and the next. He couldn't speak and saw the anxiety in her gaze as she stared at him with growing concern.

"P-please forgive me. It won't happen again. I promise."

Solo tried to put the watch away and almost dropped the wretched thing, concentrating on fumbling it into his pocket and adjusting the chain to give himself a moment.

"I didn't mind," he said, his voice sounding too loud, too strident in this elegant room, with this woman who was all delicate limbs, so very fragile, like a fairy queen. Lines from a Shakespeare sonnet came to mind and he had to bite his tongue to stop the words from tumbling out like he was some lovesick swain.

If I could write the beauty of your eyes
and in fresh numbers number all your graces,
The age to come would say, 'This poet lies;
Such heavenly touches ne'er touch'd earthly faces.

"Waiting," he added, before realising he'd paused too long to add the clarification. "I didn't mind waiting," he repeated, cursing himself. God, what a damned buffoon.

"May I offer you some tea?" she asked, daring to come a few steps closer.

"No," he said, with a brisk shake of his head, and then wanted to take it back. If he took tea with her, he could draw the visit out and stay longer. Too late now. Blasted idiot. He dared look at her again, to see her hands were knotted together, the slender fingers white. Poor little creature was scared witless. Damn his eyes, he was a mannerless brute.

He cleared his throat, making a concerted effort to keep his voice gentle. "I hope that everything is to your satisfaction, Miss Fernside."

At that her soft lips curved into a dazzling smile, and the air was knocked from his lungs. It was like falling from a great height and hitting the ground with a thud and he felt dazed, disorientated. Good grief, a smile like that should have a five minute warning go off ahead of time so a fellow could prepare himself for the impact.

"Oh, my lord," she said, the warmth of her words soothing him like a cleansing balm. "It is quite perfect. I've never... My goodness, I feel the need to pinch myself whenever I look about me for I cannot believe I shall truly live here. Your kindness as well, in taking such care to make it a home for me. I… I am so very grateful to you, for everything."

"Kindness?" he queried, unable to look away, trying desperately not to stare at her mouth.

"Why yes," she said, moving a few steps closer. If she came any nearer he'd be able to reach out and touch her, to pull her into his arms and kiss that soft mouth, to feel her warmth through her gown, to put his hands upon that tiny waist. "The watercolour paintings, and the books and ornaments, and oh, a dozen little touches that have made such a difference. It was so good of you."

Solo swallowed, trying to hold onto the thread of the conversation with difficulty. "Nothing of consequence," he muttered, frowning a little. "You must remove anything that doesn't suit. You have turned a this rather humble abode into something of refinement and elegance and I should hate to be responsible for spoiling it."

"Oh, no!" she said at once. "Good heavens, no. Your additions have been wonderful, perfect, and I should like you to feel at home here." She hesitated, two high spots of colour burning on her cheeks as she lowered her gaze. "After all, it… it is to be your home too, after a fashion."

Solo clenched his fists as the desire to lay his hands on her became overwhelming. If he stayed a moment longer, he was going to do something reprehensible and forget she was a lady. A wicked voice in the back of his head told himself she was no longer a lady, that he'd paid for her, paid for every stitch she was wearing and the roof over her head. He had rights. He silenced it, sickened and revolted. Miserable bastard. He wasn't fit to be in the same room with her. If not for circumstances, she'd not even look in his direction. What use was he to a young beauty like her? A broken down old soldier too many years her senior. God it was disgusting.

"I'd better be on my way," he said, not looking at her, stalking to the door and trying his best to hide his limp. Mrs Norrell had been right, damn her, the cold had only aggravated the pain.

"Oh, but… my lord?"

He turned, caught by the pleading in her voice.

"I… I hope I have not displeased you?"

"Displeased me?" he repeated, astonished. "Whatever put that maggoty idea in your head?"

"Well you seem… you… Are you angry with me?"

She blinked at him, her grey eyes wary and he noticed her eyelashes were long and thick and several shades darker blonde than her hair. He wondered if the hidden curls beneath her gown, those nestled in the secret place between her thighs, were that same dark gold shade and felt a wash of colour creep up the back of his neck at indulging such a wicked thought when she was obviously distressed.

"No." He shook his head and tried to remember he was a gentleman, dammit. "It's my fault. Abominably rude. Ought to have given you time to settle in. Didn't want to intrude. Just to see all was as it ought to be. Shan't keep you. Off now." This eloquent little speech made him feel an utter imbecile and he took himself off, barely stopping to snatch up his coat and hat from Bessie and hauling his protesting leg back out into the cold.

Available April 24, 2020

Pre-Order your copy here: To Bed the Baron

Want more Emma?

If you enjoyed this book, please support this indie author and take a moment to leave a few words in a review. *Thank you!*

To be kept informed of special offers and free deals (which I do regularly) follow me on *https://www.bookbub.com/authors/emma-v-leech*

To find out more and to get news and sneak peeks of the first chapter of upcoming works, go to my website and sign up for the newsletter.

http://www.emmavleech.com/

Come and join the fans in my Facebook group for news, info and exciting discussion...

Emmas Book Club

Or Follow me here......

http://viewauthor.at/EmmaVLeechAmazon

Emma's Twitter page

About Me!

I started this incredible journey way back in 2010 with The Key to Erebus but didn't summon the courage to hit publish until October 2012. For anyone who's done it, you'll know publishing your first title is a terribly scary thing! I still get butterflies on the morning a new title releases but the terror has subsided at least. Now I just live in dread of the day my daughters are old enough to read them.

The horror! (On both sides I suspect.)

2017 marked the year that I made my first foray into Historical Romance and the world of the Regency Romance, and my word what a year! I was delighted by the response to this series and can't wait to add more titles. Paranormal Romance readers need not despair however as there is much more to come there too. Writing has become an addiction and as soon as one book is over I'm hugely excited to start the next so you can expect plenty more in the future.

As many of my works reflect I am greatly influenced by the beautiful French countryside in which I live. I've been here in the South West for the past twenty years though I was born and raised in England. My three gorgeous girls are all bilingual and the youngest who is only six, is showing signs of following in my footsteps after producing *The Lonely Princess* all by herself.

I'm told book two is coming soon ...

She's keeping me on my toes, so I'd better get cracking!

KEEP READING TO DISCOVER MY OTHER BOOKS!

Other Works by Emma V. Leech

(For those of you who have read The French Fae Legend series, please remember that chronologically The Heart of Arima precedes The Dark Prince)

Girls Who Dare

To Dare a Duke

To Steal A Kiss

To Break the Rules

To Follow her Heart

To Wager with Love

To Dance with a Devil

To Winter at Wildsyde

To Experiment with Desire

To Bed the Baron (April 24, 2020)

To Ride with the Knight (May 29, 2020)

Rogues & Gentlemen

The Rogue

The Earl's Temptation

Scandal's Daughter

The Devil May Care

Nearly Ruining Mr. Russell

One Wicked Winter

To Tame a Savage Heart

Persuading Patience

The Last Man in London

Flaming June

Charity and the Devil

A Slight Indiscretion

The Corinthian Duke

The Blackest of Hearts

Duke and Duplicity

The Scent of Scandal

The Rogue and The Earl's Temptation Box set

Melting Miss Wynter

The Winter Bride (A R&G Novella)

The Regency Romance Mysteries

Dying for a Duke

A Dog in a Doublet

The Rum and the Fox

The French Vampire Legend

The Key to Erebus

The Heart of Arima

The Fires of Tartarus

The Boxset (The Key to Erebus, The Heart of Arima)

The Son of Darkness (October 31, 2020)

The French Fae Legend

The Dark Prince

The Dark Heart

The Dark Deceit

The Darkest Night

Short Stories: A Dark Collection.

Stand Alone

The Book Lover (a paranormal novella)

Audio Books!

Don't have time to read but still need your romance fix? The wait is over…

By popular demand, get your favourite Emma V Leech Regency Romance books on audio at Audible as performed by the incomparable Philip Battley and Gerard Marzilli. Several titles available and more added each month!

Click the links to choose your favourite and start listening now.

Rogues & Gentlemen

The Rogue

The Earl's Tempation

Scandal's Daughter

The Devil May Care

Nearly Ruining Mr Russell

One Wicked Winter

To Tame a Savage Heart

Persuading Patience

The Last Man in London

Flaming June

The Winter Bride, a novella

Girls Who Dare

To Dare a Duke

To Steal A Kiss

To Break the Rules

To Follow her Heart (coming soon)

The Regency Romance Mysteries

Dying for a Duke

A Dog in a Doublet (coming soon)

The French Vampire Legend

The Key to Erebus (coming soon)

Also check out Emma's regency romance series, Rogues & Gentlemen. Available now!

The Rogue
Rogues & Gentlemen Book 1

1815

Along the wild and untamed coast of Cornwall, smuggling is not only a way of life, but a means of survival.

Henrietta Morton knows well to look the other way when the free trading 'gentlemen' are at work. Yet when a notorious pirate, known as The Rogue, bursts in on her in the village shop, she takes things one step further.

Bewitched by a pair of wicked blue eyes, in a moment of insanity she hides the handsome fugitive from the local Militia. Her reward is a kiss that she just cannot forget. But in his haste to escape with his life, her pirate drops a letter, inadvertently giving

Henri incriminating information about the man she just helped free.

When her father gives her hand in marriage to a wealthy and villainous nobleman in return for the payment of his debts, Henri becomes desperate.

Blackmailing a pirate may be her only hope for freedom.

Read for free on Kindle Unlimited

The Rogue

Interested in a Regency Romance with a twist?

Dying for a Duke

The Regency Romance Mysteries Book 1

Straight-laced, imperious and morally rigid, Benedict Rutland - the darkly handsome Earl of Rothay - gained his title too young. Responsible for a large family of younger siblings that his frivolous parents have brought to bankruptcy, his youth was spent clawing back the family fortunes.

Now a man in his prime and financially secure he is betrothed to a strict, sensible and cool-headed woman who will never upset the balance of his life or disturb his emotions ...

But then Miss Skeffington-Fox arrives.

Brought up solely by her rake of a step-father, Benedict is scandalised by everything about the dashing Miss.

But as family members in line for the dukedom begin to die at an alarming rate, all fingers point at Benedict, and Miss Skeffington-Fox may be the only one who can save him.

FREE to read on Amazon Kindle Unlimited.. Dying for a Duke

Lose yourself in Emma's paranormal world with The French Vampire Legend series…..

The Key to Erebus
The French Vampire Legend Book 1

The truth can kill you.

Taken away as a small child, from a life where vampires, the Fae, and other mythical creatures are real and treacherous, the beautiful young witch, Jéhenne Corbeaux is totally unprepared when she returns to rural France to live with her eccentric Grandmother.

Thrown headlong into a world she knows nothing about she seeks to learn the truth about herself, uncovering secrets more shocking than anything she could ever have imagined and finding that she is by no means powerless to protect the ones she loves.

Despite her Gran's dire warnings, she is inexorably drawn to the dark and terrifying figure of Corvus, an ancient vampire and master of the vast Albinus family.

Jéhenne is about to find her answers and discover that, not only is Corvus far more dangerous than she could ever imagine, but that he holds much more than the key to her heart …

FREE to read on Kindle Unlimited The Key to Erebus

Check out Emma's exciting fantasy series with hailed by Kirkus Reviews as "An enchanting fantasy with a likable heroine, romantic intrigue, and clever narrative flourishes."

The Dark Prince
The French Fae Legend Book 1

Two Fae Princes
One Human Woman
And a world ready to tear them all apart

Laen Braed is Prince of the Dark fae, with a temper and reputation to match his black eyes, and a heart that despises the human race. When he is sent back through the forbidden gates between realms to retrieve an ancient fae artefact, he returns home with far more than he bargained for.

Corin Albrecht, the most powerful Elven Prince ever born. His golden eyes are rumoured to be a gift from the gods, and destiny is calling him. With a love for the human world that runs deep, his friendship with Laen is being torn apart by his prejudices.

Océane DeBeauvoir is an artist and bookbinder who has always relied on her lively imagination to get her through an unhappy and uneventful life. A jewelled dagger put on display at a nearby museum hits the headlines with speculation of another race, the Fae. But the discovery also inspires Océane to create an extraordinary piece of art that cannot be confined to the pages of a book.

With two powerful men vying for her attention and their friendship stretched to the breaking point, the only question that remains...who is truly The Dark Prince.

The man of your dreams is coming...or is it your nightmares he visits? Find out in Book One of The French Fae Legend.

Available now to read for FREE on Kindle Unlimited.

The Dark Prince

Acknowledgements

Thanks, of course, to my wonderful editor Kezia Cole.

To Victoria Cooper for all your hard work, amazing artwork and above all your unending patience!!! Thank you so much. You are amazing!

To my BFF, PA, personal cheerleader and bringer of chocolate, Varsi Appel, for moral support, confidence boosting and for reading my work more times than I have. I love you loads!

A huge thank you to all of Emma's Book Club members! You guys are the best!

I'm always so happy to hear from you so do email or message me :)

emmavleech@orange.fr

To my husband Pat and my family ... For always being proud of me.

Printed by Amazon Italia Logistica S.r.l.
Torrazza Piemonte (TO), Italy